# THE CLEANSE – MALA

A Novel by A. N. Perry

"I alone cannot change the world, but I can cast a stone across the waters to create many ripples." -Mother Teresa

D1714651

# PROLOGUE

Ross Witherspoon stood barefoot in the sand, looking out to sea. He was in turmoil. A pair of old blue jeans, long since cut-off just above the knees, was all he wore. His shoulder-length hair just about reached the top of a tattoo that had been etched into his shoulders and neck. The tattoo depicted two stylized sharks on either side of a large sea turtle, and it took almost an entire day of agony to complete, but that was well over a year ago.

The reason he was in turmoil was that Ross Witherspoon was living with a truth he knew about himself. He had tried to rationalize it, then excuse it and finally ignore it. It clung to him like a sweaty tee shirt in the summer but was far more difficult to be rid of.

His mind drifted back to the triumphant days in Canada almost seven years ago. He had been a geologist back then, and he worked for a company so small that he had to provide many of his own supplies each spring as he charted yet another route into the Western Ontario wilderness, once the snow melted enough to travel. He had graduated top of his class at McGill University and was eager to achieve as much success in the field as he had in the classroom. His discovery of Jericho kimberlite, and the diamonds contained in the three pipes he found near Twin Lakes, gained him fame and financial freedom. It was what he did after the excitement of the discovery wore off, and the drudgery of mining began, that caused his turmoil.

Like entrepreneurs who work tirelessly to start a business, but abhor running it, Ross Witherspoon wanted to do it all over again. Exploration, not mining, was what was in his blood. The problem was that his wife had given him a daughter, now almost two years old, and when he left to search the world for the next big diamond deposit, he told her he would be back in twelve months. That was five years ago. When he first arrived in Honiara on a rusty old freighter he had booked passage on, he knew from talking to the locals that the area was ripe for possible kimberlite discovery since the islands had been formed from volcanoes millions of years ago. He wired his company, Lucarana Mining, that he would narrow his search to the nearby island of Malaita, and that he could be reached there.

It was the message he received the day before that caused his turmoil. His wife, Margret, had contracted a rare form of brain cancer, and passed away after a mere six months, the last four of which were in a hospital bed in Toronto. The message from his company was already two months old just getting to him. It said that a nanny had been retained to look after his daughter, but since he had reported no new discoveries, he should consider returning to the desk job that would be waiting for him and be a father to her.

What the company did not know was that he had, in fact, made a tremendous new discovery. A rare small pipe that formed inside an older, active volcano, transported diamonds of exceptional color and size all the way to the surface millions of years ago. It was just that he no longer cared about diamonds, mining, or even the company itself. As a geologist, he had died, but in so doing, he had discovered something of far greater value. With the help of Kepa Kai and Luti Mikode, he had found himself.

Now, thoughts of that little girl being raised by a stranger shattered the tranquility he had cultivated and enjoyed. "How could I be so selfish?" he thought to himself. "What a bastard I am." Tears of shame washed down his cheeks and into the warm clear water of the lagoon he was standing in. He took out the pocketknife given to him by his father just before he left to go exploring. Pushing the little button that released the blade, he began hacking the hair at the back of his head. Then he started to work on the beard that had grown over the three years since he first knew mining was in his past. The hair fell into the water and was slowly drawn away from shore and out to sea. Something he would soon do as well.

Ross Witherspoon was ready to return home to raise his daughter.

# CHAPTER ONE

Adam Baines slid into the chair in his typically controlled manner, a decaf coffee in his left hand and a backpack in his right. Samantha barely had time to register his arrival before he planted his sneakers on the Nelson-style slat bench that served as a coffee table next to the café's front window. The table worked well because when coffee spilled, which happened all the time, it went directly through the slats and onto the floor, avoiding the laptops and cell phones lying around.

"Hey Sam, where's Tom?" Adam asked in his watered-down but still detectable Welch accent.

"Late as usual," Sam said. "I told him I'd have a surprise to announce so you'd think for once he'd be on time!" She sipped her cappuccino after taking a nibble on the oatmeal raisin cookie that was just about gone.

"Right. So, what about this surprise? What's going on?" Adam asked.

"I'll wait until Tom gets here so you both can hear it together. You guys are gonna be blown away!" Sam said.

"But I'll give you a hint. Remember how we were all talking about what we were going to do with the break coming up? Well, I have the answer, thanks to my mom."

Samantha Lewis, or Sam as her friends called her, was the daughter of a single mom. She had grown up on the coast of Maine in the small tourist town of Boothbay Harbor, about an hour up Route 1 from Portland. Bearing right off the "highway" just past the Wiscassett Bridge, it was about fifteen miles straight down towards the ocean, ending in her driveway right on the rocks, looking toward Spain. Her mother, Liberty Lewis, whom everyone referred to either as Lib or Libby, had always been a hard worker and ran her own business at one point. Later, after a stint as a nurse for five years, she had applied for a job as a personal assistant to a woman who was quite wealthy, and after a rough start, they got along famously. Lib traveled the world with her employer and friend, Blaire, and the experience transformed her from a typical rural "townie" into someone with a degree of sophistication and an acquired sense of taste. It also provided Sam with the opportunity to "get off the peninsula," as they say, and go to a private school that was a tradition in Blaire's family. Then on to the University of New Hampshire for undergraduate work, all paid for by Blaire Hoffman and the family trust. Later, when Blaire was diagnosed, Lib called on her nursing background and took it upon herself to care for Blaire right to the end. Blaire had made it clear that she didn't want to die in some nursing home somewhere. Rather, in her own bed, looking out at Squirrel Island, hearing the foghorn, and watching the waves breaking on the rocks in front of her window. Lib devoted over fourteen months of her life twenty-four/seven to make that happen.

Sam's mom knew that Blaire Hoffman was never married and therefore had no children. But what she didn't know was that she had been named in her will. Although Ms. Hoffman had often mentioned leaving her substantial fortune to various charities, especially those which sought to save wildlife and nature, she had simply never gotten around to creating a will that would dictate that outcome. But she did mention Lib, to the tune of a few million dollars. Come to find out, when no one else is named, and even when other family members challenge, the courts decide who gets what and, in this case, ruled Lib to be the sole beneficiary since she was the only one specifically mentioned. That is why a bright red Range Rover Evoque was sitting outside of Hot Shot's Café, a popular spot for graduate students attending the University of California-Berkeley.

"Here he comes now. I can always tell by the hat!" Sam said as she waved to the ruggedly good-looking guy who seemed plucked right out of a Marlboro commercial. In an age where baseball caps were notoriously worn backward, Tom McDonald stuck out like a sore thumb with his Stetson-style cowboy hat. And he couldn't care less.

"Hey, Tom, lovely morning, good to see you!" Adam said. "Did you walk or take the bus?" He gulped the last of his decaf even though it was barely lukewarm.

"You should be able to tell by now, Adam, just by looking at my feet. See the Converses? Yeah, I walked. Those cowboy boots wouldn't cut it. Hi, Sam, you look like a cat with a mouse. What's that grin on your face all about?"

Samantha, sitting cross-legged in a chair with a computer in her lap, unwound herself, and turned the laptop around. "This is what my grin is all about," she said.

"Where the bloody hell is that, Sam? It's beautiful, but what's it got to do with us?" Adam had his nose about three inches from the laptop trying to determine where in the world that beautiful beach with those magnificent waves could be.

"That, boys, is where we're going for seven days of surfing! The Solomon Islands. Malaita, to be specific. Whadda ya think about that?"

"Let me see." Tom took the laptop. "Wow, this is beautiful, but I can't afford a trip like that, Sam. Hell, I don't even have a car."

"Nor me, Sam. That kind of cash? No way," Adam chimed in.

Samantha frowned. "Now hold on, guys! You know I wouldn't bait a hook without being able to cast it in the water. Mom is giving us the trip all expenses paid for my birthday, and we're using the Citation X to get there. All you have to do is get your sorry asses up a set of flight steps, and away we go. Besides, what else have you got going on that could compete with seven days of sun and fun on one of the most beautiful and remote islands in the world, and me?"

"Sam, your mother has a private jet? I thought she just likes it up there in Boothbay, doing not much of anything. That must cost a fortune," Tom said.

"She doesn't own the jet, she has a NetJet account, and yes, even that costs a fortune," explained Sam. "But as she always says, she didn't ask for what she got, and I'm not going to try to talk her out of it! Besides, she has so many hours of use billed to her each month whether or not she goes anywhere, so she figures she might as well put them to good use."

"I've heard of NetJet," Adam said. "Fractional ownership, but as much as I love to surf, I'm no pro, just a hacker who likes to ride a wave now and again. Seems a bit extravagant to me."

"Well, you'll both just have to get over it." Sam pouted. "Because we're going, and that's all there is to it, or you guys go tell Mom you shot down her idea, not me."

With his lean, wiry body bent over the laptop and his chin in his hand, Adam said almost to himself, "Well, I can't think of a better place to do a little research on microplastic contamination, and I don't need much gear to do it."

"Sure, Adam," Sam piped in. "We can't be on the waves all the time, and don't think I won't be bringing some of my research material along as well. My thesis needs refinement, and this will be the perfect chance to clear my head for some new perspective."

As Tom looked over Adam's shoulder at the pictures of Malaita, he said, "Me, I would just appreciate getting away from the labs and clearing my head for a while. It sure looks to beat Hampton Beach, doesn't it, Sam?"

Tom and Samantha had met while both were attending the University of New Hampshire, and while the waves at nearby Hampton Beach were not necessarily a surfer's dream, they did develop a camaraderie that began in wetsuits and evolved into a deep friendship. Platonic, to be sure, but deep.

"Sam, isn't that Guadalcanal?" Tom asked

"That's right, Tom. Guadalcanal is part of the chain of over nine hundred islands, and there are all kinds of World War Two relics there, but this is Malaita, which is one of the bigger islands. It is remote, and it's considered one of the last surfing frontiers, and by some, to be the new Bali because of its pristine natural and cultural environment. The flight takes about eleven hours."

Adam lifted his head off his chin and sat up arrow straight. "Sam, tell your mom she's outdone herself, but flying over the water for eleven hours scares the crap out of me! "

"What difference does it make if it's over water or land, Adam? If you come down from thirty thousand feet, it better be on a runway, or your goose is cooked either way!"

"I suppose you're right, Tom. As long as I can get a Creamflow or two onboard, I can probably endure the journey!" Adam said.

"What the heck is a Creamflow, Adam? A milkshake?"

"Piss off, Tom! Of course it's not a bloody milkshake. It's beer. Ale, actually, and great ale at that! Haven't you ever heard of Worthingtons? Smooth as silk, and it'll knock you on your ass. Just what the doctor ordered for a long plane ride over the ocean!" And then he said, "The first to the mill grinds. When we leavin' Sam?"

"That's the spirit!" Samantha said with a big smile. "We leave in two days, so you don't have a lot of time to get your stuff together. Just one thing, though. The plane can't handle boards, but they have them on the island. So, all you need to do is plan on seven days in paradise and pack accordingly.

Samantha looked at her watch and stood up. "Hey, I gotta run. Pick you up in the Rover Tuesday morning at ten a.m. sharp! Deal?"

"Deal!" both answered with one voice.

# CHAPTER TWO

Julia Witherspoon stood hunched over old banker's boxes which were strewn across a century-old library table in the dank and dark basement of the Lucarana Mining Company. For weeks she had been systematically working her way through the archive of company records that had been stored pre-digital age, and which no one ever ventured down to the company dungeon to look at anymore. This was not a random search. Rather, she was looking for something very specific, and something she believed rightfully belonged to her.

Julia was the daughter of the company's first and only rock-star geologist, the man who almost single-handedly put a tiny Canadian prospecting company on the map as a respected player in the international diamond mining business. He was as close to a real-life Indiana Jones character as one could imagine, and his daughter Julia was driven to follow in his footsteps. What she needed however, was to find out where, exactly, those footsteps had trodden. That was why, when she dug down through yet another stack of musty trade periodicals and saw the crusty brown leather book bearing a handwritten "Ross Witherspoon" on the cover, she said, "Got It!" and slapped her hand down hard on the old oak table.

What she had been looking for and which was now being tucked discretely into the back of her tight jeans, was her father's diary. It was leather bound and ancient-looking due to where it had been and how it had been handled, even though it was no more than fifty years old. But none of that mattered to Julia Witherspoon. All she cared about was where he had traveled after the big discovery in the Northwest Territory gave him the wherewithal to explore anywhere in the world he wished to go. Although he never made another find like the three kimberlite tubes he'd found at Lookout Lake, he used to tell her stories as a little girl of a mountain of diamonds he had discovered in the South Pacific on a remote island. Her father in general, and that story in particular, had fueled her thirst to prove herself in what was a very male world of gemstone exploration. When he retired, all his records were considered company property and were either stored or disposed of since he apparently had found nothing to justify all the travel expenses the company had underwritten. Although long since deceased, he had enthralled his young daughter with stories, and told her that he kept a detailed personal journal of his travels. Her hope that it might have been saved as a historical item was just realized.

"You're coming home with me, Dad. Back where you belong!"

She trudged up the stairs and through the heavy steel

door. The security guard was a rotund, middle-aged man who sat in a comfy chair surrounded by monitors behind a glass wall.

"Find anything, Julia?" he asked.

Julia smirked as she said, "No, John, I'm afraid not. I'm not going to give up on it, but I think I may take a break for a while. It gets discouraging, you know."

"I know, honey. Just come back when you get your spirits back up. You'll find it!"

She cringed at being called honey, but said sweetly, "I hope so, John. Bye for now."

Julia Witherspoon could hardly contain herself as she walked through the monumental brass and glass front door which John had just buzzed open. Outside, she breathed the fresh air and wondered what the air her father had inhaled smelled like at the diamond mountain. Jungle air. Rich and humid, and full of life. Not the piercing, bitterly cold air of the Canadian Northwest where she had been stationed by the company as she was climbing the corporate ladder.

"Well, now they can all go frig themselves," she thought to herself, remembering the constant humiliation that being the only woman on a Canadian field team inevitably imposed. Julia Witherspoon was attractive, thirty-four years old, and not afraid to use her many charms to get what she wanted. And what she wanted, above all else, was success. Not just the financial security that a major discovery would convey, but validation that she was indeed worthy to be Ross Witherspoon's daughter. To that end, nothing was going to stand in her way. Absolutely nothing.

# CHAPTER THREE

The red Evoque pulled up gracefully to the curb outside the rather drab brick building housing Adam's basement apartment. His cell phone lit up, and he saw Samantha's text, "Let's roll," so he slung a duffle bag over his shoulder and picked up a sleek dark blue hard-shell case. A quick look over his shoulder, and he was out the door. After stowing his gear in the back of the Range Rover, he pulled the front passenger door open and looked at Samantha. "Hi, Sam. You look great this morning!" he said with a broad smile breaking across his usually tightly controlled features.

"Why, thank you, Adam! I feel great too. I think this is the beginning of a big adventure for all of us, and I'm so excited!" Sam said with a giggle. Despite seeming a bit little-girlish in her demeanor, which was very endearing to everyone who knew her, Samantha Lewis was a brilliant scientist and could be as serious as a heart attack for weeks on end doing gene sequencing. However, when she was off duty, she played without dragging the lab with her, and if you didn't know better, one might assume her to be an excellent waitress in an upmarket fine dining restaurant. Affable and attractive, her effusive personality had lured many a student and professor to underestimate her.

"That's an interesting-looking case, Adam. It looks like it holds more than just socks and shorts. What's up with it?"

Adam debated for a moment whether to share the full extent of his multi-functional case, but in the end, decided candor would serve everyone best. Besides, they'd know what he was up to soon enough.

"I put together a small test lab to take a look at the level of microplastic contamination in Mala. Nothing fancy, but it will be able to give me some great data from a place I doubt has been studied much by the scientific community."

"You've got to bring me up to speed with this whole micro-plastic research you've been doing. I had no idea it was such a big deal to someone studying evolutionary biology. Speaking of Tom, here we are. Let's see if he's ready to catch his plane."

"I doubt it, just not in his DNA, but he more than makes up for it once he gets going on something, he doesn't let go. Remember last year when he got in that argument with the undergrad at the pub about global warming caused by cow farts? What a hoot. And it almost got him in the jam jar too. That guy was a bit into his beer."

"Yes, and as I recall, he managed to squeeze out a couple of his own right on cue just to make his point. It was hysterical."

"Speaking of the bloke, here he comes now!" Adam

pointed over to the alley where Tom was striding away from the door he had just locked.

"Adam, quick, wind down the window! Hey Tom, aren't you missing something? If you think you're going to the beach for seven days and not bringing your Martin, you've got another thought coming. Now get your ass back in there and get it!"

Tom said, "Wasn't sure we'd have the room for it."

"Are you kidding?"

"I'm glad it's okay!" he said as he turned to go back and get his forty-year-old Martin 000-28 guitar that he loved so dearly and played so well.

When everything was loaded in the back of the car, Samantha headed the Rover down Interstate 880 towards OAK. Adam turned back towards Tom and said, "I never saw anything like this coming, eh, Tom? This should be the adventure of a lifetime, absolutely brilliant!"

Tom, who was still getting to know Adam said, "Adam, for a while now I've had the strong sense that something remarkable was going to happen, and when Sam first sprung her surprise on us, I knew immediately that this was what I had been anticipating."

"Have you been having visions again, Tom?" Samantha asked.

Tom said, "Not visions this time, Sam, just a deep feeling, almost like a knowing. Knowing that something is coming, but not knowing what exactly."

"What were the visions about, Tom?" Adam was starting to become intrigued with his new friend, but the spell was broken by Sam saying, "Okay, guys, we'll have to pick this up later, we're at OAK, and it won't be long till we're in the air."

After parking in a long-term lot, they caught a small shuttle that drove them right out to the tarmac between two hangers. The Citation X+ was sitting on the runway looking for all the world like it was the fastest private jet in the world. Which it was. Waiting for them at the bottom of the stairs was the co-pilot, Denny Johnson, dressed sharply in a dark blue uniform. He stowed their gear and welcomed them aboard graciously. They entered the cabin and settled into comfortable facing recliner seats.

The intercom came on, and a voice said, "This is your Captain, Ben Wilde. We've just completed the pre-flight check on our trusty Garmin G-five thousand and will be ready for departure in a few minutes."

The low whine signaled that the flight was about to begin as the engines quickly came to life with an ever-increasing pitch. Denny made sure everyone was buckled in properly and then slipped back into the cockpit as Captain Wilde eased the jet forward to his take-off position on the runway, just one back. As the big Rolls engines wound up to full thrust, off they went with a palpable feeling of G-force in rapid acceleration. As the nose went skyward and the gear went up, the awesome power of the engines could be appreciated. With an initial climb rate of 3500 feet per minute at a speed of 300 knots, they just kept on climbing and climbing. Finally, after little more than twenty-five minutes, they leveled off at an astonishing 51,000 feet, much higher than commercial aircraft fly. High enough to make out the curvature of the earth.

"Wow!" said Adam. "That's enough to change my mind about flying! One minute we're on the ground, and the next, we're in a fighter jet going straight up! What a ride!"

"You can say that again," Tom said, "I wouldn't have believed how much that raw power can be felt to your core. Very cool!"

"See, boys, I told you Lib does things right!" Samantha said. "I've ridden in her a few times, and believe me, it never gets old!"

Tom asked, "So, Sam, do we fly straight to Malaita?"

"Nope, too far, not enough legs to make it in one go," replied Samantha. "So, we're heading for Hawaii where we'll refuel, grab dinner and stretch our legs. Then it's off to the Solomons. Since this bird flies so fast, pretty near Mach One, we can probably get to Honolulu in a little over four hours. The second leg to Honiara will be a bit longer, about six hours, but we'll probably all be sacked out."

After Samantha raided the galley for beer and snacks, they settled in for the first leg of the journey, while the drone of the engines lulled them into a gentle peace. Adam decided to break the ice in the conversation by taking up the question he had asked Tom right before they had arrived at the airport.

"Tom, Sam mentioned you had visions, and you were describing what they were like a while ago. I've always been interested in psychic phenomena, let's say, although nothing strange ever happens to me. If it's not too personal, could you share a little about what you see or experience?"

Tom sat silent for a minute or so. Finally, he looked up and took a deep breath. "Well, Adam," he began, "it's been a mixture of things that I've finally reconciled enough to call gifts. I've told Sam a little about it over the last year or so, but it's hard to describe, really. See, I used to train horses for this lady back in Florida, and I taught her and her daughter how to ride quarter horses."

Adam said, "Me, I was never into horses, although I did enjoy seeing the wild ones back home up to their necks out in the bay at high tide."

"What I did was to find the exact right horse to fit with the personality of each rider."

Adam shot Tom a thoughtful look and asked, "How were you able to know which horse to connect with which rider, Tom?"

Tom popped a cracker in his mouth and washed it down with a swig of water before replying in a low voice, "I asked them, and they told me."

Samantha, who had remained quiet all this time, now looked Adam right in the eyes and said, "Tom is what has become known as an animal communicator, Adam. It's a rather remarkable gift and one which took me, personally, quite a bit of convincing to accept."

Adam remained silent. Finally, he said, "So you're telling me that you can have a conversation with a horse, Tom?"

Another silence hung directly below the smooth vibration of the two Rolls Royce turbines that was a felt thing more than a heard thing. Again, Tom, in a thoughtful low voice, said to Adam, "Not just horses, Adam. I can communicate with dogs, cats, birds, and many others. It's just that I first realized what was going on in Susan Belter's stable where I worked. The first time I ever heard a non-human voice inside my head was from Red Bar, a gentle quarter horse mare, which was Susan's favorite."

Adam sat, elbows on knees, leaning in the seat,

enthralled. "What did the horse, I mean Red Bar, say to you, Tom?"

Tom looked up at Adam and said slowly, "She told me that she loved Susan and was sorry she was in so much pain since Peter, her husband, had passed away. Red Bar asked me to tell her that she will be able to move forward in life because she is strong, and that love will come to her again." Tom shuffled a bit in his seat and then said, "So I asked Red Bar, inside my mind, how could I possibly expect Susan to believe that it was you that told me to give her this message? She'll probably think I am trying to patronize her in some weird way." Red Bar's voice came back to me, '"Tell her I said that when I was just born, still wet and feeble as a new foal is, she sat in the hay and held me. She told me that I have the most beautiful eyes in the world and that she would love me like her own daughter. Tell her that she said that out loud."

Tom looked out the window. "I have always thought of that conversation as an awakening in my life, or maybe more like the beginning of a new direction that I knew would change everything."

"And so did you tell Susan what Red Bar asked you to say to her?"

"Not right away. It was about a month later, and we were having a snack before dinner after cleaning the stalls and finishing chores for the day. She was pouring us a glass of wine and said that this had always been one of her favorite times of day that she enjoyed with Peter, just relaxing on the porch, and looking out at the fields and the barn. But she said it in a pained, and I can only say a defeated-sounding way. Sad really. So, I took that moment to give her Red Bar's message."

"Did she think you were making it all up, or did it freak her out?"

"At first, she said nothing, just stared into her glass of wine and kept swirling it around. After a minute or two, she looked up, and her eyes were a bit moist. She stood up and moved to the porch rail and told me over her shoulder that almost every night, late after everyone was in bed, she used to go into the barn and walk down between the stalls and ask out loud, "What am I supposed to do now, what am I supposed to do?" She would walk down one side and back up the other, patting her horses, ending with Red Bar, who would always be there without fail, waiting for her. She said she would stop and put her head alongside Red Bar's, sometimes until she almost fell asleep on her feet. Then she'd head back to the house and back to bed and try to get through another day."

" I guess Red Bar helped her with her grieving process."

"What she didn't realize was how much that horse knew what she was going through. There was so much she wanted to say to Susan."

"What got you started training horses?"

Tom said, "I've been around horses ever since I was a kid. My sister and I used to go to Four-H events and then county fairs showing our horse Mack. It was the one thing my dad did growing up that kept me off the streets after school since I wasn't really into sports, and later I got a job at the Belter place that was about a mile down the road from us.

Adam asked, "So how did you first know the horse was talking to you? Was it in English or pictures or what? That is, if you don't mind me asking."

"No, I don't mind, and yes, it was in English, but if I happened to be German, I think it would have been in German. I can't count the number of times I have been in that horse's stall cleaning or grooming and just doing all the stuff that goes with looking after horses. But that time was different. I was really in a different space emotionally, you might say, and I just looked Red Bar right in the eyes and quietly asked her, what will we do with Susan? Then, I just sort of stepped aside inside my mind. That's the only way I can say it. I wasn't into meditation then, but I think I must have entered a different state, similar to what a good meditation is like now, deeply relaxed, and long spaces between thoughts. It was in one of those long spaces that I heard Red Bar for the first time."

Samantha, who had been taking all this in, finally leaned forward and said, "You know Tom, I went to the Catholic church with Mom every week growing up, and we were a Christian home, I guess you could say. The big white church overlooking the harbor was much more than just a pretty postcard or a place to bless the fleet. But what gets me going with your story, and believe me, I don't doubt you a bit, is how does it fit into what we've been told by our church priests, pastors, and ministers all our lives?"

Adam added, "I don't go to church at all anymore. I got so sick of being dragged to that chapel by my mum, that even the smell of frankincense makes me ill! I always figured we're born, we live, and we die. And that's it. But this story throws a real curveball at me. Tell me, Tom, what do you think of all this?"

Tom thought for a moment and then said, "When you look at a horse or a dog, Adam, what do you see?"

"I see a horse or a dog," Adam said. "Maybe young or old, black or brown, but an animal we call a horse or a dog. What else would I see?"

"That's exactly the point. When most people look at a horse, they mentally say to themselves, in a conversation inside their head, 'this is a horse,' and then they define through their mental construct what that means. They limit their ability to experience anything other than what that mental construct tells them a dog, or a horse, is."

"Well, what else can it be other than a dog or horse?" Samantha asked.

"Energy," Tom replied, "or more to the point, consciousness. Conscious energy, perhaps you could say spiritual energy, expressing itself as 'dog' or 'horse' but which is individualized, self-aware, and able to communicate. If only we, as humans, could stop pigeon-holing everything we perceive into these mental constructions, a whole new world of direct experience might open up to us. Including us being able to communicate on non-verbal levels with animals."

"I've come to understand that everything—and I mean everything—is made up of conscious energy. It is what the world is made of, only slowed down to a level of vibration that we call matter. But it is energy, nonetheless, and that energy is in all of us. You, me, dog, horse, flowers and, yes, even trees and stones. All made from one substance, conscious energy, which expresses itself in infinitely creative ways."

Now Adam was slow to gather his thoughts, but said, "What you're saying is something akin to the Gaia theory."

Sam asked, "What's that? I've never heard of it."

Adam said, "If I recall, it postulates that living

organisms interact with their inorganic surroundings in a synergistic and self-regulating way. This creates a complex system that maintains and perpetuates the conditions for life on Earth. I now realize it was this theory, in part, that drew me to the study of Earth system science, although I wouldn't have made the connection then. It's just that I felt that the planet was itself a living organism and that it was, how shall I say, suffering and in pain from the many abuse's we humans have been inflicting on it. But never have we, or I should say I, been able to hear another life form communicate what their experience has been due to our thoughtlessness."

Tom added, "The sad thing is that the conversation is all around us, we just can't hear it."

Adam asked, "So do all animals talk all the time? It must be crazy noisy to have a gift like that."

"No, Adam, it requires 'intention' to hear and communicate, and not all species can do it anyway. From what I can tell, it requires individualized consciousness within an animal as opposed to group or species consciousness."

"So, like ants can't communicate the way dogs can?'

"Exactly. They seem to have a 'hive' or collective sense of self rather than an individualized consciousness. In fact, for example, not all birds can be engaged, but some can. I think, at the end of the day, it's not that different in some ways from people. Not everyone has evolved to the same level of consciousness within the human species, and not everyone wants to engage in conversation outside their comfort zone or with folks they don't know or trust. Same thing with animals."

Adam said, "It would be fascinating to kind of get an

opinion poll, so to speak, from animals of all kinds as to how they feel their environment is changing."

Tom said, "From what I sense, you'd get an earful and a pretty consistent impression that we have not been the best stewards of our world. No surprise there, I suppose."

Adam said, "I suppose not. Certainly, the issue of global warming has captured the attention of the scientific world, and rightfully so, but it's a crowded space at this point. It's just that it's not the only environmental problem we face. There are others that I believe we need to be more focused on, but global warming tends to suck all the oxygen out of the room. No pun intended!"

Tom answered, "One, which I know you will say, is the proliferation of plastics throughout our environment, and it absolutely disgusts me also. Did you know that more than one point five million pounds of plastic is dumped into the ocean every hour?"

"Yeah mate, I do, and I've lugged my share out. Even though there are about two hundred and seventy million tons of that crap floating on the surface, in some ways, what's even scarier is the amount of microplastic fibers that sink to the bottom. The number is staggering, around four billion fibers per square kilometer of deep ocean. That's why I've got that case back there."

"I know, it's everywhere," Tom said, shaking his head. "For me, what is also truly terrifying is the incredible loss of insect life going on around the planet, and as a result, also the die-off of birds. I used to wake up to the sound of birds singing every morning in Florida, but now when I'm back there, the silence is noticeable and disturbing."

"You're right, Tom, plastics are my primary focus in studies, but between pesticides and micro-radiation from cell phones and satellites, insects all over the planet are dying off at an incredible rate. We all know that bees, which pollinate the flowers that provide fruits and vegetables for us, are in trouble, but what about the millions of other species that are going extinct? We have no idea how everything is interconnected, only that it is, and that is very bloody disturbing."

Samantha, who had been taking all this in, looked up to see Denny signal to her that they would be starting their descent into Honolulu soon and to begin to buckle up.

"Okay, boys," she said, "we can take this up again later, but we'll be on the ground before you know it. I can't wait to stretch my legs. Let's get the seatbelts on 'cause we're heading down soon."

# CHAPTER FOUR

Julia Witherspoon was annoyed, which was common for her, although she never bothered or even cared to understand why that was. She had pored over her father's diary for two days and still couldn't uncover where in the hell her father had been when he discovered the lava tube and the diamonds it contained. It was driving her mad.

"Goddammit, Dad, why did you write this freaking thing if you weren't going to say where you went? Idiot!"

And then there was the issue of the apes, or at least Julia assumed they were apes because what else could they be? Her father referenced very large and hairy creatures which confronted him and finally drove him off the mountain. There was something in her father's description of that first encounter that intrigued her, but she didn't know what. Irritated, she read that section of the diary yet again.

"And there, standing before me, were three of them. They were much taller than a man, and more robust in muscle. I quickly abolished the thought of my sidearm, with the realization that even if I were to kill one, I would surely perish at the hands of the other two. Or perhaps endure a fate much worse. So, I raised both hands in a display of peace, and what happened next, I still cannot believe. As my native Solwota guide stood frozen in fear, the leader of the three beasts spoke to me in perfect English."

"We are Ramo. Our home this is. Luti Mikode, I am. What here do you seek?"

I was shocked and speechless. But I summoned my wits and replied, "I seek white stones, like this." I pointed to the large diamond ring I had made to celebrate the Lookout Lake discovery and held it up to sparkle in the sun.

The beast was impassive and glanced to his right at his comrade. What happened next, I still cannot explain, but as I watched him closely, he said, glancing at my ring, "White stones are not here. This place, Ramo, it is. Leave, or this place buried you will be, Ross." Then, he picked up a boulder the size of a small refrigerator and flung it down the mountain, one hundred yards at least. I heard it crash through the forest as it toppled small trees. "Go. Return not!"

"I was shocked. Not just because the beast, impossibly, knew my name, but because his lips never moved as he spoke the words. They just flowed into my mind, but not through my ears. It was terrifying, and I left."

Julia sat back in her leather chair and laid the diary on her lap, annoyed. What the hell was she missing, other than the fact that her father must have had jungle fever and was a bit delusional? After all, large apes don't speak English and aren't telepathic, so obviously Dad was a bit touched upstairs. But the fact that they seemed to know what the white stones were, even as they denied their existence on the island, maybe that was it. No, that is interesting, but it doesn't get me any closer to where the hell he was. Then a light went off. She had already been on her computer and searched for any reference to the word Ramo, having found nothing. But what about Solwota? Dad had said, "my native Solwota guide." Why the hell didn't I pick up on that before?

Excited, Julia turned on her laptop and went to the kitchen to add ice and Jack Daniels to her glass. When the computer finished booting up, she searched Google for the phrase "Solwota people," and there it was. Numerous references to the "salt water" people of the Solomon Islands popped up, and, in particular, one island, called Malaita. She leaned back in her chair smugly, her annoyance having faded. That's it. Now how do I get there? She thought to herself. I can't believe Dad was scared off by that ape called Mikode. He faced plenty of grizzlies in his day, but I guess that it's a good thing because the white stones are there. I can feel it. But it will be me that shows them to the world, not him. A thin smile stretched across her face as, satisfied, she looked at air routes to the Solomon Islands.

# CHAPTER FIVE

The Citation gently touched down at HNL and headed for the commuter terminal, where they could relax as the plane was being refueled. Once they came to a stop and the shutdown process was complete, Captain Wilde informed them that they had two hours to stretch their legs and suggested the Mahalo Bar as a great place to grab a sandwich and a beer or coffee. The flight steps were lowered, and they were on their way.

"It seems weird walking into an airport through the doors rather than on a Jetway."

"I'll tell you, Adam, I've only flown with Mom on the jet a half dozen times, but avoiding the crowds, the sneezing and crying babies? It's worth it!"

Adam said, "Yeah, but if you had to pay for it yourself, you'd get over it in a hurry!"

As the Mahalo came into view, Tom decided it would be a good idea to hit the head and told the other two he'd be right along. Just before he turned into the hall leading to the restroom, he glanced to his left and noticed an unusual-looking man sitting on a bench, who seemed to be staring intently and directly at him. Tom crossed the aisle and stood just inside the entrance to a magazine stand. He stood behind a rack to better observe the strange fellow. He seemed ageless, yet rugged. His bronze tattooed skin had been burnished by the sun but was devoid of sags and wrinkles. A sense of power emanated from him that drew Tom closer. As he watched him, the man seemed to sit almost as if in a trance, looking forward, which gave Tom the chance to observe him and the tattoos closely. He wondered if he should make contact with him, but he was too nervous to do so. He could feel subtle vibrations coming from him, that reminded him of how he felt as he began communication with animals. His tattoos were of birds and fish, or more accurately, sharks, which were on each side of his neck, and they formed a very elaborate headband across his forehead. Tom decided that before he summoned the courage to introduce himself, he had better complete the visit to the restroom. After he downloaded his discomfort where it needed to go, he walked towards where the strange man had been, but he was gone.

Completely gone.

It couldn't have been more than a minute, and Tom could look way down each corridor to the many gates beyond, but no one who even remotely looked like that enigmatic fellow could be seen.

Tom, who was much more attuned to the subtle ways that the universe communicates information, took the episode as a message, the meaning of which would be revealed when the time was full, and the need was apparent.

It would not take long.

# CHAPTER SIX

"Alex, I found it!" Julia Witherspoon said in an excited but controlled voice.

"You found what, Julia?"

"My father's journal, you moron, the one I told you about last time at the office party. Don't you remember? I've been hunting for it for over a month, and now I have it!"

Alex Taylor was the CFO of Lucarana Diamond Company, and was almost the exact opposite of Julia Witherspoon, which served her purpose well indeed. Having received his B.A. in Mining Engineering at McGill University, he thought it might be helpful to have a second degree in Mine Finance. After all, he didn't relish being underground or even out in the cold, so now he sat at his desk in Toronto and listened with vague interest to what Julia was saying. His mind was drifting off to what occurred after the office party that Julia had just mentioned, so when she said loudly, "Didn't you hear what I just said, Alex?" he snapped out of his reverie, and left the memories of that steamy night behind.

"Of course, I heard you, Julia. What do you plan on doing with it? I'm sure that McGill would love to have it for their mining museum. After all, your dad was one of their brightest stars."

This statement had the effect of annoying Julia even more. "I know who my father was, and I'm not giving a damn thing to that school!" She didn't mention that McGill was her first choice for college, but she didn't get in. "What I'm going to do with it is none of the company's business, but what it will do for me sure as hell is!"

"What do you mean by that?"

Julia paused before answering, her mind racing. "Why don't we meet later for dinner, and I'll show you what I found? After all, it's been over a month since we've seen each other."

"I have a previous engagement, Julia, but for you, I'm sure I can reschedule it."

"That would be a good thing, Alex. For the company and for you!"

They met at Richmond Station, a cozy neighborhood restaurant known for great food and hefty prices. Alex chose it because he was sure that Julia couldn't afford to experience it on what he knew she made, and he was relishing the thought of being rewarded for his generosity later in the evening. He sat at the quiet table he had reserved which gave a great view out the giant circular window that was a centerpiece to the restaurant's décor. He waited for her with growing impatience. She was almost fifteen minutes late already, but when she finally strode in, he almost swallowed his sip of wine down the wrong way. She was stunning! Her auburn hair hung just below her shoulders on a white lacy top that was sheer enough to pique the imagination, but discreet enough for fine dining. The rest of her curves were tightly wrapped in designer jeans, supported by three-inch heels, creating a very sexy, but elegant and casual look.

"Julia, you look ravishing!" he said as he stood to hold her chair. "I love your outfit!"

"Oh, it's nothing, but thanks," she said, making sure to sit so that he could see through the sheer side of her blouse. "I don't get to places like this often. I'm glad I look okay."

"You look much better than okay, dear. Every man in the room was gawking when you walked in."

Julia winced at the word dear but didn't say anything. She knew it was better to keep a pet fed, but still hungry, than to starve it. Control was a subtle thing, and she was a master.

"Now then, shall I order you a glass of wine?" Alex asked.

"No thanks. I'll have Jack Daniels on ice with a twist."

"As you wish. I'll stick to my wine though."

They made idle talk about the state of the diamond business, international supply, and rumors of new deposits. After his meal of trout almondine, and her ribeye steak were finished, he remembered what the occasion for their dinner meeting was. He thought that before getting her back to his place for a nightcap, he should indulge her with a question about Ross Witherspoon's journal, just to get it out of the way.

"So, Julia, you mentioned that you were looking for

your father's diary and that you finally found it. Where was it, and what was so important about it?"

The last thing Julia Witherspoon was about to tell the CFO of Lucarana Diamond Company, was that she found the diary twenty-eight floors beneath the desk of Alex Taylor. But what she would tell him is what it revealed.

"Oh, it was in an old trunk of Dad's in a small storage unit where I still keep his stuff, although I don't know why I do. It was wrapped up and I must have missed it last time I looked."

"I see. And what did you find in it that was so exciting? Do you have it with you?" he asked.

"Yeah, it's right here," she said, pulling it out of the clutch purse that barely held it.

She placed it on the table in front of Alex. He looked closely at it and remarked, "This really does look like it should be in a museum, Julia. May I look in it?"

"Sure, just be careful how you handle it."

"I will, don't worry," he said as he picked up the chocolate brown leather book. "Really cool that it says Ross Witherspoon on the cover in his writing. He really put Lucarana on the map. This should be in a glass case in the executive conference room!"

"The only case that will be in is on my bookcase in my apartment, so don't go getting any ideas, Alex!"

"Oh, I just meant it has historical interest, that's all."

Julia smirked slightly as she said, "It has more than just historical interest, Alex."

"Oh? Why is that?"

"When I was a little girl, my father told me stories of where he traveled after the Lookout Lake find, and—"

Alex cut her off, "And as I recall, that wasn't much.

Which is why one of my predecessors pulled the plug on him."

"Let me have the book, Alex."

He slid the journal to the daughter of the man who wrote it, and she immediately opened it to a page she had nearly memorized. She read it aloud.

"As I climbed higher, I was rewarded by a most remarkable sight. The jungle gave way to a view of the sea in a great flat clearing, that was completely unexpected. Gazing down, I could make out villages perched on stilts as if seen from an aircraft. Then, as I turned to resume the climb, something caught my eye on the side of the steep mountain in front of me. High up, perhaps two hundred feet above, something was reflecting the sunlight in a dazzling reflection. I moved to my right and then back to my left. It was like a mirror, only clearer and more intense. It could be only one thing. I knew I had found the mountain of diamonds that the rumors told of. Having no way to make the ascent, and my guide almost faint with fear seeing the strange relics strewn around, I decided to leave. But I would be back fully prepared!!!!!"

"He put five large exclamation marks after that last word," Julia said.

"But that reflection could be anything. You're just assuming it was a diamond. What's the big deal?"

"The big deal was that my father, as you just pointed out, was a hero to this company, and he knew what the frig he was looking for, and where to find it. Not like some I know who sit behind desks and push pencils around. If he had reason to believe that the mountain was loaded with diamonds, then it probably was."

"So why didn't he go back and get them? Lord knows money would have been no object back then," Alex asked.

"He did, but he was run off."

"Run off? From a diamond mountain? That doesn't sound like the Ross Witherspoon I've read about!"

"Well, listen to this: 'The giants were nearly nine feet in height. They did not have the appearance, nor the demeanor of apes, although they were covered in long hair, except for around the face and hands. It was obvious that they were intelligent, but when one spoke to me in English, I very nearly fainted. If I had not grabbed my guide by his hair, I would surely have had a difficult time finding my way back as he was terrified.'"

"Giants? You've got to be kidding."

"I'm deadly serious, Alex, when I say that I'm going there, giants or no giants. And you're the one who's going to get me there, capiche?"

"I think we need to discuss this over a nightcap. My place is only two blocks away, shall we?"

"I thought you'd never ask." Julia stood after placing her father's journal back in her purse.

# CHAPTER SEVEN

The take-off from HNL was every bit as impressive as that from Oakland had been, and as Samantha had said, "You never get tired of the rush!" The next leg of the journey would take just over six hours, and the trio settled in for the flight. Adam sat next to Samantha with Tom across from them. The sun had been settling deeply down the horizon, and the view from fifty thousand feet was amazing.

"Look at how those colors fade from a deep orange at the edge of the earth to violet and then black as you look up!" Samantha exclaimed, "You never get tired of this!"

"Brilliant! And the stars are starting to appear twinkling right above! How cool is that!" Adam was excited by the show Mother Nature was putting on, one which few people would see given the altitude and the direction of flight.

Adam and Samantha continued to marvel at the sunset while Tom began to gently strum his guitar. He was not playing anything recognizable, yet it sounded as if it should be.

"Tom, that's a cool sound, and you're not even using your left hand," Adam said as Tom gently finger-picked the strings in various patterns.

"Yeah, it's called open-tuning, and I've been playing around with it for a year or so. It's different than playing in standard tuning. I enjoy just creating my own melodies kind of free-form, as opposed to playing songs and singing along."

Tom formed a position with his left hand and began to fingerpick strings with his right. He slid his left hand up and down the fingerboard keeping the same frets covered, and soon a very lively jig was underway punctuated with hammered-on bass notes and connecting runs on the higher strings, often returning to just strumming the open strings to play the underlying anchor chord. He continued for perhaps ten minutes, allowing the tempo to alternate and changing the mood of the music from upbeat and lively to pensive and subdued. Finally, he returned to the theme he began with, ending by strumming the harmonics on the frets producing a distinctive conclusion to the piece. It was obvious, by the complete silence that hung in the air that his friends were impressed.

"Wow," said Samantha," that is so different than what I've ever heard you play, but it is captivating!"

"Thanks, Sam! I still enjoy singing and playing the songs I grew up listening to, but I've been finding that I can zone out and almost become part of the music when I don't have to think of words and notes to sing. A lot of artists have recorded records you would know this way. For example, many of Joni Mitchel's songs were played in what are called open tunings. Also, many early blues masters used the same technique, and any time you see someone playing with a metal or glass tube on their finger, they're probably using an open tuning. I just find it fun. I'm glad you enjoyed it!"

Tom returned his guitar to the case, sat down in the lounger, and took a sip of his wine, gazing into the glass as he swirled it. Then he said, "You know, back at the terminal, I had a funny experience. It's probably nothing, but I can't stop thinking about it."

"What happened, Tom?" Samantha asked.

"Well, you guys were just a few steps ahead of me before I went into the restroom. Did either of you happen to notice a Hawaiian-looking older man? Shorts and sandals with tattoos on his neck and forehead?"

"I didn't. Did you, Adam?"

"Nope, not me. I was just trying not to bump into anyone in the crowd. Did he seem threatening or something?"

"No, not at all. It's just that he seemed interested in me and somehow let me know that he was there. Very present and very aware."

"Aware of what, Tom?"

"I don't know, just aware. Aware of his surroundings. Aware of his place. I don't know how to put it into words. He had a powerful presence. Neither of you saw him?"

"I didn't either," Samantha said.

"He stuck out like a sore thumb. I'm surprised."

"From how you described him, I'm sure I would have remembered."

"It's probably nothing. It's been a long day, and this wine is making me sleepy."

"Me too," said Samantha, "We'll be landing in

Honiara before you know it. Probably best we all get as much rest as we can."

Adam agreed, "Right, same here. I can barely keep my eyes open."

With the cabin lights dimmed, the jet droned on with just the slightest of vibrations on a beautiful night surrounded by twinkling stars.

# CHAPTER EIGHT

Julia flew from Honiara International Airport on Guadalcanal, where she had landed late the previous afternoon, to Auki Gwaunaru'u Airport. It was about twelve miles north of Auki, the capital of Malaita Province. She really had no idea what to expect from this remote place, but she knew she wasn't far from the mountains that ran down the island's spine, and that was a starting point. Staying at the Auki Lodge near the center of town and not far from the wharves, she decided to explore a bit and headed down towards the shore to look for a bar where she hoped she might pick up some information. For the capital of a province, the place was far from a comfortable tourist resort and was depressing to her already. She noticed some tables and outside seating at a place called Dawnbreaker, that had a nice view of the dock and the water, so she wandered over and sat down.

"Hello, miss, wat can I git for ya?" a young man with an indeterminate accent asked politely.

"I'd like Jack Daniels on ice with a twist of lemon please," she replied.

"Who is Jack Daniels, miss? Never heard of the chap." The confused waiter was embarrassed.

A man at the next table answered for the young lad, "That's not a who, Tommy, that's a drink. One you won't find on this island, miss, trust me on that."

"Oh, I see. Well then, what kind of whiskey do you have?"

"We have very good whiskey, miss, very good. I bring you some."

"Don't forget the lemon, ok?"

The man across from Julia chuckled and said, "This should be good."

When he returned, the young man placed a tall glass with ice and dark viscous liquid on the table, and then put a whole lemon down next to it. "There, miss, you like, I know. Food for you? I come back," he said, placing a handwritten page of computer paper on the table which described the cafés offerings.

Unfazed, Julia withdrew a knife her father had given her, one that may well have been in this very town over fifty years ago. She flicked open the blade with one hand and sliced the lemon deftly, squeezing a little juice into her glass. Picking it up, she belted back a large swig.

The stranger said, "Oops."

The fire that was lit in her mouth traveled down her throat and boiled in her gut. She looked frantically for the waiter or some water but found neither. Almost in a panic, thinking she had been poisoned, she was grateful when the stranger next to her said, "Have a sip of Foster's mate, help put out the fire it will." Julia nodded and reached for the mug, downing the entire contents. When at last she knew she would survive, she said, "Thank you. The next one's on me. What the hell was that shit anyway?"

"I should'a warned ya, miss. I'm not sure what it is exactly, but they keep it mostly for Friday nights when the boys come in from fishing all week. It has to be at least one hundred and sixty proof. I tried it once, just one sip, but that was enough to cure me. I'll stick to me Foster's thank you very much! By the way, my name's Tony" he said extending his hand. "What brings a beaut like you to a place like this?"

Julia shook his hand and introduced herself, careful not to answer his question. "Oh, I had some vacation time coming and wanted to do some traveling. I wanted somewhere remote to visit instead of the usual tourist traps, and I read about these islands on the web. They called them the land that time forgot if I recall. I don't know about time, but it sure looks like a lot was forgotten around here. Like Gentleman Jack!"

"Yeah, there isn't much here other than hard scrabble livin' and good waves. The surfin' is what brings 'em here," Tony said a bit wistfully.

"So, what do you do here? Is this your place?" she asked.

"Mine? Hell no. Wish it was. I work as a chef at the Mala Surf Camp over on the other side of the island, although I guess cook would be more accurate with what I have to work with. It's about sixty-five miles down the coast and a three-hour drive in the jeep, but it's quite dardy when ya get there. We have a party comin' in from the states tomorrow, so I had to run here to stock up. It's too long to come and go, so I'll stay the night and head back tomorrow. What about you? How long are you staying here for?" he asked.

"Well, that depends. My father visited here almost sixty years ago, and I kinda wanted to retrace his steps. Thought it would be fun." She wanted to open the door just a little, and see what might come in.

"Sixty years ago? Musta been a logger or miner, right?"

"He was a geologist from Canada, a pretty famous guy back in the day. He came here to see if diamonds might be found. That usually means where volcanic activity has taken place." She was being coy, but the gamble seemed to have promise.

"Well, he came to the right place, that I can tell ya! On the other coast the mountains come up right out of the ocean and rumor has it that a lake in the middle of the island rises and falls with the tides. That tells me one thing..."

"Lava tubes!" Julia couldn't help herself cutting him off.

"Yeah, miss, lava tubes. It's the only thing that can explain it. The whole island was made by volcanoes. Thank goodness they're not active."

Julia was lost in thought for a minute before saying, "Ummm, tell you what Tony, how about I buy the chef dinner for a change? I'd like to hear more about the island and your surf camp. Sound good?"

"Dinner with you sounds great, Miss Witherspoon, and I'd be right happy to tell you about the place."

"Friends call me Julia. Where shall we meet?"

# CHAPTER NINE

After a nap and freshening up back at the Auki Lodge, Julia walked to the little restaurant that the Australian had suggested. There really weren't that many choices in such a small town as Auki, but she was pleased to see that the Coconut Crab Cafe at least appeared to be clean, and even a bit cute. It was painted in bright tropical colors reminding her of the week she spent in Key West a few years back. He was sitting at a small table on the porch and stood as she arrived saying, "Always like a lady who's on time! Nice to see you again, Miss Julia."

"Same to you, Tony! This place seems nice. Good call!"

"Well, there isn't a lot to choose from, so I usually eat here when I'm in town. They do a good job back in the kitchen, but I'd stick to the Fosters if I were you."

"No need to remind me on that score. If I don't see a bottle being opened, I'm not having anything on faith. That whiskey, or whatever the hell it was, was like drinking gasoline, so Fosters sounds great. That guacamole looks great as well," she said nodding towards a dish that had just been served to a neighboring table. "Let's have some, I'm starving!"

They enjoyed the appetizer and then, at Tony's suggestion, shared two orders of tacos, one fish and one pork. As they finished Julia asked, "So, Tony, tell me about that lake up in the mountains near your surf camp that moves with the tide. Have you been there?"

"No, miss, not me, but I know someone who has. It's in a very remote area, and it's about to be incorporated into the trust."

This last bit got Julia's attention. "What do you mean, trust? What's that all about?"

"Well, the surf camp is what brings in the bacon for those of us who work there, but the trust brings in the dollars to help preserve the island. They've got some heavy hitters who don't seem to know what to do with all their money, so they give it to Bryan and Susie, who run the trust and the camp, to help protect the island. I guess they get a tax break or something. Anyway, I think they're about to close on the purchase of a big chunk of the middle of the island which includes the lake. In fact, from the scuttlebutt I heard, the daughter of the lady who donated the money is arriving at the camp tomorrow, which is why I'm here. Don't want to run out of anything while a V.I.P. is here! That wouldn't be cracker, now, would it?"

"I suppose it wouldn't." Julia paused, and then asked, "Say, Tony, when my father was here, he mentioned in his journal that he encountered big hairy apes, which he called Ramo. I know it sounds crazy, but I was wondering if you ever heard of such creatures. I think Dad was probably overtired or maybe had a touch of malaria or something, but I'm still curious."

Tony Perkins had been around in life, and he sensed there was a deeper purpose than idle curiosity to the question. He thought for a moment before saying, "Oh that's just an old wives' tale told by the Solwata natives. They say there were giants here hundreds of years ago, but they also say they see lights in the sky that fly into the ocean. Superstitious lot they are by cracky. Actually, miss, I've seen the lights meself, just not going into the water. But giants, nahhh, nothin' like that."

There was something about the way the Aussie turned his head and looked at his beer when he said that which tipped Julia off to the possibility that maybe Tony was holding something back. If Ross Witherspoon really had been run off by giants, and they were still here somewhere, she had to find them. Finding them would mean finding diamonds. And finding diamonds would mean finding her future. This was exciting.

She decided to change the subject, "Could you suggest a place I might stay at over on your side of the island? Auki is getting old real fast. I'd love to see what really brings folks to this place in the middle of nowhere. Any extra room at your surf camp? I can afford as much as I need to spend to be comfortable. Or if there is an inn or another surfing camp, maybe they have a room available."

"Well, Miss Julia, I'm not sure if the Mathew's would want an extra guest in camp while the Yanks are here, but I can ask them for you when I get back in the morning. I've got to get the truck back early cause Bobby, their right-hand man, is picking them up in Honiara and needs the jeep. There is another surf camp, our competition, I suppose you could say, that's not too far from us 'cause the best breaks for surfin' are right there. If you can rent a vehicle, you could follow me over in the morning. If Bryan says he doesn't want another guest, it's only six or seven miles and two villages up the coast to Denny's Digs, the other surf camp. It's nowhere near as nice as Surf Mala, but beggars can't be choosers, right?"

"No, Tony, they can't. I'm fine with anything that keeps the rain and bugs out. I saw a place that rents vehicles on my way in, near the airport. I'll catch a ride over and see what they have. I noticed a couple of small pickup trucks, hopefully they're still there."

Tony agreed, "Yeah, miss, a pickup would be cracker 'cause the roads are really more like trails in places. There's nothin' paved on that side of the island."

Julia paid the bill, which considering how much they ate and drank was ridiculously small, and asked, "Tony, do they have any kind of taxi service in Auki? It seems like it was a bit of a hike from the airport to town."

"I can give you a lift, Miss Witherspoon, no worries. Wouldn't want you in back of a stranger's car by yourself now, would we?"

"I can handle myself Tony," she said, instinctively patting her right pocket where the knife her father gave her years ago rested, "but I appreciate the offer, thanks!"

"No worries, Miss Julia. Let's go."

# CHAPTER TEN

The next day, Julia followed Tony Perkins in a fifteen-year-old Mitsubishi Raider pickup truck that was at least thirty years newer than what he was driving. The sun was just beginning to paint a faint pink glow behind her, as the first leg of the trip would be west across the southernmost part of the island where hills later became impassable mountains. Then they would turn north and head down the island to the surf camp, about fifty miles away. She thought to herself how strange it was to say they were going "down" the island as they would head north. Being from Canada, she always knew that one went "down" to the states, or "down" to Florida, and that meant going south, not north. "Oh well, that won't be the only thing that'll be different than Canada," she thought to herself, remembering the whiskey that nearly took her life. "I just have to roll with whatever comes and not get side-tracked."

Tony Perkins, up ahead in the Toyota, was deep in

thought and almost driving on automatic pilot. He didn't feel like he was doing anything wrong, but he didn't have his usual mellow demeanor about him either. It was that Witherspoon woman. There was something about her that was unsettling, something that wasn't right. He knew, being the camp chef, that he was an integral part of the operation, but he had never brought a potential guest to the camp before. Especially at a time when the daughter of a major donor was arriving. And then there was that question she had asked about giants. Of all the things she might have said yesterday, that was the last thing he expected to be asked, and, having spent the last eight years learning from Grandfather, he was sure that it was no coincidence. But what did it mean? Was he doing the right thing leading her to Surf Mala? Well, what he'd told her about Denny's Digs was true, she could always crash there, and she seemed like the type that was going get to where she wanted to go with his help, or not. He would just let Bryan and Susie make the decision and then he'd be off the hook. If they didn't sense an issue, then there probably wasn't one. Also, he had to admit that she was a dardy, and seemed to enjoy his company at the café. "Who knows?" he fantasized to himself. "Maybe she'll like my cookin', and me too. That'd be cracker, it would!"

The time passed quickly, and the sun was barely blazing through the trees when he noticed a lane leading off to his left which he knew would end in a village just ahead of where Denny's Digs was located. He slowed to a stop, got out of the Toyota, and walked back twenty feet to the truck. He motioned to Julia, and she rolled down the window.

"Yeah, miss, this here's a trail that takes you down to

a Solwata village. If you keep going just past it, you'll end up at Denny's Digs, the other surf camp I told you about. Surf Mala is about eight miles down where we're heading now. Do you want to stop in and see if they have a room? Or drive back if Surf Mala isn't available? Just remember what this looks like because I won't have the jeep to guide you back."

"Thanks for checking, Tony, that was thoughtful. I've spent a lot of time in the bush, so I'm pretty sure I can find my way back. After all there aren't that many branches off this road, and it's not like it'll be getting dark anytime soon. Let's go see what your boss says. From what you described, that's where I'd like to stay, but if not, no problem."

Tony was disappointed with her answer, but there was nothing he could do now, so he got back in the jeep and continued north. He slowed at the next fork in the trail so that Julia could recognize another Solwata village and use it as a reference for the one they just passed. Then the beautiful entrance to Surf Mala came into view, with its tasteful sign and its subtly beautiful, landscaped appearance. He stuck his arm out the window and gave a thumbs up to the pickup behind him as he turned left down the lane.

Bobby Berry, the camps all-round Mr. Fixit and right-hand-man to the owners, Bryan and Susie Mathews, was sitting on the porch of the main lodge waiting for him, coffee in hand.

"Hi, mate, right on time! Get everything you needed? Get the petrol?"

Tony answered, "Yeah, Bobby, no worries. Easy trip it was."

"Who's that in the pickup truck? Did he follow you here?" Bobby asked.

"Actually, mate, it's a she, not a he. And yeah, she followed me here. Her name is Julia Witherspoon, and she's looking for a place to stay on this side of the island."

"Tony, you know who I'm about to go fetch, don't you?"

"Yeah, Bobby, I do, and I know what you're sayin' mate, but I thought that Bry and Susie can make the call. I showed her the road to Denny's if they decide it won't work. She seems nice enough and she really wanted me to ask them. I guess I bragged on the place and got me knickers in a bunch I did."

"Well mate, let's get the supplies unloaded, then you can go talk to Bryan. I've gotta get outta here real soon!"

Tony walked back to the truck and told Julia he'd just be a few minutes.

There was a noticeable tightness in his stomach as he walked in the main lodge where the office was located. They were taking a break and enjoying a glass of iced tea on the back porch, so he went out and stood awkwardly for a moment before Bryan noticed him and said, "Hey, mate, quiet as a mouse you are, I didn't hear you come in. How was the run to Auki? Get everything we need?"

"Yeah, Bry, no worries on that score, but I brought along something else as well. Or I should say someone else, a sheila."

Bryan's wife Susie said, "A girl, Tony? I'm not sure we really want any other guests right now considering the three who are arriving this afternoon."

"I know, Susie, but I told her - her name is Julia, I told Julia that I would ask, and if the answer is no, she already knows where Denny's place is, and she's cool with that. I guess I just went a bit over telling her about this place and she took a fancy to coming here she did. She's out in a rental pickup truck waiting. She'll be apples either way so no worries."

Bryan replied, "Why don't you let us have a word, Tony, and we'll come out and meet her and let you know what we decide in a minute or two."

"Works for me, Bry. Thanks!"

Tony was relieved as he walked back to the truck where Julia had gotten out to stretch her legs. "Beautiful place this is, Tony. What did they say?"

Tony said, "We'll find out in a bit. They just wanted to discuss it between themselves."

"That's understandable."

Bryan Matthews stood up and paced on the porch before speaking.

"So, what do you think, Suze? Bit of a curveball this one, eh?"

"Yeah, Bry, it is. My first instinct is to say come back another time. We'd love to have you as a guest, but something is nagging on me about that."

"Same here, and I'll bet it's the same thing. Grandfather always says that things happen for a reason, doesn't he?" Bryan asked.

"My thoughts exactly. No coincidences. So maybe she's supposed to be here, who knows? We certainly have plenty of room."

"Do you think Samantha Lewis will be upset that she doesn't have the camp to herself?"

Susie said, "Maybe, no way of knowing though. Why don't we invite Tony's sheila? Julia is her name, right? Why don't we invite her to stay the night and if it's no problem with the Lewis party, she can stay as long as she likes. Agreed?"

"Sounds like a plan. Let's go meet her."

They walked out to where Tony and Julia were waiting and warmly greeted their wayward guest. Tony was visibly relieved when they offered Julia accommodations for the night with a promise to extend the invitation if the new arrivals were agreeable.

# CHAPTER ELEVEN

The Citation banked steeply over the azure waters of the South Pacific and lined up on the glide path into Honiara International Airport, formerly known as Henderson Field. The Japanese began construction of the airfield in 1942. Later, it was captured by the 1st Marine Division. It was named Henderson Field in honor of the first naval aviator killed in action at Midway, Major Lofton Henderson. After years of neglect, the facility was renovated in 1969 and reopened as a civilian airport.

Once on the ground, the trio bid farewell to the two pilots, both of whom were retired from the military and looked forward to visiting the many historical sites. Inside the terminal, they hadn't taken half a dozen steps before a very tan and very wiry man about thirty years old or so strode right up to them and introduced himself, "G'day, mates, my name is Robert Berry, but friends just call me Bobby. And you, miss, must be Samantha Lewis, and there's Adam and Tom if I'm guessin' right, but which is which?

"Hi, Bobby, I'm Adam Baines, and this is Tom McDonald. Nice to meet you!"

"Beauty! Nice meeting you as well! Yeah, I'm here to get you over to Mala. We've got a puddle jumper to catch in twenty, so we'd best be at it. Is this all your gear?"

Samantha jumped in, "We were told to travel light since we'll be in the water a lot, and from what I understand, five-star dining isn't in the cards."

"Well, Miss Lewis, I wouldn't say you won't enjoy five-star cooking, but it'll be in a shack on poles, with big mobs of fresh seafood and some Fosters, but no white linens and one- hundred-quid tips. So, let's get moving. It'll take us a couple of minutes to walk over to the plane."

As Bobby bent down to pick up Sam's bags, his dreadlocks fell forward and revealed a tattoo that spanned from shoulder to shoulder. Centered on his neck were stylized bird wings or perhaps more like two triangles which met at the base, and on either side facing in, was what had to represent fish, or more likely, sharks. Tom was stunned, and he stared at the images until Bobby hefted the duffle bag and stood erect. It was the same image, albeit larger, that he had seen on the strange man's forehead who had been watching him in Honolulu, and it sent chills up his spine. Tom decided that this was not the time to remark on the tats, but he still felt that he needed to find out what was going on because sometimes coincidences weren't, as far as he was concerned.

"So, Bobby, how far is it to Malaita?" Adam asked.

"It's about eighty clicks. Take us thirty-five minutes once we get airborne, and then another twenty clicks to the camp."

"When you say 'clicks,' you mean miles?"

"Oh, no mate, a click means a kilometer, little over half a mile. So, you can reckon on forty-five miles give or take, and then we take the jeep out to the huts about ten miles up island."

They boarded the twin-prop "puddle jumper" which seated about the same number of passengers as the Citation, only in considerably less luxury, and were soon in the air climbing to a few thousand feet over the Pacific. "I saw that bird you folks came in on and although this will get us where we're going, that one sure was a beaut!"

"You can say that again, Bobby. What a rush when it takes off, and fast, bloody hell it's fast. Say, Bobby, back at the airport you said quid, not dollars as I would expect an Australian to say. Also, I hear something else in your accent which leads me to think you spent time there but not as a youngster. Am I right?"

"Good ear Adam, and yeah, you're right. I grew up in Preston, Lancashire. I got so sick of the grey and the damp all winter that I jumped at the chance to travel with a friend to visit Brisbane and meet up with his sister who married a bloke from down there. My friend went back home, but I loved it and stayed on. That was sixteen years ago, and that's where I got into surfing. Cracker beaches, great breakers, and nice people. Why leave?"

"Don't blame you a bit. That's why I left Wales to study in California. I wanted to get into the warm sun and warm water. At least that was the plan, although the water is pretty chilly where we are, but no regrets! Someday I'll go back to Gower, but not till I finish up at Berkeley, and then who knows? What brought you to Mala from Brisbane?"

"A job, mate, plain and simple. I got pretty good in

the surf and heard about this place as the next big thing. A friend of mine came here to check it out and told me the camps were looking for some help to run the place, so I packed up to give it a go. I probably wouldn't have stayed on for so long except for Grandfather."

At this point, Tom, who had been listening to the conversation with interest, perked up. "Who is Grandfather, Bobby? I know you can't mean your actual grandfather."

Bobby laughed. "No, my gramps is long gone, bless his soul. I'm referring to Kepa Kai, who is kinda like a holy man, or some might say a shaman. Everyone calls him Grandfather out of respect, at least those who understand who he is do. He means a lot to me. I really can't imagine leaving these islands now."

Tom looked at Bobby and quietly asked, "He doesn't by any chance have a tattoo across his forehead, does he?"

Bobby turned to Tom and said, "How the blazes did you know that, Tom? Yeah, mate, he has the symbol of the frigate bird and sharks made to look like a headband. Very traditional images for the South Islanders."

"And that's what you have on your shoulders and neck, right?"

"Yeah, Grandfather is what they call the Dinky-di in Australia, the real deal or the genuine article. I got the tats out of respect, and I guess you could say, love for him. That's all to it."

Adam explained, "Tom saw this strangely handsome man in the airport as we were getting refueled in Honolulu. Sam and I must have just missed seeing him, but Tom seemed pretty tweaked by the experience because he just seemed to vanish seconds after he saw him. He described his tattoos just like you have, only smaller. But how is that possible, Bobby? We flew on the fastest thing in the air outside the military."

Bobby looked out the window, lost in thought. Finally, he turned back and said, "Listen, mates, I don't expect you to believe me, but what you saw was real, and it means something. Don't ask me what, 'cause I don't know. But what I do know is that you're on a journey, and it's about more than just surfing. Grandfather has, how shall I say it?...abilities, which are very hard to accept at first, and he does NOT use them lightly. Most folks around here just know him to be a really funny, but very wise man. He's kind of a ballbuster sometimes, excuse the phrase, Samantha, but he always helps people see things in a certain way. He forces you to look at life from a higher perspective. A few of us have taken, I guess you could say, his teachings, to heart and from what I understand, he travels throughout the islands visiting folks he knows, and that's a lot of islands. To some, he is a legend. To others, a mystery. You'll have to make up your own mind when you meet him."

"What makes you so sure we'll meet him?" Adam asked.

"Well, for one thing, Tom already has, in a way. And for another, Grandfather never does anything, and I mean anything, without purpose and intention. If he revealed himself to you in that way, then I know as London to a brick, he has something deadset in mind, and that will mean face to face for sure. He's really nice, so no worries!"

Samantha craned to see through the small window as the plane was banking and said, "Yikes, Bobby! We're descending, but where the hell is the runway? There's nothing but jungle down there!"

"Don't worry, Miss Lewis, Mala has the nicest grass runway you'll ever set down on, piece of cake!"

"Grass? Are you sure it's safe?"

"Been in and outta here a hundred times picking people up for the camps, no problem! Auki has a paved runway and is much more commercial, but it would mean a lot longer ride in the jeep."

And no problem it was. The wheels touched down smooth as silk. The plane taxied up to a jumbled collection of what looked like ex-military Quonset huts and came to a standstill close to the largest of the bunch, which had a primitive hand-painted sign saying, "Welcome to Malaita" over the arch. After the twin props shut down and the door opened, Bobby doubled down with, "There you go, mates, welcome to Mala. The landing wasn't so bad, eh? Jeep is right over there in the parking lot."

The "parking lot" was nothing more than compacted sand about seventy-five yards wide with a fence to pull up to that separated it from the jungle. Rusted machinery lay strewn about. What it had once been used for, was anyone's guess. The "jeep" was a circa 1970 Toyota FJ55 Land Cruiser which looked tough and all business with the full-length roof rack on top. Bobby threw the duffels up on the rack and stowed the hardcases in the rear. Then he hopped in the driver's seat and fired up the engine.

"Right, mates, now be sure to use the belts 'cause it can get bumpy, and you don't want to get thrown about!"

He did not exaggerate. The road was a one-car affair with just enough room to pull over when confronted with oncoming traffic. Dodging the ruts, and puddles, and wild pigs, the trip took over a half-hour. Eventually, they came to an intersection that had a nicely carved sign which said, Mala Surf Camp. An arrow pointed down the lane to the right.

After all the jungle they had driven through, it was obvious that this area was under constant attention from humans, who endeavored to keep Mother Nature at bay, but with a deft and aesthetic touch. The jungle had been thinned, and native flowers were everywhere. Enormous, exotic trees had been pruned so that one could behold their great age and beauty. After about a quarter of a mile, the first of the thatched lodges came into view. Finally, the road circled in a clearing surrounded by huts and lodges of differing sizes and then continued, roughly paralleling the road they had been traveling on. In between two of the biggest lodges, the beautiful sight of breaking surf and sky-blue water could be seen, off in the distance.

"Welcome to Mala Surf Camp, mates," Bobby said. "Home sweet home for me, and a great spot for going off for you three! I know you'll be stoked with the waves, but I hope you'll also appreciate what isn't here as much as what is." And with that, Bobby grabbed Samantha's duffle and said, "This way, guys, I'll show you to your digs."

He led them down a winding path from where the truck was parked. Two rustic thatched lodges nestled against the thick tropical vegetation, and a beautifully kept path along a lagoon trailed in slightly from the beach. Twisted roots had been cleared, and crabs scurried to get off the path just ahead of them. Several delightful huts were built on poles set into the sand, and a man-made island had a thatched cottage perched on it, providing the most beautiful view of the breakers rolling off the beach in front of the main lodge.

"Bobby, this is breathtaking! No wonder you decided to stay!"

"That it is, Miss Lewis, and I can't see leavin'. That's deadest."

The entire resort created the impression of a small upscale native village. Exactly what was intended when it was built over twenty years ago. The lane they had driven in on continued for a mile along the shoreline, to a real village, consisting of forty or so dwellings and some three hundred native Solomon Islanders. Their lifestyle was a mix of traditional subsistence farming, fishing, growing organic vegetables, and selling their excess produce and fish in local markets.

"Miss Lewis, this is where you'll be stayin'. I hope the accommodations please you," Bobby said as they came to the first hut.

"Bobby, I can't cope with a week full of 'Miss Lewis'. Please just call me Sam, and it looks divine!"

"Beauty! I'm glad you like it, Miss, err Sam. Now, you've got fresh spring water that comes down from the hills on tap and an outdoor shower just 'round the corner there that's warmed by the small black tank on the roof. And inside that little door, there is a composting loo, or I guess I should say toilet, but no matter, you get the drift, and they work great. We've got rechargeable battery lanterns off the solar panels just over here, and the mattress and sheets are first-rate and washed by hand every day. As long as you keep the door closed, you'll have no problem with bugs or critters at all, so make sure it is! If there's anything you need, just let me know. And that hammock on the porch is a great place to nod off after paddling all day!"

"Thank you so much, Bobby! It's perfect!"

"As for you gents, there's where you'll be stayin'." Bobby pointed through the palms and out to the lagoon. What looked like a large rock served as a foundation for a palm-thatched cabin which molded itself into every crevice of the mini-island for support. "Ain't she a beauty! My favorite spot in the camps it is, just like your own private island 'cept built from scratch by hand with coral. Don't worry, mates, the water's only up to your knees, and it never gets rough in the lagoon, so it's an easy walk out. If you're all set, Sam, let's go, guys."

"Sam, do you mind if I leave my travel lab here? I'll be using it along the shore anyway."

"And my guitar, Sam, if you have the room."

"No problem, guys. Adam, I'm interested to see what you have and how it works, so that would be perfect. I'll be fine, Bobby, but I'm starting to feel my stomach growl. What time is dinner served?"

"Meals here are always on island time, Sam. Dinner's around sunset, breakfast just after sunrise, and lunch will be with us on the boat."

"I love it. Living with the light!"

"But feel free to swing over early for a beer or a glass of wine. There are a lot of great folks to meet.

"What is the native cuisine anyway?"

"Come by and watch. It's a show unto itself! Come on, lads, let's get crackin'. It's getting near sundown, and you'll want to settle in a bit, I reckon."

After dropping Sam's large duffel on the floor, Bobby headed out the door and down the steps to the water. The cabin was about fifty yards out in the lagoon and looked for all the world like something Robinson Crusoe might have built. Funky but beautiful with round log framing and sago palm thatching, it sprouted all sorts of weird angles and had a wide porch complete with three hammocks, assorted chairs, and small tables. Perfect!

"Hey, Adam, can you believe how cool this place is?" Tom giggled like a little kid. "This is right out of *Robinson Crusoe*!"

"If the world was ending soon, I can't imagine a better place to be than right here. It's self-sufficient, peaceful, and absolutely beautiful! It reminds me of home, only much warmer and, obviously, a different environment altogether than Wales."

"You kinda lost me on that one."

"Well, where I'm from, it's all about nature, just like here. We have huge, beautiful beaches with big tides and rich fertile farmland that rolls down to the cliffs where you can see for miles out to sea. The folks in the village have lived there and scraped a living off the land and sea for a thousand years or more, and they have their ways of seeing things like I'm sure the natives here do. The climate being so different changes things, like stone cottages, instead of pole huts, but the essential elements of subsistence living are probably more alike than not."

"I never would have guessed! It sounds like Wales is a place I'd like to see someday, but first, let's get our gear stowed and get back to the lodge. I'm starving!"

"I'm all for that!"

# CHAPTER TWELVE

Adam and Tom waded back to shore as the sun started to paint the sky in stunning tones of yellow, red, ochre, and purple that only sunsets on the open ocean can deliver. After just a few steps on the shoreline, the smell of wood smoke mixed with the pungent odor of garlic, onions, and ginger wafted towards them and quickened their pace.

"Does that smell great or what, Adam?" Tom said, "I don't know what we're in store for, but from here, it sure smells five-star!"

"You can say that again. I can't wait to see what's cooking and how they're cooking it."

As they rounded the corner of the largest lodge, they could see smoke rising from behind a small hut right next to it, and they headed over to check things out. To their surprise, Samantha was sitting on a log next to a native girl, about sixteen years old. They were chatting like two high school kids in any cafeteria back in the states. In front of them, there was a fire pit, rectangular in shape, and about six feet long. It had both a steel grill and a flat steel cooking plate, like a commercial stove propped up on stones for height adjustment, and a device used for smoking various things was set off to the side. At each end of the fire pit were live coals, and they could be raked under or pulled away from the cooking surfaces to provide the right amount of heat for the dishes being prepared. The entire outdoor kitchen nestled in the center space between four of the main camp lodges, which created a shelter and windbreak during what were usually brief afternoon squalls. The sago palm thatching well above the fire pit worked well to keep the workers dry, and along with rustic prep tables and strategically placed logs for sitting, the whole affair looked remarkably efficient and inviting.

Adam sat back on his haunches next to Samantha and was pleasantly surprised when she leaned into him as an acknowledgment of his arrival. The cooking crew consisted of two Solwata girls, salt-water people as the native islanders are known, and an older chap who quickly revealed himself to be Australian as he asked one of his helpers to move some more coals under the plate steel griddle. He introduced himself as Tony Perkins, but never even looked up, as he was concentrating on the meal he was crafting. In the coals were foil-wrapped sweet potatoes becoming soft and infused with the smell of the dry jungle hardwood charcoal they were cooking in. On the grills were fish kabobs slowly charring over low heat and mixed vegetables on the griddle sautéing with onions, shallots, ginger, and spices, and being steamed a bit with a ladle of white wine occasionally added to the mix. The smells emanating from the cooking hut were intoxicating.

When the aroma became almost too much to bear, a handsome man strode into the "kitchen" and introduced himself. "Hello, mates, and welcome to Surf Mala. My name is Bryan Mathews, and along with my lovely bride Susie, who is in the dining lodge getting things set up, we'll be your hosts for the next seven days! We're mighty glad to have you, and we look forward to showing you the beautiful sights as well as the fantastic waves that this enchanted place has to offer. Right now, though, I'm sure you must be starving after your long journey, so let's shake a leg and grab a seat inside. Miss Lewis, may I have word with you?"

"Certainly Bryan, what is it?" Samantha replied. "And please, call me Samantha or Sam."

"Oh, it's no biggy. I just wanted to tell you that our chef here brought along a guest he met on the run to Auki for supplies. We hadn't planned on anyone but you three being here, but we said it would be fine for one night, until I had a chance to run it by you. Her name is Julia Witherspoon and she's from Canada. I guess she's on a sabbatical of sorts, I really don't know much about her, but she seems nice enough."

"I didn't expect we'd have the place to ourselves, Bryan, so no need to ask. Of course, it's fine with me. I look forward to meeting her."

Bryan added, "I asked her to have dinner in her hut, which is two down from where you are so that we can get to know each other tonight a bit. So perhaps you'll see her in the morning or when you get back from surfing with Bobby. Anyway, that's that. Shall we go inside?"

The group strolled the fifty feet or so on the crushed shell path over to what was a combination eating hall, game room, and bar, complete with funky décor ranging from old beat-up surfboards and fishing rods to native wood carvings reminiscent of tiki bars everywhere. An interesting eclectic mix of kitsch, coupled with comfortable lounge chairs grouped around low coffee tables that looked out onto the lagoon, completed the picture of what one instantly sensed was a place to relax and share company with kindred spirits. The fourteen-foot-long dining table was hand-hewn from one gigantic board three inches thick, having a "live edge" along both sides. The cantilevered base construction allowed the maximum number of chairs to be placed since there were no table legs to get in the way and looked as if George Nakashima had visited the island.

Bobby arrived just as everyone was getting seated and grabbed a chair with a quick, "Hello, mates. Smells pretty five-star, ya think?"

"Hey, Bobby! Yeah, I think!" said Tom.

An elegant woman walked out the door behind the bar. She wore a flowery cotton blouse and shorts with a twisted palm headband holding back her long strawberry blonde hair. Smiling at everyone, she placed two bottles of Australian pinot grigio on each end of the table and said, "Hello everyone, my name is Susannah, and I'm Bryan's better half, but everyone here calls me Susie. I thought this pinot would work well with the fish, and we get it from a friend of Bryan's dad back in Australia. If anyone would prefer beer, let me know. Like the wine, we keep it cool in the spring water."

No hint of Aussie accent was in her voice, more a mild southern drawl spoken with a confident, educated demeanor that immediately left the impression of a serious yet affable persona. "And no, I'm not Australian, as I'm sure you can tell. Rather, an ex-Texas cowgirl turned ecopreneur thanks to Bryan's dream!"

Before they began their meal, Bryan asked the group to hold hands, and he said, "We honor the life energy which has been provided to us, and we pledge our energy back in return, for the benefit of all that lives. Ah Ho."

Each person in the group acknowledged the words spoken as grace in their own way and then began to dig in. The absolute silence gave testimony to how delicious the meal was and how hungry the guests were. After taking an opportunity to complement their hosts on the food and wine, Samantha asked Bryan the question all three had been wondering.

"Bryan, I'm sure you've been asked a million times, but how did you put this all together? What was the inspiration for it in the beginning?"

"You said you prefer to be called Sam, so, well Sam, it's a long story, but since we only enjoy at most ten guests here at a time, not as many people know it as you might think, and many of those that do have helped build it. It begins with my father and our family history back at the station."

"What kind of station, Bryan? Was your family in the railroad business in Australia?"

Bryan chuckled at the question and said, "No, not railroads, Sam, cattle. A station is a true-blue proper ranch in your terms, and my family has been on Clear Spring Station, since the late eighteen hundreds. Clear Spring is one of the biggest in what we call the 'woop woop,' up in the Northern Territory."

Susie explained, "Woop woop means in the middle of nowhere, Sam, and believe me, it is. As a girl who grew up on a large ranch in Texas, it was astounding to me the first time I visited Clear Spring. Our family spread in West Texas is a little over three thousand acres. Clear Spring is just a bit under four thousand square miles, isn't it, Bry?"

"Yeah, I think they're running around fifty thousand head now. We're what's known as pastoralists, in that we have a perpetual lease of Crown land to graze our stock. The same arrangement was established under the Taylor Grazing Act of nineteen thirty-four back in the States, and many large ranches operate under that stature, but not your family, right?"

"No, we own the land we graze on, and it's just enough to keep the family with plenty to do, but not so much that they have to hire an army to do it."

Samantha was astounded. "Four thousand square miles? That is unbelievable. How is it even possible?"

"We're by no means the biggest station, Sam. I've got three older brothers, and they have houses and kids spread out over the station. They all help out when needed but also might not see each other for weeks at a time. Dad still lives at the main house and looks after most of the financial affairs of the station, and it's the reason why we're here."

"How's that, Bryan?" Adam asked.

"Well, mate, my dad, Mason Mathews, is a third-generation pastoralist, but he is also a great admirer of American history. He especially loves how so many humble but hard-working immigrants of all nationalities created great wealth with only their hands and brains. But most of all, he truly admires the unique tradition of giving back to the people, immense levels of their wealth for the common good. Things like museums, educational institutions, research centers but most of all, your national parks. Get him going on that, and he won't shut up for hours. Susie and I met when we were both going to Texas A&M, and I fell in love the minute I laid eyes on her, and we got married before we graduated. The problem was, where would we settle down? Since we both were in families that already had plenty of kids to run the show, we were a bit stumped. Australia or Texas, right, babe?"

"And it was Mason that offered the solution."

"What my father suggested was for us to consider doing what the great American philanthropists had done. Find a worthy site in the so-called third world and find a way to acquire and preserve it. After all, he said, you've both been on the business end of a cow all your lives. Why not try something different? And if it doesn't work out, you'll always have a home on Clear Spring Station."

Susie continued the story, "So Mason said that if my folks felt the same way and gave their blessing, he would match any contribution they would make for the seed money to help us locate and purchase our preserve. My family was very supportive both emotionally and financially, and so we had enough to be fairly ambitious out of the gate."

"We sure put some miles in the air before we found Malaita."

"If you don't mind me asking, how did you discover this hidden gem?" asked Tom.

"When I could get away from the station, I enjoyed going up to Brisbane for some beach time and began to enjoy surfing, not that I'm any good. But I met some nice people and heard stories of great waves off the beaches of 'the land that time forgot,' which is here. So, we came to have a look. Although we both fell in love with Mala, it was Grandfather who convinced us that this is what we'd been searching for."

"Grandfather," Tom blurted, "he played a role in all this? Incredible! Bobby told us a bit about him on the flight over, and I saw him in Honolulu, although I still can't see how that was possible. What did he do to help you get started?"

"Tom, he didn't do anything. He just was. By that, I mean it was just his aura or presence that was so special. That and the fact that he told us he'd been waiting for us for years!"

"That's right, Tom," Susie said, "and it still gives me shivers when I remember how he said it, even though now it's all old hat. He told us that we had a purpose in coming here and that the purpose would be revealed over time. He said that he would help in all ways he possibly could. He said that Mother was sick and that he had dedicated his life to healing her."

"Wow, what a story!" exclaimed Tom. "So, does Grandfather speak English? You really can just talk with him like this?"

"Yeah, he does speak English mate, and other languages too, but it's more that he communicates in uncanny ways, I guess you could say. It's almost like he knows what your thoughts are before you say them, so he's always prepared to give the answers you need. I don't know if that explains it. It's hard to put into words. You'll just have to see for yourself. But to finish the story, we set Surf Mala up as the economic base and logistical center for the Solwata National Preserve Trust, our station, you might say, and as of last week, we now have approximately one hundred and ten square miles in trust for the native islanders. Over the years, many of our guests have decided to make contributions, and most recently, Liberty was enormously helpful."

"Liberty!" Sam cried out. "How the heck does Mom get in the story?"

"We have a presence on the internet as an ecological charitable giving possibility for those who wish to give to those kinds of causes. Liberty's very generous donation to the non-profit SNP Trust, allowed us to close on a large parcel of mountain forest, which we've been trying to save from loggers for the last two years. We'd had an option on the thirty-five-mile strip of virgin forest, but it was running out until your mom stepped in. Didn't she tell you about that? I assumed that's why you came, to check us out and make sure we are who we represent ourselves to be."

"No, Mom never let on a word about any of this. She just told me she had a surprise birthday present, a trip she had been planning for a while, and that she wanted my closest friends to go along with me for a surfing adventure. That's all."

"Liberty is a remarkable woman, and she embodies the spirit of giving back that my father so much admired. I was chatting with her this morning about another parcel that is about to become available soon, one which will become the jewel in the crown of the Solwata Preserve and which is full of artifacts of great archeological significance."

"Chatting with her? How do you do that?"

"In either one of two ways, Sam. We have a forty-kilowatt solar array, a battery bank, and an inverter capable of providing us with most of the creature comforts of home, including satellite uplink and internet connectivity. We also use a satellite phone such as you would see on ocean-going yachts for direct communication anywhere in the world. We don't encourage and don't advertise this because the point for our guests is to experience this place in the most remote sense possible. But for safety and business reasons, we require modern communication and computing capabilities. This morning we emailed back and forth a bit."

Adam, who had been taking all this in, asked, "I must say, Bryan and Susie, this is much more than just the remote surf camp I had been expecting. I am amazed by the scope of what you have going on here. I'm curious, though, what kind of archeological artifacts does this new parcel contain? Were there battles fought here or downed aircraft?"

"No, Adam, nothing like that at all. Guadalcanal is where the WW Two action occurred, and there's plenty to see over there. Umm, let's just say that there is significant evidence of a species of hominid that is unknown to western science, but which the Solwata people are quite familiar with."

"Really? That's remarkable! What characteristics do the bones possess that make them unique?"

"Well, Adam, it's not about bones. You'll never see that."

"What is it about then?"

"If you ask any native you see about the giants who live here, they will point up towards the mountains and say, up there."

"Wow, you mean they're not extinct. They're still living on the island?"

Samantha asked, "Are they dangerous, Bryan?"

Bryan said, "The mountains are all volcanic in origin,

and there are vast unexplored cave systems and deep inaccessible valleys which are said to hold substantial populations of these creatures, and no, they are not dangerous, at least not now. The Solwata people just accept them as a given, no big deal. But there are places where huge stone bowls and other artifacts exist, which are completely unexplainable. The tract we are hoping to purchase is right in the middle of where the sightings and artifacts are concentrated. So, you can see how excited we would be to provide a permanent sanctuary to the area by including it in the Preserve. Hopefully, thanks again to Liberty, we'll be able to do that soon."

Tom exclaimed, "It sounds like Sasquatch live on this island in numbers. Have there been any reports of what they look like or how tall they are?"

"Yes, Tom, many reports. I am not trained in the field, but I'd say there is some similarity to what I used to hear of when I was in the states. These are taller, though, usually estimated to be around nine feet tall, very muscular, and extremely strong. They are reported to have long brown or reddish hair, pronounced eyebrows, and very human-like eyes. You're welcome to use our computers and research the subject yourself when you have a break from surfing. There is a lot of information on the internet and numerous eyewitness reports, and Grandfather has very personal knowledge of them. We take it seriously, especially when spoken about by Grandfather. However, I don't want a bunch of scientists from *National Geographic* coming down and tramping all over the place, which is why we're hoping to close on the purchase soon. Protection for the land and whatever may be living on it."

Susie emerged from the door with a pot of tea and

some small cups of what looked like sherbet. "Here you go, gang, a little sleepy tea and some frozen coconut milk with fruit to finish the meal for a good night's sleep. Tomorrow y'all will be on the waves, so make sure you turn in early, not that there's late-night television or room service! Anyway, I've had a busy day myself, and that's what I'm going to do right now. See you in the morning!"

Bryan added, "I'm right behind you. Goodnight, mates. And you too, Bobby! Get them on some good breaks tomorrow!"

They finished their tea and made their way back to the sleeping huts as the evening darkness began to creep in from the jungle. The silence during the walk was testimony to the many revelations which the extraordinary dinner revealed. Each was lost in thought, trying to assemble the whole picture of what was going on in this remote corner of a very big world. Samantha said goodnight as the men waded out to the island and fell asleep almost immediately upon climbing into bed. Tom and Adam chatted quietly for a short while on the porch, then turned in themselves, to the sound of the small waves lapping the coral all around the cabin. Neither moved a muscle till the first light of dawn crept in through the screened windows, and the birds and fish began breaking the surface looking for a meal.

# CHAPTER THIRTEEN

The sun rose early over the horizon, framing deep purple clouds with an orange-yellow background, giving the impression of a spectacular distant mountain range. Adam climbed out of bed and was surprised to see Tom sitting cross-legged on a small pillow, watching the breaking waves off in the distance. He walked over to the steps leading down to the sandy bottom eighteen inches below the surface and sat with his feet in the clear warm water. After a few minutes, Tom got up and stretched and then sat down next to him.

"You meditate every morning?" Adam asked.

"I try to, although life doesn't always allow it to happen. Here it's just perfect with the gentle sound of the waves lapping the coral, the breeze, and the silence. It will definitely be part of my experience of this place while we're here! Did you ever try it?"

"Try what, meditation? Not really. I never knew how to do it or actually what the benefits are. Of course, I know what's said about the health benefits from slowing the mind down and all that, but I just never got into it, I guess. What do you get out of it the most, Tom?"

"Well, aside from the health benefits as you say, I think the biggest thing for me was in realizing that there is as much space inside, as there is outside, and by consciously stilling the mind, that space or you might say reality, can be accessed and explored."

"What do you mean by 'as much space'?"

"I mean, there is depth and substance to inner space, just like there is to physical space all around us, but we never permit ourselves to focus enough on it to allow it to become real. Do you remember how I tried to explain the process I go through when I communicate with horses? I said I needed to 'step aside' inside my mind to allow communication to occur. That stepping aside is what I'm practicing during meditation. You can do a little experimentation on yourself if you're interested. What you want to observe is how long or short your gap is."

"My gap? What do you mean my gap?"

"The gap of time between your thoughts, the space where there is no thought, whatsoever. For most people, it is very brief, and for many, it is almost non-existent. One of the goals of meditation is to stretch that gap, and ultimately to be able to experience it while walking around during life, and that allows direct perception of, I guess you could say 'reality,' without filtering everything through the mind, which is highly conditioned."

"How can you experience reality without thinking, Tom? That's how we have evolved and survived as a species. Remember the famous postulation from Rene' Descartes, 'I think therefore I am?' It is the one way to prove that we, as individuals exist. We think. We learn. We live. Don't you agree?"

"Only in a limited context. I would be more inclined to say, 'I AM. Therefore, I think.' Once you realize that unlike what most religions preach, which is that we're humans who are having a spiritual experience by going to church, rather, we are spiritual beings in the physical world having a human experience. That paradigm shift, if you can make it, profoundly changes how you perceive everything."

"How long have you been into all this, Tom?"

"Kind of hard to pin down exactly when, but even as a young kid, I always felt there was more to the story than we were told. I guess I started a search to find out what that is quite a while ago. I've read a lot, done different practices and methods to expand my understanding, and now I'm just working with what I've learned."

"I'm going to think about all this. There is a ring of truth here that is elegant and undeniable. But tell me, how does one observe their 'gap,' as you call it?"

"Well, a simple way is this; next time you lie down to sleep or rest, try counting very slowly backward from a hundred and be alert to when you realize you're no longer counting. A stray thought will inevitably derail your progression, and it may well happen quickly. Like at ninety-six. At that point, recognize what happened, and start over again. If you find yourself counting AND thinking, start over as well. Most people won't be able to get to eighty-five before starting over. This will give you some insight into how compulsive your thinking is. Try it. You might be surprised!"

"I'll do that, Tom, thanks! Now though, I think we'd better get over to breakfast, I'm hungry, and we have an active day ahead of us!"

"Roger that, Adam, let's get going."

Samantha had been awake for almost an hour before the sun was fully over the horizon. Being the inveterate beachcomber that she was, she slipped into a pair of shorts and waded along the shoreline, enjoying the feeling of the sugar-soft sand between her toes. The natural world was waking up around her and she felt at peace with it and herself. She skirted a large mangrove and was surprised to see another woman doing the same thing she was. It could only be the Julia that Bryan spoke of the night before. Once they both noticed each other, there was nothing else to do but to make acquaintance. Samantha continued down the shore until she was close enough to be heard.

"Hi, my name's Samantha Lewis. Are you the Julia who Bryan told me about last night?"

"Yes, I am. Julia Witherspoon, nice to meet you! Thank you for not objecting to another guest. I really like it here and I'm glad I didn't have to go back to Denny's whatever the name was. Tony said your party was important to this place. Do you come here often?"

Samantha answered, "No, I've never been here before, and didn't know until last night that my mom even had a connection here, but I'm glad we do. Isn't it beautiful?"

"You can say that again. And so peaceful, like the world stands still!"

"Yes, I slept like a baby last night. I don't usually get up this early," Sam said.

"I slept better than I have in a long time too, although I had a strange dream that kept playing over and over all night."

"Sometimes dreams mean something, what was it?"

"It was weird. It was just an image of a hut. A hut like you see here, only not as fancy, and it had a blue door. I kept trying to go into it. I saw the door open, and I walk in, but then I disappear. Nothing. Then I'm at the blue door again. Like I said, it was weird."

"Well, it's probably just your subconscious reacting to a strange place. Anyway, I've got to get back. Are you into surfing?"

"No, not me. I just wanted to see this side of the island and the only place to stay is at surfer's lodges. The cook, Tony, told me about this place. Glad I landed here, it's really nice."

"Well, I'll see you when we get back. What are you going to do today?"

"I thought I'd do a little exploring, maybe walk up to the next village Tony pointed out. It's only a mile or so. Have fun!"

"See you for dinner. Nice to meet you!"

"Same here!"

Adam and Tom walked to the shore and headed to the kitchen. Once again, the aroma of what was being prepared set their mouths to watering. Omelets filled with onions and peppers and gooey cheese complimented true, American-style, hash brown potatoes. After the meal, they were told to meet at the boat dock in thirty minutes, and everyone left to get into swimwear and sunscreen. On his way back from the cabin, Adam stopped by Sam's hut, and knocked on the door. She invited him in, and he went right to the plastic travel case he had left off the day before.

"I'm not sure I'll get a chance today, but if we do take a break and get to shore, I'd like to start getting some samples to test, so I'm just going to bring along the sieve and a couple of collection bottles."

"That makes sense, but judging from how clear the water is here, it doesn't seem you're likely to find much."

"I hope I don't, but I suspect it may be you who gets surprised. Microplastics are found virtually everywhere on the planet; on top of mountains, in the Arctic and Antarctic, as well as inside most living things, so I'd be quite surprised if they weren't here, just a matter of the concentrations."

"What do you mean inside most living things? Come on. You're exaggerating!"

"You think? A study of twenty-five hundred children in Germany from twenty fourteen through twenty fifteen found that ninety-seven percent had microplastic traces identified in their blood and stool samples. Of course, virtually all sea creatures consume it in one way or another, and it just works its way up the food chain."

"But the water seems so clean."

"I know, and that's why I want to test some samples here to see how bad the situation is in an otherwise pristine environment."

"Well, I hope it doesn't take too long to collect samples because I, for one, am looking forward to getting in the waves!"

"No, it doesn't, nothing to it, and I am too, so let's get over to the boat."

The boat was a beamy twenty-six-foot outboard, rigged to hold over a dozen surfboards of various types; longboards, fish, shortboards, and a couple of guns, plenty to choose from. The mid-section of the boat provided utilitarian seating for up to ten surfers, and the stern had a console to drive the boat, with its 115hp Yamaha four-stroke. An aluminum frame supported a canvas top, which shielded the guests and the driver from the direct rays of the sun. Miscellaneous coolers, tool kits, and soft bags held everything from towels and waxes to lunch.

Bobby fired up the Yamaha, which was so quiet and smoke-free that you could barely even tell it was running, and said to them, "Righty, mates, hope you all had a great brekky 'cause we're going over to Charles Right for the day. A beaut she is too, not too gnarly right now, but you'll be seein' fours to sixes and with some crankin' carvers for sure! The wind is just offshore, and how we like it, so you should have a clean go of it. It'll take us about forty minutes to get up to Charles, but you'll see some pretty cool sights along the way. If anybody wants a coke or a bottle of water, it's all in the cooler just aft the last bench. Plenty for all, so don't be bashful and remember to stay hydrated!" With that, he got the boat up on plane by briefly gunning the throttle and then backed down to a comfortable cruising speed to conserve fuel.

Leaving the lagoon, they headed north around a small island but stayed in the protected inshore waters for a smooth ride. After about ten minutes, another island came up on them quickly, but it turned out to be an island made of houses. Bobby saw the astonished look on his guests' faces and said, "Yeah, mates, now you know why they're called Solwata, which means salt-water people. They've lived this way for centuries, and gradually these islands build up until whole villages can live on what are like artificial atolls. Musta taken hard yakka and heaps of coral to build these, for sure!"

"Bobby, what the heck is 'hard yakka?' For God's sake, can't you speak real English?" Sam was only kidding, but they all wanted to know what the heck he said.

"Oh, sorry, mates. 'Hard yakka' just means hard work, that's all, and last time I checked, Australians do speak English. You blokes just gotta get with the program. We'll make proper Aussies out of you yet!"

"Thanks, but no thanks, Bobby. It's all I can do to remember what everything means when I'm back in Maine. I'll pass on being true-blue Aussie thank you very much!"

As they passed the village, one could easily see how connected the people were to the sea. It encompassed virtually everything they did, everything they saw, and everything they ate. The village began on the shore, with thatched houses on wooden poles driven into the sandy shallows, and further out consisted of several man-made artificial islands completely covered with thatched pole huts. Kids played in both traditional dugout and modern aluminum canoes. Women cleaned the morning catch, and everywhere there was a sense of unhurried activity.

Bobby pointed to the shoreline to the left of the main group of huts. "See that hut over there, off by itself? The one with the painted blue door? That's where Grandfather lives when he's on island. He grew up in this village and always comes back, and judging from that little flag, he is back." Samantha was startled by the connection of the blue door she was looking at and the dreams that Julia had just shared but didn't say anything. "We can come back over tomorrow if you want and have a walk-about so you can meet some of the people and see how they live. They are the most friendly and good-natured folks in the world!"

"That would be wonderful, Bobby!" Sam said, "I can't wait to do that! It seems so romantic, though I'm sure looks can be deceiving."

About fifteen minutes later, they rounded a point and before them stretched a beautiful white sand beach configured in a giant half-circle three miles long before melding back into the shoreline jungle further up the coast. About a half-mile offshore was one of the most stunning breaks any of the three friends had ever seen. The banks threw up waves that broke right with near-perfect tubes and produced set after set.

Adam could barely contain himself. "Oh my God, will you look at that!"

"Meet Charles Right, mates, one of the nicest places to ride this side of heaven!"

Bobby guided the boat to where the white water from the breaking waves flattened out before racing to shore and dropped anchor in about six feet of water. The boat swung round, stern to the waves, and Bobby snapped the swim ladders into the slotted guides on each side of the engine. Next, he removed the canvas which shaded the boards. Since part of his job was to wax them before the trip, he didn't want them to melt in the sun. He let them choose what they wanted. Tom chose a shortboard, while Sam and Adam both went with longboards. The water temperature was around eighty, so there was no need for wetsuits. Sam looked stunning in a stylish Roxy Pop one-piece bi-color suit, and she wagged her finger at Adam and said, "Stop gawking!" But she couldn't take her eyes off Adam's chiseled physique either.

All three slipped into the water, climbed on their boards, and began paddling. "Have at it, mates!" Bobby said, "It's a soft bottom here, and no rays to worry about, so just have a great time. I'll be out after a little bit."

"Thanks, Bobby!" Adam said, "Amazing waves, and incredible to be the only ones here! See you soon!"

Once the trio had either duck dived as in Tom's case, or Eskimo rolled through white-wash and incoming breakers, they paddled further out and sat up on their boards, waiting to pick their waves. It didn't take long before Tom began stroking furiously to match the speed of an incoming wave. With two final strokes, he pushed up and got his back foot in the "chicken wing" position, before popping up onto the board and taking off backside down the wave. He executed a shallow angle bottom turn and gained speed while decompressing and rode up the shoulder to the lip, where he turned his head and changed direction back towards the curl. Once there, he attempted to ride the lip but lost his balance and fell into the white water as his board shot several feet past him. When he surfaced and got back on his board, he pumped his fist and shouted a loud, victorious, "YEEEESSSSSSS!" that no one could hear but which expressed everything he was feeling.

Samantha and Adam were riding high on long, smooth carves in and out of the green room, just getting used to being back in the waves. But after a couple of runs, both headed back to the boat and switched to the smaller fish, which, like Tom's shortboard, would allow much more creativity in the ideal conditions. After a couple of hours trying all the tricks they knew, they decided it was time to grab a bite to eat and check in with Bobby back at the boat. Lunch was served under the protective canopy, and after a light meal of sushi and herbal tea, the three rested for twenty minutes or so before they grabbed their boards and began paddling back out. This time Bobby was with them, and the way he carved through the tunnel and up the lip, riding the crest and shooting back through the green room provided a clinic by a master surfer.

The time flew by, and after one last acrobatic ride, Bobby rode the whitewater to the boat, and one by one, the others followed. When they had stowed the boards, a light snack of fried sweet potato chips dipped in mango salsa and sparkling water restored their energy. Bobby pulled the anchor and fired up the Yamaha. Within minutes they were in the calm inner waters again, protected by the string of small reefs and islands. They passed near one of the larger islands that had vegetation on it but no signs of inhabitants.

"Say, Bobby," Adam said. "Small favor. Any chance we could put ashore over there? I'd like to spend a few minutes getting some samples of the sand and check how much plastic is on the beach."

"Sure, mate, we've got plenty of time, and that little spot is a beaut. I've put in there before myself."

Bobby eased the bow into the quiet water and onto the sandbar, and Adam hopped out with the bowline and tugged it up securely. Tom and Samantha followed him onto the beach after passing him the collection kit he had brought along.

"We won't be long, Bobby, thanks!"

"No worries, mate, take your time. I'm just chillin' island style!" With that, he popped the top on a can of Fosters, kicked his feet up, and waved after them. "I'll be here, have a good walkabout!"

The protected cove was a perfect spot because the island narrowed, making their trek across to open water a short one hundred yards. As they headed towards the sound of the waves breaking on the beach, Tom noticed something unusual off to the left in the sand.

"Hey guys, what do you think that is over there?" he said, pointing at a large white object in the sand.

"I don't know, let's go have a look," Adam said as he pivoted in the direction Tom had pointed.

Tom reached the object first with the other two right behind and exclaimed, "It's a bird, a big dead bird. It's been dead for quite a while, judging by the remains."

"I think it's an Albatross." said Samantha. "I remember reading about them when I was looking on the web about what these islands had to offer. They mostly stay out at sea but come ashore to the same islands each year to hatch new chicks."

"Let's take a closer look." Adam bent over and picked up a small stick and carefully pried some of the feathers and bones aside. The three were amazed at what they saw.

"Look there, Adam, it almost looks like cut-up credit cards or something. Look at that pile of plastic chips. That must have been what killed this guy. What a shame!"

"Yeah, it sure is Sam, and I'll be willing to bet it's not the only one we'll see."

"But why would it eat plastic, Adam? These birds don't forage for food on the ground."

"No, they don't, but they do eat fish and other marine life like squid, octopus, and shrimp. When they dive for food, a floating piece of plastic, could easily be mistaken for any of those. Also, the fish they eat may well have consumed something they thought was prey, and so it concentrates going up the food chain."

"I think I read that the Albatross is a threatened species, and now I can see why!" Samantha said sadly.

"Well, I'll take some of these bits for samples. Let's

get over to the beach and see what we find there. Whoa, you don't have to look far to see another one, and lots more, look over there." He pointed to numerous other piles of what could only be more Albatross casualties.

"Oh, this is so sad. I had no idea it would be this bad."

On the beach Adam used his mini manta sieve to sample the water being churned by the waves, emptying it several times into a covered bowl. Then he filled a container the size of a soup can with actual sand from the beach itself and twisted a secure lid onto it as well. As they walked the beach, they realized that this island may have been remote but was by no means immune from the piles of junk that washed up on beaches worldwide. Everywhere they looked, they saw buoys, pieces of fishing net, bottles, and little shards of plastic that had been broken down by the sun and waves. Similar to what remained in the Albatross. It was disgusting how much of modern societies' waste ended up in the sea and washed ashore.

"This is why I joined the SAS back home," Adam said. "No matter how much we used to pick up, just as much washed back in. Bloody criminal it is!"

"Well, something needs to be done about it! The politicians are all about making laws about gas mileage and plastic straws. How about banning anything which isn't recyclable?" Samantha blurted out.

Tom jumped in, "It isn't that simple. We in the west actually do a decent job protecting the environment, but it was a long process for us, and most developing countries aren't there yet."

The three friends headed quietly back to the boat, each contemplating what they had witnessed. When they told Bobby what they had seen, he acknowledged the horror, "Right mates, I should'a warned you about that. Real nasty that is. It's all that plastic that just gets into everything. It's Grandfather's biggest concern, actually. That and preserving the island itself."

They stood on the beach, silently observing the disaster washing up in front of them while the sun began to drift to the horizon. The boat ride back to camp was mostly a quiet one.

# CHAPTER FOURTEEN

Julia waded back to her hut and sat down on the bed. She reached over to the little bamboo nightstand and picked up the only reading material she had brought along. Her father's journal. Absently, she turned to near the end of what had been entered. Something was bothering her. She began to reread what she didn't pay any attention to when she was searching for clues of the location of this place. After all, who cares what he experienced after he was scared off?

"I left the mountain with my guide in disarray. Both physical and mental. I had planned to spend several days exploring the region that I could see towering above the village I stayed in. But now, I felt defeated. The three-hour hike back was depressing. After coming all this way, only to have creatures that were impossible to exist, prevent me from discovering what I was certain would pale Lookout Lake. Yet I knew my life would be forfeit if their warning I did not heed."

Julia hadn't noticed that the journal had a few more

pages to it than she realized, having thought that was the end. Now she could feel the page or two which seemed stuck together, and she freed them with her thumb and forefinger. She began to read again.

"When we returned to the village, I was desperate to understand what had happened. My very sanity depended on it. There was activity by the water's edge, and I went to observe fishermen returning with their catch. One man seemed to be superior to the others, and I walked over to meet with him. I asked if he were the chief, but he said that was not the case. Not knowing what to do next I blurted out the question of giants and pointed at the mountain. The man seemed to freeze in place. I asked who can tell me. He pointed to a path leaving the far side of the beach and just said, "Blue door."

Julia put the book down. She felt a shiver somewhere deep in her being. She wanted to wrap it up, put it away and not finish reading to the end. But she knew better than that. She had to know what happened, because the Ross Witherspoon who returned to Canada was very different from the one that left. Julia turned the page.

"The path ran along the lagoon for several hundred yards. It was well kept and pleasant, and I passed numerous village huts until I could see only one more where the trail seemed to end. The path wound around the side of the structure as it was angled to take full advantage of the view out into the lagoon. I climbed the three stairs up onto the porch and stood in front of a crude bright blue door. As I raised my fist to knock it, the door opened. Standing in front of me was a very handsome native man of indeterminate age, but with one remarkable feature. He wore an elaborate headband of sharks and birds tattooed onto his forehead. I started to form a sentence of greeting in my mind, but he said, 'Hello, Ross, I have been waiting for you.'"

Julia closed the diary because that was the last entry, he had made in it. She closed her eyes and tried to visualize the hut she had seen all night in her dreams. "Yes, there were three steps up to that porch, and the door was a bright blue not dark, and Dad went in."

"What am I supposed to do?" she thought to herself.

# CHAPTER FIFTEEN

They arrived back at the lodge and tied up to the short pier which jutted out into the lagoon. The two men waded over to their island hut while Samantha climbed the stairs to her porch and swung into the hammock for a quick nap, letting the gentle sea breeze quickly lull her to sleep.

Tom asked Adam what the process was for determining the concentration in the samples he had collected, and Adam replied, "How about you give me a hand and see how to do it yourself? It's easy and fun actually, and who knows maybe this whole subject might interest you as well. We can pick up the rest of the gear over in Sam's place after dinner."

"It's one thing to read about all the junk we create but it's another to see it way out here killing wildlife up close and personal. Seems everywhere we go we leave a mess, and yeah, I'd love to help out!"

Adam said, "Sad to say, and that's bloody well why I went into Earth sciences, to begin with, just hoping to play a part in humans doing something to help nature for a change, although it does seem hopeless. Just the scale of it is bloody overwhelming!"

"One thing I do know is that an empty stomach creates an empty mind, and there's too much to think about to allow that to happen! Let's see what kind of magic they're cooking up at the lodge."

When they arrived at Samantha's hut, they called out to her, but she had woken up and wandered over to the lodge a bit earlier. As the two friends got closer to the main complex and the cooking hut, they could sense different energy in the air. For one thing, there were numerous native islanders and lots of children sitting, playing, and just socializing with the staff and each other. Tom and Adam smiled and introduced themselves to parents and kids alike as they made their way to the cooking hut. When they turned the corner, they were astounded by all the activity they saw, and at the center of it all was a gentleman dressed in white cotton trousers, a floral short-sleeved shirt, and wearing sandals and a Panama-style hat. He was a handsome man of what appeared to be Polynesian decent, just about six feet tall. His body conveyed a sense of strength, yet he moved with the ease and deliberation of someone who might have studied martial arts or yoga. At the moment he was smiling and speaking with Samantha, who waved the two of them over immediately.

Samantha called out, "Guys, I'd like you to meet Kepa Kai. Kepa this is Tom McDonald and Adam Baines."

With his right hand, Kepa took off his hat and placed it under his left arm, and then extended it in greeting to Adam, who shook it warmly. Then he turned to Tom and smiled. Tom was just standing there motionless, looking directly at the forehead of Kepa Kai or rather at the tattooed designs of fish and birds which created the faux headband he had first seen in Honolulu. As his hand was grasped by the right hand of Kepa Kai, he snapped out of his reverie and said, "I am so pleased to meet you Kepa, or should I call you 'Grandfather'?"

"It is I who am most pleased and honored to have you three here, and you may address me in whatever manner spirit guides. Here on this island, Grandfather is what my children usually call me, but from where I just came, Mr. Kai was how I was addressed and Kepa Kai was how I signed my name. It always amuses me to be in two worlds, but in many ways, of neither. I have been looking forward to this meeting with you three. Welcome to Malaita."

His voice was rich and melodious, but it was his eyes that were so captivating, being a shimmering light brown with an almost golden hue, like two deep pools of honey. They conveyed at once a sense of warmth and high intelligence. Although his face showed the lines and the looks of someone older, his obvious good health and vitality radiated an almost palpable aura of energy.

Several children made their way up to him and in recognition, he placed his hand upon each one's head for a brief moment, a small but intimate gesture of affection that had the effect of lighting up their faces in broad toothy smiles. Soon it was time to eat, but the process was completely different from the night before.

Each person, whether they were staff, native, owners, or guests, was given a broad banana leaf and fell in line for heaping servings of rice, shrimp, vegetables, and slow-roasted wild boar. One by one they wandered off to congregate with their families, or in the case of the guests and Kepa, slipped into the dining lodge and grabbed a seat at the long table.

The occasional visit of Kepa Kai merited a feast of sorts and attracted those islanders who did not share their village with him to gather for both the food and the personal attention he bestowed on them. This night, however, was a bit different due to the three guests, and as they sat down Grandfather stood. After a brief pause, he said, "In the fulfillment of time, all is possible. With the intention of love, all is healed. Through the path of knowledge, all is realized. In the way of spirit, all is made whole. Let us pledge ourselves to the process. Let us prepare ourselves to serve. For those who have been chosen, there is no surprise. For those who have been chosen, there is no turning back. Within the deepest mysteries, lie the simplest truths. Let us honor the mysteries and the truths, the pain and the healing, the love and the intention. As we begin a new journey to a place we already know, let Mother guide our way home."

The people gathered around the table sat still. Quietly so. Not sure what to say or what was meant by Grandfather's somber statement, each of them stared awkwardly at their plates until Grandfather laughed and picked up a piece of fruit and popped it in his mouth saying,

"This wonderful food isn't going to eat itself, and once made shouldn't be wasted! Come now, eat up!"

The silence of a minute before was replaced with the satisfied murmurs complimenting Bryan and Susie on the great meal. Before long a pleasant banter ensued as it would at any family gathering over a sumptuous meal. As the pace of eating slowed and tea or coffee was offered, Samantha turned to Grandfather and asked,

"Grandfather, earlier you said that where you had been today required signing your name and implied being in the outside world. Do you have a business or a profession here in Mala?"

"My business here is the protection of these islands, and all that lives upon them, people included. I have represented and defended the Solwata people in many ways over the years. From developers to miners and especially loggers, many would seek to change what we see and enjoy here now. It is thanks to Mason's vision and to caring people of wealth such as your mother that we have been able to achieve as much as we have. First and foremost, it takes the vision, and I mean that quite literally. As the wisdom seekers have known and scientists are now proving, it is the thought which creates the reality. Actual visualization attracts the energy which becomes the matter to make it real. The outer world of circumstances shapes itself into the inner world of thought. This is the great secret which is just now being discovered or perhaps I should say rediscovered. Thought appears to be empty of substance. But thought and spirit are made of matter, but of a much finer substance than dense physical matter. As the being becomes purified the matter can be seen and understood. You are where you are in life not from chance or mere serendipity, but rather as a consequence of the purity and totality of your thoughts. This is a law which is immutable in this world and beyond."

"Have you spoken directly to my mother?" Samantha asked quietly.

"Yes, Samantha. Thanks to the sky phone, as we call it, I have spoken to Liberty many times over the last few years. She is one whose purity and intention is blossoming and whose thoughts are helping grow this sanctuary. I am very fond of your mother and was most pleased by her wisdom in planning this trip for you three to come here. However, even she does not fully realize where it will lead. But for now, the signing of the deed granting the trust an additional three hundred and thirty-five thousand acres was extremely important to both the goals of the trust and to me personally. What Liberty viewed as a modest contribution resulting in tax relief, will have a profound effect on this island and certain of its inhabitants."

Tom used a break in the conversation to ask a question which he had been wrestling with since Honolulu.

"Grandfather, when we were refueling in Honolulu, I saw you sitting in the waiting area by the gate, or at least I saw someone who looked like you and had the same band across his forehead. This has been on my mind ever since. Can you help me to understand?"

"I will help you, Thomas, but now is not the time or place. For now, let us enjoy the company of kind spirits and good food. Perhaps tomorrow you three will visit me in the village after you enjoy riding on Mother's back! There is someone there that I would like you to meet. An old friend."

With that, the first introduction to the mystery known as Grandfather closed as he rose to wander amongst the remaining islanders before walking the mile or so up the trail to his village. Gradually the villagers and the staff dispersed onto the paths and trails leading them to where they belonged for the evening. Tom chatted with the Masons as Adam and Samantha strolled back towards the lagoon.

Upon reaching her hut Samantha invited Adam to sit with her and watch the sun finish its journey west. They sat together on the bench on the porch, and Sam spoke first,

"You know, Adam, I think there is more going on here than we bargained for."

Adam said, "I had relished the chance to gather samples as you know, but my intuition tells me even that isn't the whole story. Tell me, what did you think of Kepa... errr Grandfather? He's something else, no?"

"You can say that again. I've never met anyone like him! I can't believe my mother never mentioned him. That's just not like her. She doesn't even try to keep secrets!"

"Well, she must have had her reasons, and I suspect that she may have wanted you to form your own ideas about this place and people with no influence from her at all. It almost seems like Grandfather should be up in a cave in the Himalayas or something. You can definitely pick up on his energy, that's for sure!"

"Speaking of energy, I'm feeling a tiny bit chilled. How about sharing a little with me?"

Adam put his arm around Samantha, pulled her close, and said, "How's that? Better?"

"Wonderful, what took you so long?"

"Incorrigible gentleman that's all, but you won't have to ask again!"

After another hour of small talk discussing the events of the day, they both decided it was time to hit the sack and get ready for another full and probably unpredictable day. As he left Adam leaned in and gave Sam a gentle kiss and hug which was warmly returned, and he waded out to the island. Thoughts ran through his mind in many directions.

Exciting thoughts. Thoughts of purpose and thoughts of emotion. Nice for a change.

Adam lay down in his bunk. He began counting backward from one hundred.

# CHAPTER SIXTEEN

Julia had decided that since she didn't know yet for sure whether the one-night offer would be extended, that she should have a back-up plan. Also, there was one line in her father's journal that intrigued her. It was "the three-hour hike back was depressing." She reasoned that if he could see a village from where he met the three giants, and it was a three-hour hike back, then this had to be close to where he was almost sixty years ago. So, she decided to take the truck up to the furthest village, and check out Denny's whatever it was, Digs, that was it. And who knows, she thought to herself, perhaps there is still a trail that goes up into the mountains. Maybe I can get lucky.

She stopped by the cooking hut to pick up something to nibble on. It was obvious that Samantha and her two escorts were already off to their day's surfing adventure, but Tony Perkins was still there.

"Hello, Tony, another day in paradise, eh?"

"I imagine that's deadest for the three Bobby took out in the boat. For me, it's kinda the same old same old, if you catch my drift."

"Well maybe a change would do you some good. I'm sure the camp could manage without you. Have you ever thought of opening your own restaurant someplace? From what I sampled last night you certainly seem to have the talent for it," Julia said.

"Talent is one thing, dollars are another. It takes lots of those to open something even as modest as the Coconut Crab, and that's a bloody oath!"

Julia was thoughtful for a moment, and then asked, "Say, Tony, yesterday you mentioned that this place has a foundation or a trust. You said they're about to close on a large land acquisition. Do you know if the deal went through?"

Tony was again put on guard by the Witherspoon woman. "Why do you ask? It's above my pay grade, but I believe it's in process or even closed, but I don't know for sure."

"I ask because I have my father's journal, and in it he made some very interesting observations. The kind that would make funding a top-notch dining experience child's play."

Tony looked up. "What kind of observations?" his voice barely squeaked.

"He observed what he believed to be a diamond deposit on the side of a mountain. A mountain that's not very far from here. In fact, I'm going to do a little exploring myself this morning, want to come?"

"I probably would, but this place will be choc-a-bloc with people tonight and it'll take me all day to get things ready."

"Well, next time then. But if your own restaurant is really your dream, maybe I can make it come true. I just need a little help doing it." Julia was going for the kill, and she knew it. She held her breath waiting for what the Aussie cook would say next.

"Well, miss, I have dreamed of my own place, that's deadset. What is it that you need from me?"

"Your eyes and ears Tony. Maybe a bit more. I want to find the place my father discovered before he was driven away by some kind of giant ape, as unlikely as that sounds. And if it's inside that purchase you mentioned yesterday, I may need to see if other bids are still possible. We can even make some promise to preserve part of that place ourselves. After all, it's only the little white stones that I'm interested in and that will be in specific areas. If my company makes the purchase, your lack of dollars will be a thing of the past."

"Yeah, but I've seen what places look like when the miners have a go at it. Not pretty."

"Didn't expect a tree-hugger in you, Tony. Mining has changed a lot from years ago. It can be more environmentally responsible than you might think."

"Yeah, right. Maybe in the States, but not here. No one would give a roo's ass what happened here, and you know it, Miss."

"Well, if you don't want to help, I can probably find someone else. It's your future either way."

Tony quickly said, "I didn't say I wasn't interested, Miss Julia. I'm just a bogan from the outback, but I like to keep me eyes wide open, that's all."

Julia resisted a victory smirk. "See what you can find out about the status of the trust's big acquisition you mentioned. That's the main thing we need to know for certain. If it isn't settled, it will be ours because money will be no object. Trust me on that."

"I'll see what I can find out."

"One more thing. Is there any way to get online here? I need to send someone an email. This place must have some way of communicating with the outside world or how would they book reservations. Right?"

"Yeah, we have a satellite dish that runs off the solar panels. The office in the big lodge has wi-fi, although Bryan and Susie don't really advertise the fact. You can probably log on there."

"What's the password, Tony?"

"I haven't a bloody clue. Don't have any use for a computer and never have." Tony uttered this with a certain tone of pride. But that quickly changed.

"Well, if a fine-dining chef in your own restaurant is what you really want, a computer and knowing how to use it is what you'll need. Lucky for you I can help you get set up. Get me the password Tony and find out about that purchase. Now, I've got to get going. I'll see you when I get back. Don't let me down."

# CHAPTER SEVENTEEN

Adam and Tom waded over to Sam's hut, and after making sure she was up and about, Adam picked up the lab case and carried it out onto the porch. Tom carried the sand and water samples that had been collected the day before, and together they began walking over to the main lodge complex, with Samantha assuring them she'd be right along.

When they got to the lodge Adam found Susie helping to get things ready to serve breakfast.

"Morning, Susie! Is there a worktable someplace where I can set some things up?"

"Sure, Adam. Follow me."

Tom said he'd catch up in a minute and headed towards the cooking hut to grab a piece of fruit. He turned the corner between the buildings and bumped a bit harshly into a woman dressed in western clothing that he hadn't seen before. Because they hit almost head-on, they stood there for a moment awkwardly. Tom looked into the face of a woman almost eye to eye whom he felt had great beauty, both inside and out, but whose face was hardened and whose energy was severe.

"She seems very tightly wrapped," he thought to himself, but he extended his hand in a relaxed manner and said, "Oh, I'm sorry. I should have paid more attention. My name is Tom McDonald."

Julia felt surprisingly at ease standing in front of the man who had just about knocked her over. Instead of getting rattled and using it as a way of asserting herself and her importance, which was her norm, she said, "Well, you know the old saying. It takes two to tango."

She grasped his hand as she looked into his face, which seemed at ease, and she thought, I wonder why? Where she came from everyone was stressed in some way or another and it showed, but this man didn't seem to be. Not only that, but he's also my age. How is it possible?

"My name is Julia Witherspoon, nice to meet you. Are you with the Samantha Lewis group? I bumped into her this morning. She seems nice." The thing she noticed about the man standing in front of her, and it took a second to realize, was that he was actually listening to her, and paying close attention. His eyes didn't wander to her chest, and he didn't seem to be thinking hard on what to say next. He was a quietly handsome man but didn't seem to know it. Interesting.

"Yes, there are three of us. Adam Baines is the other. We're research scientists from Berkeley. Sam and I have been friends since college, and we met Adam in California. We're here for a holiday courtesy of Sam's mother. It's her birthday in a couple of days."

Julia felt a tinge of - what was it? Disappointment? She knew that people were never just friends. Lovers or exes, colleagues, or bosses, but not just friends. But why should that matter?

She asked, "What field of science do you study, Tom?"

"Sometimes I wonder. Earth science is the department, but I'm not sure how long I'll continue with it. What about you? What brings you here? Seems like someone would only come here with a purpose. Like surfing, for instance."

She felt totally disarmed, yet comfortable, and uncharacteristically replied with candor, "My father was a geologist and came here almost sixty years ago, and I wanted to see what he saw."

"You mean see if there are any gems or minerals worth exploiting?"

She was a bit taken aback by his directness, but again, answered strangely. With candor.

"Honestly? Yes, that was something that interested me since I followed in the same career. I'm a geologist too. Dad found an area that he thought had great possibilities for diamonds and I just couldn't give up trying to find where he was." What am I doing, she thought to herself? Get a grip.

The man just stood there, saying nothing. Not looking at her, but past her. After a moment, he took a deep breath and said, "Well, one thing that I am beginning to learn is that not all wealth is in a bank, or in the ground, and everything is a trade-off. Companies make a fortune selling soda, but the plastic bottles end up in the sea and kill everything. Diamonds may be a girl's best friend, but I don't think this place would ever look like this again. Trade-off, right? I guess I'm starting to look for a different kind of wealth, but I'm not sure where to find it. Anyway, I've got to get going. Maybe we'll bump into each other again. Nice to meet you."

"Nice to meet you too, Tom. I hope we do."

Susie led Adam out of the dining lodge and over to where the camp had their office and business space. On two of the walls separated by offices were large tables that could be used for a variety of purposes such as presentations or displays, but which were cleared at the moment.

"Will this work?" she asked.

"I couldn't have asked for a better space, Susie! One thing though, do you have any type of cover I could put over the table. I would feel awful if this lovely wood got a water spot on it on account of me."

"No problem, I'll go over and grab something from the dining lodge. We have waterproof table spreads which we use occasionally. Also, there is a standard one hundred and fifteen-volt outlet just under the top of the table. As Bryan said yesterday, this whole business of plastic being everywhere is something Grandfather has been talking about for years now. Anything we can do to help, don't hesitate."

Adam laid the case on the ground and unsnapped the latches. He separated the two sides and unzipped the protective covers on each and folded them back to reveal what he had packed for the trip. Each item was carefully secured in its compartment, and he began with the right side of the case. The first thing he removed was a small digital scale, followed by an equally compact lab-quality hot plate that could control temperature up to boiling in precise increments. Next, he produced several items which were homemade out of common PVC plumbing pipe. There were three of these, each of which had three inches of two-inch pipe inserted into a collar meant to couple two pipes together, leaving a short piece of pipe protruding. He had super-glued nylon mesh to the end of each pipe in five mm, one mm and 0.3 mm mesh size, and that was sealed inside by the coupling. The net effect of all this was to provide an easy way to screen samples of water into capturing three different sizes of particles, simply by inserting the three pipes together with the largest mesh on top and the finest one on the bottom. Each segment of pipe and mesh had been labeled and would retain subsequently smaller pieces of whatever had been captured in the manta sieve the day before as they were heading over to the island. The final items packed on the right side of the case consisted of a variety of stirring rods and one large glass beaker which had been carefully wrapped in newspaper.

On the left side of the case was a foam-lined compartment that cradled a compact 40X magnification dissecting microscope, forceps, a pipette, funnels, and various other lab paraphernalia. In the bottom, were several sealed and zip-bagged bottles of chemicals. One by one he took everything out and set it up on the table which by then had been covered in a foam-backed waterproof tablecloth. The bottles he placed off to the left of his set-up and contained distilled water, 30 percent concentrated hydrogen peroxide, Iron ( Fe(ll)) solution, lithium metatungstate solution, and finally a jar of high-grade sodium chloride, otherwise known as salt.

Tom and Samantha entered the room quietly and were observing Adam at work. They couldn't help but be impressed by the efficiency, care, and forethought he had exercised in putting his mini traveling lab together. Tom finally broke the silence by saying, "Adam, I know you understand what you're doing, but it seems like a lot of gear just to see small pieces of plastic in the sand."

"It is, but it's both what's in the sand, and free in the water, that needs to be understood and there are two similar but different methods to determine that. I have to separate the plastic from the sand and any organic material which may be in the sample or the water from the plastic, to get an accurate count. Also, it's not simply a matter of seeing the plastic, because much of it is too small to see, but also quantifying the amount, determining the type of plastic and its probable source. That way we can attempt to understand the level of contamination at any given location, and maybe pinpoint where it's likely coming from, like fishing nets, plastic bottles, cosmetics, etcetera."

"Cosmetics? You mean like all the lipstick containers and suntan lotion bottles?"

"No, Sam, I mean like the tiny little plastic particles called microbeads that are so widely used in the cosmetics industry for all kinds of things such as lipstick, exfoliates, moisturizers, shampoos, and much more. Every night they get washed off and flushed down the drain and ultimately out into the ocean. It's bonkers how much of it there is. Also processes like media blasting, which is how hulls of ships and many other surfaces like graffiti on walls are cleaned, all end up in the ocean. It's just an insidious and almost intractable problem, but we've got to start somewhere. As far as this kit goes, I've used it many times and have been refining it to give me the exact data I need. Believe me, I'm not lugging one bloody thing more than I have to!"

"So, what do you do now, Adam? What's the first step?" Samantha asked.

"It's different for the two different sample types. If either of you wouldn't mind, after I weigh this beaker of sand, I would appreciate it if you could see if the kitchen could spare some space in the oven while we're off for the day to completely dry out the moisture."

Adam proceeded to weigh out exactly 400g of wet sand which had been collected on the beach into an 800ml beaker which he had previously weighed and labeled back at Berkley. He sealed the beaker and gave it to Samantha with instructions to remove the lid and to make sure no one disturbed the sample till they returned.

As she hurried off to complete her task she said, "Don't take too much longer, Adam. I can smell breakfast now, and we've got a busy day planned. Also, the oven you're going to use is a solar oven and it doesn't get much hotter than two-hundred-and fifty-degrees Fahrenheit. Will that be ok?"

"That will work. I'm not interested in cooking the samples, just drying them out completely. This next step won't take but a jiff. Where is the solar oven located? I'll put these in on my way to breakfast."

"It's on the south-facing side of the dining room. You can't miss it."

"Okay, see you in a bit."

Adam took the three PVC filters and inserted the three mm into the five mm, and the 0.1 mm into the three mm to create the stacked arrangement for the separation of the material. Next, he carefully poured the large container of seawater which he had collected the day before during lunch break, through the top sieve slowly. He was careful not to let any of it overflow since he knew exactly how much water the container held and would therefore be able to determine a ratio of the number of particles of plastic per liter of seawater, the standard of comparison for wet sample analysis. When it had all filtered through, he took each of the three sieves apart and carefully transferred the material into three small, labeled beakers, even using the squirt bottle and pipette to collect every single tiny piece of material. When he was satisfied that he had all the samples properly prepared, he covered the bottles, secured his makeshift lab, and headed to the kitchen where he placed the three small bottles in the oven with the other bottle.

Tom, who had returned and was assisting Adam as needed, headed to the dining table with Adam right on his heels. They both sat down to a hearty plate of eggs, fruit, homemade toast, and jam with coffee, regular for Tom, decaf for Adam.

Samantha spoke up after the guys got a few bites down. "Bobby left for the boat, and it sounds like we're going to have an interesting and fun day. He'll have us back on Charles Right for the morning, but after a late lunch, we're going to stop by Grandfather's village for a visit. He says it's a really neat place which is actually like a second home to him, and he's looking forward to showing us around. I, for one, can't wait!"

Tom said, "Ever since I saw Grandfather in Honolulu, I've wanted to know more about what's going on with him. It's like I'm drawn to wanting to know. I think the world is full of mysteries and there's so much I'd like to ask him!"

Adam agreed, "He is an impressive chap! As Bobby said when we first got here, he does seem like the Dinky Di, the real deal, and I too wonder where all this is going. One thing for sure, this place is a lot bloody more than just a surf camp!"

# CHAPTER EIGHTEEN

Julia headed back south in the pickup truck. She saw the turn-off to the other village Tony had pointed out and felt drawn to take a right and check it out. As she slowed to a stop a voice inside said to stick to the plan, so she continued on. Fifteen minutes later she took a right turn past the old sign crudely painted on a derelict surfboard, which proclaimed that Denny's Digs was, indeed, somewhere down the lane. The old Raider pickup handled the ruts well, but it was obvious that whatever lay at the end of this road did not receive the care and attention as where she had just left. Not even close. She instinctively patted her leg to be sure her knife was with her, but that was just out of habit.

The lane ended abruptly in a circular cul-de-sac of sorts, where anyone with a vehicle just left it and walked to wherever they were going. In her case, the rack of surf boards out in front of a group of huts built on poles near the water's edge made the decrepit sign over the door unnecessary. She got out of the truck, threw one strap of her fanny pack over her shoulder, and climbed the steps of the run-down hut which served as the main "lodge." She thanked her lucky stars that she had bumped into the Lewis woman in a pleasant way because she felt sure that she wouldn't have to return to this dive later in the evening. Thank God!

"What can I do for you, honey? Looking to catch some waves? You've come to the right place," said a voice coming from a heavy, shirtless middle-aged man holding a beer in his hand. "My name is Dave, welcome to my surf camp!"

She cringed as she answered, "I thought this was called Denny's Digs. My name is Julia Witherspoon."

"Yeah, well Denny sold it to me a few years back, and the signs were perfectly good, so why make work for yourself, right?"

"I can see you don't like making work for yourself. Where are all your guests?"

"Oh, it's a bit slow right now, but we've got a couple of parties out on the waves. Got me some locals to help out with the boat and the cleaning, so the place almost runs itself."

He had an accent that Julia couldn't quite figure out, but she took a guess. "You don't sound Australian, and you're definitely not from the states. Are you from England?"

"Naw, miss, I'm from South Africa, but I bounced all over before swallowing the hook and landing here. So, what can I do for you? Need a place to crash or get out on the waves? We've got it covered."

"No, I don't know how to surf, and I'm staying at Surf Mala."

"Well then, what the hell are you doing here? You

look like you'd be right at home down there, no offense. Just didn't seem like the type we usually get."

"My father visited here almost sixty years ago and must have stayed at one of the villages on this part of the island. I read in his journal that he had hiked up a mountain and could see a village from a clearing pretty high up. I'm just taking a vacation and retracing his steps, that's all."

"That's a first, and I doubt that's all to it. Again, no offense. This is a place that attracts two kinds of people, surf bums, and money hounds looking for anything that glitters or can be chopped down. You don't surf, so which one are you?

"Well, like I said, my father was here a long time ago, but to be truthful, he was a geologist."

"And you're following in his footsteps, right?"

For someone who didn't appear to have much on the ball, this Dave guy is pretty sharp, Julia thought to herself. "Well, maybe you could say that. I am a geologist, but that's beside the point."

"Seems to me that is the point! So once again, what are you here for? What do you want from me?"

"I'm trying to find some information that might lead me to where my father actually was when he.....was uh..." Julia didn't know how to finish her thought and she uncharacteristically stumbled mid-sentence.

"When he what, died?"

"No, nothing like that. Like I said, he was somewhere up there," she said pointing vaguely inland, "and he met some kind of large creatures who convinced him he wasn't welcome. I'm just trying to verify what he wrote and maybe figure out where he was. Of course, he might have had a touch of malaria or something, because he called them giants in the diary."

"I doubt he had malaria, 'cause if he did, he probably wouldn't have been able to make the climb. Had it myself once, and it wipes you out. As to the giants, it's common knowledge amongst the islanders - they're called Solwata people, that something large and mysterious lives up there. I think they call them Ramo, but that's about all I know. They don't bother me, and I sure as hell don't go up there!"

"I see. Is there anyone you can think of that might be able to give me more information about them? I just need to understand what I'm dealing with."

"The only person that comes to mind, is a man that comes to this village every so often. I think his name is Kai.. uh Kepa Kai, that's it. He's kinda like a shaman or something and they all call him Grandfather, whatever that means."

"Any idea how I can find this Kai fellow? This Grandfather?"

"Yeah, no worries on that score. He lives in the village you drove past when you came here. Just pull left and drive down and ask the first person you see where Grandfather lives, 'cause that's what they all call him. You'll find him."

Julia was anxious to leave and said, "Thanks, Dave. You've been a big help. See you around."

"I'd love to see you around, Julia. Why don't you stop back? We'll have a few drinks. Got my own bar here!"

"I'm sure you do, but it's a bit of a hike. Thanks again."

She wasn't afraid, or even remotely close to it, but just wanted to get away from there, the sooner the better.

It gave her the creeps and made her think that civilized society really did suit her much better. Thankfully, she didn't think she'd be knocking on Dave's door for a place to stay. She passed the old surfboard sign and headed north, down the island.

# CHAPTER NINETEEN

J ulia was glad to be driving away from Dave and his digs. Something was mildly revolting about him, but he did provide her with an important clue, and she was excited to pursue it. The turn-off that had drawn her on the way down was quite a bit nicer than where she had just been, and everything seemed better maintained. A mile and a half, and ten minutes later, the jungle began to thin out. Then she drove into a clearing, where she beheld numerous thatched huts standing on poles, both on land and out in the lagoon. She pulled over and parked alongside the four or five other vehicles that were there and got out of the truck. This place had a totally different "vibe" than where she had just been, and she took off her fanny pack and slid it under the seat and locked the door.

It was still only mid-morning, yet there was a relaxed sense of activity in the village. Children were playing or helping their mothers with different chores and canoes could be seen out in the lagoon. Men had come in from early morning fishing and were unloading their catch, so she walked over to see what they caught. As she walked past them, some of the children came up to her and playfully circled her, encouraging Julia to a kind of dancing game. She smiled and held her arms up and jumped up and down, but she really didn't have much to do with kids, so she walked through them and looked for someone to ask what she had come to ask.

A handsome young man about her age was speaking with an older man who was sorting some fish on a plank laid across the bow of his dugout canoe. He seemed to be speaking in English, so she walked over to him.

"Hello, my name is Julia Witherspoon. Do you happen to speak English?" she asked.

"Sure, mum. Most of us around here do. Ma' names Seth. What can I do for ya?" he said smiling.

He was very disarming, and she said, "I'm looking for information about where my father might have been when he was here many years ago. I was told that someone called Grandfather might be able to help me. Do you know him?"

The man named Seth stood passively for a moment, as if lost in thought. Then he replied, "Ya, mum, I know him." The smile was a bit diminished, but still there.

Julia said, "Do you have any idea where I could find him? I just want to speak with him for a couple of minutes."

Seth replied, "See over there?" he said pointing towards some mangroves. "There's a trail that leads through the village it does. Just follow it to the end and you'll find him. Last hut, he is."

"By any chance do you happen to know if he's home? It's important."

Seth replied softly, "Sure, mum, he's there, no worries."

"Ok then, thank you," she said, and started in the direction the young man had indicated.

The path began on the other side of the beach which was the hub of the village. She made her way through a maze of canoes, nets that were drying, and fish that were being prepared for market. The path was obvious, and like the rest of the village, well maintained. Julia felt a nervous excitement in her being. She had traveled for days to find where her father had been, and now she was almost certain she would find out. She walked past numerous huts, all on stilts. Some were out in the lagoon, and some she almost had to walk underneath right next to the beach. Villagers waved or said "g'day" and were pleasant to say the least.

At last, there were no more huts to be seen, other than the one another hundred yards down the trail, and she knew it was the one. She walked around to the front steps and stopped in her tracks. The three steps before her would take her to the front door. A door that was brightly painted a light blue. Memories of her dream flooded back into her conscious awareness...." What the hell? she thought to herself. A chill went down her spine as she realized that this might have been the same door her father had entered in the dream she kept having. After all, what were the odds? She was rattled.

Julia thought of turning back and maybe coming another time, but she rejected the idea. She climbed the steps and stood for a second in front of the door before raising her hand to knock. Before she did, the door opened.

"Hello, Julia, Grandfather has been waiting for you.

Please come in. My name is Arihi, nice to meet you," she said, extending her hand and smiling.

The tension that had been building was released in a heartbeat, and Julia grasped the young woman's hand. "How do you know my name? And how did this Grandfather know I was coming?" she asked.

The beautiful young island girl replied, "Grandfather has his ways of knowing things, Julia. Come, follow me. He has been looking forward to meeting you."

Looking forward to meeting me? Julia felt a shift was taking place. She felt disoriented, unsure of herself. She followed the girl called Arihi through a curtain and into a large comfortable room. Arihi motioned to a chair and said, "Wait here. I'll go fetch him."

Julia sat down and made herself comfortable and looked around. The décor was not what she expected to see in a villager's hut, more like what a Japanese home might look like, she thought. It was immaculate, if a bit austere, and there were pieces of art and sculpture all over, yet it did not look cluttered.

Arihi appeared back in the room, having come through a door leading somewhere out back. She walked past Julia and said, "Grandfather is on his way. I have an errand to run, but we will meet again, I'm sure. Bye for now." She smiled and closed the blue door behind her.

Julia sat alone, not sure what to expect, mildly apprehensive. After what seemed a much longer wait than it probably was, she could hear steps approaching on the wooden floor.

Then a man entered the room.

He wore three-quarter length white, baggy pants and a white loose-fitting cotton shirt. Wearing sandals and a blue and white bandana, he reminded Julia of Mr. Miyagi from a movie she had seen as a child, only this man was more robust and seemed more fit. It was hard to tell his age. He held two cups of what she assumed was herbal tea, and he extended his right hand to offer her some, then sat down across from her.

"Hello, my child, I have looked forward to seeing you. Welcome to Mala."

'My child'? she thought to herself. Who calls a stranger "my child" the first time they meet? Maybe he just gets off on impressing people with a wise-man act, although she had to admit that wasn't the vibe she was getting.

"I believe I was told that your name is Kai. Nice to meet you, Mr. Kai."

"You may call me Kepa, my dear, and the pleasure is certainly mine. It's been a long time since a Witherspoon has graced this hut. That is why you've come so far, is it not? To follow your father, my son, Ross."

Julia Witherspoon was being shaken to the core, and she knew it. She was frantically trying to process what this old man was saying, even though he had spoken very little. How did he know that I was following Dad? And even more mind-blowing, he called him "my son." What the hell could that mean?

"What did you mean by that, Mr. Kai?"

"Mean by what, my child?"

This was beginning to get out of control and Julia needed to ground the conversation. The "my child" bit was going just a little too far.

"You know. What do you mean by saying that a Witherspoon has been here, and then calling my father your son? I never knew my granddad, but I know my dad did. He gave him some things when he left to go exploring, including this knife I have here." Julia patted her pants pocket where her trusty knife always lay.

"Do you mean the one with the stag handle and the initials 'RW' carved into it? It's been a long time. May I see it?"

Julia, who was taking a sip of the tea from the cup she held, almost choked, but she recovered quickly. She set the coconut cup on the table and extended her right leg so that she could retrieve the knife. Her hand was shaking. She slid it across the table.

"Ah yes, you're back," the old man said, and he cradled the knife in his closed hand. Then he pressed a tiny button as if he had owned it as long as Julia had. The blade immediately snapped open with a click.

"Your grandfather gave this beautiful knife to your father, that is true. He told Ross that when needed, a knife should be able to open, with just one hand. A switchblade, I believe it is called. I have enjoyed many knives over the years. I use them for carving. I have always admired this one. It's the only one of its type I have ever seen." He closed the blade and slid it back to Julia.

Julia was even more bewildered. The man sitting in front of her was no spring chicken, and, doing the math quickly, she knew he couldn't possibly have sat with her father all those years ago. Yet, as she closed her eyes for a second, the image of the three steps, and the blue door flooded back. And there was something else. What was it?

"When I first met your father, he had come down from the mountains and was seeking answers to questions he did not know how to ask." Having said that, the old man seemed to absently remove his blue and white headband.

Julia stared at Kepa Kai's forehead. The tattooed headband on the man's forehead was exactly the one she had seen in her dream, as her father entered the hut with the blue door. She was reeling. Her head was exploding.

"I believe you are seeking answers to questions also, my child."

# CHAPTER TWENTY

Tony knew that Bryan and Susie tried to maintain an important part of their routine no matter how busy they were. They loved to walk along the trail which led from the road that traversed the island, down to the camp, about a mile each way. When things were slow, they were the ones who maintained the pruning and shaping of the jungle, keeping it at bay with an aesthetic touch. It was their way of relating to nature. So, when he saw them walking down the trail hand in hand, he knew he had his chance.

He felt very strange. He was nervous and there was a noticeable tightness in his stomach as he headed towards the lodge where the office was stationed. Once inside he walked across the large room where meetings were occasionally held and peered out the window to make sure his boss was still walking down the trail. Then he turned and walked to the office.

Tony was forty-six years old and had been at the surf camp for almost five years. He was generally content with his lot, but like many people looking towards the future, he wondered if this was enough. Was this what he'd be doing at sixty-six years of age? The chance meeting with the Witherspoon woman had wetted a desire, long held, but unattainable. Until now.

He stood in front of Bryan and Susie's private sanctum feeling like he was about to become Judas and betray the only people he really loved in the world, his dear friends at Surf Mala, and Grandfather. He tried the door, but it was locked.

It was locked, but in only the most casual of ways, having a hole in the public side, like a bedroom door, which required nothing more than a small nail to unlock. He returned from his kitchen with a skewer. He took a quick peek up the trail before easily opening the door, then shut it after himself. He stood for a moment almost trembling with guilt, fear, and excitement. There were two wooden tables facing each other, that served as desks and had laptops and a printer on them. A horizontal style filing cabinet displayed pictures and mementos of a personal nature, while the walls were adorned with pictures of guests and memorable events of the past.

A quick search of Bryan and Susie's desks revealed nothing, so Tony turned to the filing cabinet. As he bent to open the drawer, he saw a picture. One with his image on it. He was sitting on a log tending his fire, surrounded by guests and friends. Bobby and Arihi were there, Bryan was standing behind him and another man was sitting to his right. Grandfather. Susie must have snapped the picture at one of his visits in the last couple of years, but Tony didn't know it. A feeling of belonging and family washed over him, and he started to turn to leave, but he didn't.

Pulling open the file drawer, he quickly searched the file folders which were neatly arranged in alphabetical order. Scanning through, he noticed a file with four letters on it, SNPT, which he knew stood for Solwata National Preserve Trust. He pulled it out. It was an accordion file and had a lot of papers in it, but the ones he was looking for were right on top. It was a purchase and sale agreement for the large purchase SNPT had negotiated and was signed by the Solicitor General of the Solomon Islands. There were pages describing the property geographically, since it had never been surveyed, and a page with the agreed price and method and time of transfer of funds. The price was eighteen and a half million dollars, and it was for a one-hundred-year lease on the vast tract. He saw references to something called "The Protected Area Bill of 2010" and noticed the signature, "Kepa Kai, Solicitor" signed at the bottom. The deal looked final to Tony's untrained eyes, but he continued to read to the end of the last page where he saw, "All parties shall respect a seven-day right of rescission, in accordance with the laws governing customary land rights."

That was it! The date showed that it was signed yesterday, but that left six days until the deal was locked in. "Now it's Witherspoon's problem," he thought to himself. "I just want to get the hell out of here." He caught himself before simply walking out the door and stopped. Instead of pushing it wide open, Tony opened it just a crack and peered out the window at the far end of the lounge. He was horrified to see Bryan and Susie no more than one hundred feet away, and if he had simply opened the door and walked out, there was a good chance he would have been noticed. So, he barely opened the door, dropped to his hands and knees, and crawled quickly around the corner where steps leading to the kitchen area were not visible to anyone entering the office lodge. In less than ten seconds he was back where he might be expected to be found, fussing with the cooking fire.

Now all he had to do was find out the wi-fi password. On that score, he hadn't a clue, yet something occurred to him. He knew that visiting guests used the office area to stay in touch with business or personal responsibilities while here, so why not just ask Bryan and Susie what it was? What's the big deal? He went back to the office lodge and was told by Susie that the password had eleven letters.

They spelled "Grandfather."

# CHAPTER TWENTY-ONE

Bobby was waiting at the boat with the motor already running and ready to shove off. He had only stacked the three boards that had been settled on by the group the day before, and of course, he had waxed and racked his own board as well. They got underway in a more subdued manner than before, quietly and peacefully motoring through the lagoon at slower cruising speed allowing a more relaxed view of the scenery and a bit of conversation. He pointed out various features of the landscape such as the mountains which could be seen rising seemingly right out of the ocean off in the distance, and the local names of the numerous small islands which dotted the coastline. After a few minutes of silence, he said, "You know, mates, Grandfather said he wanted you to meet someone at dinner last night, and I know who that someone is. I'm feelin' that a bit of a warning might be a good thing to maybe prepare you for something you might think a bit strange."

"What could be so strange about meeting someone I assume must be a Solwata villager, Bobby? We're starting to feel right at home here, or at least I am."

"Well, Sam, if it were only that I wouldn't even bring it up, but in fact, you're going to meet a turtle. A very bloody big and very old turtle. One which is dying I might add."

"A turtle? How does one meet a turtle, Bobby? I mean I suppose you could visit a turtle or go to view one but meet one...that's nuts!"

"If we were going to see anyone other than Grandfather, you would be deadset, but he has known this turtle for who knows how long. I mean a really, really long time, and he's been caring for his friend for about a year."

Tom had been listening to the conversation with intense interest. He turned to Bobby and asked quietly, "Bobby, what kind of turtle are we talking about, and how old is it?"

"It's a sea turtle and a big one at that. A she, actually. Her name is 'Kahiko Aukai,' although Grandfather usually just calls her Kahi. As to how old she is, that's anybody's guess. Her name means 'Ancient Seafarer' in native tongue, and from what Grandfather tells me, she goes back to the days of sailing ships, and I'm not so sure Grandfather doesn't as well if you can believe that. She's a leatherback turtle, used to be very common in these parts, but now you don't see them too often. She has to be at least ten feet long and must weigh close to a thousand kilos, but she's tired and getting ready for her final voyage, what Grandfather calls her 'moeroa' or long sleep."

"A thousand kilos, that's about a ton. I had no idea turtles could get anywhere near that big," Samantha said. "How do you know it's a female?"

"A couple of ways; first Grandfather speaks with her, and second only female leatherbacks ever come ashore, and only then just to lay eggs, which is how Grandfather met up with her in the first place. But I don't want to say anything more. It's Grandfather's story to tell. I just wanted to prepare you blokes for an experience which could blow your mind."

At that point, they were once again passing the village where Grandfather lived and all three turned to see as much of it as they could, anticipating being there in the next few hours. They rounded the point and again beheld the magnificent crescent-shaped beach and the fabulous breaking waves half a mile off the shoreline. Charles Right was as perfect as it had been the day before and all four were eager to get out and start paddling. The anchor was dropped, and this time Bobby was in the water straight away. For the next several hours, four young people enjoyed what few others in the world have done. Riding wave after perfect wave, shooting through the barrel and carving the shoulder only to kick out, paddle back, and do it all again. The amazing thing was, they realized, that of all the people in the world who surf, probably less than a thousand had ever been here, and to have a spot like this all to yourself was surely surfers' heaven.

As muscles tired and stomachs growled, Bobby signaled the last ride, and one by one they rode the whitewater back to the boat. Once aboard, they all just sat back in the seats and marveled at the perfection of what nature had provided on this remote island, and how lucky they were to be there to experience it.

"Doesn't get much better than this, Bobby, in so many ways! I can see how you could come here and never want to leave, but I'm dying to know what you brought along for lunch because I, for one, worked up an appetite!"

"Tell ya the truth, guys, I didn't bring anything but water. Here, have some, mates, don't want to get dehydrated. As for lunch, I think they got that one covered back at the village, so let me get this engine started and off we go!"

Ten minutes later Bobby beached the boat in a cove a short distance from the heart of the village; they pulled it up to the high tide mark and set off towards it. As they walked amongst the pole huts in the shallows and the various thatched dwellings strewn along the shoreline, several children ran up to Bobby who picked each one up and twirled them around. They were radiant and beautiful people with pearl-white toothy smiles, mostly long curly hair of different colors, some almost blond, and a strong and healthy demeanor both of body and spirit. The most prevalent sound to be heard was that of laughter, and the whole experience being there could be described as simply disarming. They immediately felt relaxed since there was absolutely no sense of aggression or discord to be seen or heard anywhere. Adults smiled and waved to them, and many came up to Bobbly to speak to him quietly for a moment before they moved on. If the truth was told, Bobby was seemingly more at home here than he was at the camp, and when they arrived at Grandfather's hut the reason became instantly apparent. A stunningly beautiful young lady of mixed descent laid down a tray of food and went straight to Bobby and embraced him in a huge hug.

"Hey, babe, you keepin' the ole man happy?"

"As always!"

"Whatcha make for lunch? Here's a box of lollies I got for ya pickin' these blokes up."

"You gotta cut that out or you'll have me out jogging on the beach! Who are your friends?"

Bobby said, "This here is Samantha, and that one's Tom, and here's Adam. And this mates, is my wife to be, Arihi. Arihi Mathews to be exact."

Samantha asked, "Are you Bryan and Susie's daughter?"

Arihi said, "Nice to meet you all! Yes, I am legally Bryan and Susie's daughter, and in exactly ninety-two days soon to be Mrs. Robert Berry! Has a nice ring to it, I think!"

"Pleasure to meet you," Samantha said extending her hand. "I would never have guessed by your voice that you were from these islands. Did you grow up here?"

"Yes, I did. In fact, just the next village up."

"But you must have left for schooling?"

"My mother grew up in this village and met my father who was surveying the forest for a logging operation. Fortunately, the loggers didn't stay, but neither did my father. Bryan and Susie took me in and treated me like their daughter, which I am. After medical school, there was nothing I wished for more than to come back to this island and help care for the villagers along the coast I grew up on."

"Medical school, so you're a doctor?" Samantha asked.

"Well, yes and no. I started on the path of traditional

western medicine intending to become a family doctor, but I changed direction and received my degree in Osteopathy. Once I realized that I would be returning to these islands I felt that a more natural approach to healing would be more appropriate to what I would encounter here."

The hut which Grandfather lived in had one large room strewn with comfortable chairs and several low tables, and numerous cushions stacked against the wall. It created a feeling of comfort and relaxation and could certainly hold a crowd when pressed into service, which occurred regularly. A small room off to the back was where Grandfather slept or retired just to be alone. A cooking station in the rear was a smaller version of what was at the camp.

"Arihi, tell me, you said you will be married in ninety-two days. How come such a specific timeframe? Is there a special traditional significance to it?"

"Well, when Bobby asked me to be his wife, I said yes immediately, but with one caveat; that we would wait one year to be sure. That was exactly two hundred seventy-three days ago, and as you can see, nothing has changed between us! Right, Bobby?"

"I wouldn't say that, Ari. Without being too much of a mush, I can say that we're stronger now than a year ago. It's been like waiting for a good thing, and seeing it get better each day."

"So, if you guys have had enough to eat, why don't we go drop in on Grandfather? he's in his workshop just 'round the bend there."

As Arihi turned to lead the group out through the

back of the hut, Samantha and Tom followed closely. Both could just see the top of a tattoo rising from the small of her back, up to the bottom of her neck. They turned to each other with a knowing glance, as it represented the head of some creature. The group filed out of the hut and strolled the twenty-five meters to an interesting-looking structure nestled against the trunk of a giant Banyan tree just a little way in from a quiet lagoon. On the porch facing the water was a small platform raised a foot off the deck and covered by a roughly woven cushion stuffed with dense filler such as sago palm leaves.

"This is where he often sits, and when the breezes blow, he'll nap here as well. Duck your head, Adam, or I'll be looking after you for a bump!"

They entered a pleasantly strange room. It had the wonderful odor of tropical woods, almost like incense lingering in the air. All around the perimeter were shelves that had exquisite carvings of myriad birds and animals, some mythical and others realistic in their design. Where there might have been a large window at one time, there was an opening created by sliding a panel back into the wall similar to a Japanese shoji screen, which could let light in when closed, but which now allowed a beautiful unimpeded view of the lagoon. Another structure could be seen right at the shoreline which looked like a small, thatched shed of some sort. Grandfather sat in a comfy chair which was low to the ground and was dressed completely differently than he was at the surf camp, wearing sandals, shorts, and no shirt, just a headband across his forehead. He was concentrating on a carving and did not look up, but simply said, "Welcome to Santa's workshop. I see you've met my chief elf! I am just about ready to take a break. Ari, do you think a pot of tea might be possible?"

"Anything is possible for you, Grandfather, as if you didn't know! Be right back. Want to give me a hand, Samantha?"

"Sure, Ari, and call me Sam. Tea would be great, actually."

They strolled back the way they had just come while Tom and Adam pulled out the stools and set them around a low table near the center of the "studio" and waited for teatime. Tom wandered over to the opening where he gazed out at the lagoon. Grandfather was meticulously carving an object which was hard to see since he had it covered with burlap to guard his hand against the slip of a knife or chisel, revealing only the exact spot he was working on. Adam was fascinated with the carvings and admired the level of detail and skill involved in his work. Many were fantastical or perhaps mythical creatures, but most were realistic and highly artistic renderings of animals and creatures of the land and sea. A subtle but very effective multi-color staining technique brought the features to life, and they had the warm glow of some kind of wax polish. Grandfather set the piece wrapped up in burlap aside, cleaned his bench, and put his tools away. He rose from his low chair and sat back down at the coffee table where several chairs and stools had been arranged waiting for tea. Just then Arihi and Samantha returned with a large teapot and mugs for all.

They all sipped the tea quietly for a few moments before Adam asked, "Grandfather, how long have you had the hobby of woodcarving? The pieces I looked at on the shelves are amazing, almost like sculpture really. Bloody good!"

"What has now become my art, shall we say, was my survival in the beginning. Like Arihi, I too was abandoned as a child. My mother died in childbirth, and my father shipped out on a trading ship from Honiara, leaving me with my sister who was thirteen years old. He gave me a pocket knife the day he left, and I never saw him again. I began whittling small figures like shells and fish and sold them at the market for food and clothes. Later, after I spent time in the mountains with my "grandfather," my inner vision became more and more acute, and I could visualize each piece in minute detail and study it before I even picked up a tool. It was then that I began looking for the "vaite" in each piece, which is the native word for "spirit." I give most of what I carve to the children for birthdays, or ceremonial days or even weddings. Isn't that right, Arihi?"

"I know, Grandfather. I still haven't told you what Bobby and I would like. We'll come to a decision soon, I promise."

"Unlike thought forms which require mere concentration and intention to manifest, something substantial enough to adorn your home will require sharp blades and many hours to produce. Your one-year wait is surely worth my best effort, but please don't have me begin on day three hundred and forty!"

"We won't, Grandfather, we promise! Hey, Bobby, let's take a stroll through the village and let our friends have this rascal to themselves."

"Yeah, babe, I reckon that's a good idea, but where'd I leave my sunnies? Oh, there they are, let's go." As Bobby put his sunglasses on and headed to the door he turned to the group and said, "Be sure to work out what we're doing tomorrow, 'cause right now I reckon I haven't a clue! Bryan said to just keep the schedule flexible, so that's what I'm doing until further notice."

"I think I will be able to help you with that, Bobby. Why not stop back later in the afternoon and see what plans have emerged? I suspect you will be interested as well."

"Works for us, Grandfather! Bye for now."

"Now then, Thomas, I believe you wanted to ask me something last night?"

"Yes, I asked you if the man I saw in the airport was really you. I mean I know it was, but my mind can't cope with how it could be possible even though I know it happened."

"Well, think of the many people who have heard you tell them what their animals are thinking..."

"How do you know about that?" Tom interrupted him.

"I know about that gift, or better yet, that ability I would call it, but how can you explain to people what you do within the context of their current understanding? It is very much the same for me."

He rose from his chair and walked over to the far end of the shelf and pulled down a wooden box about twenty-four inches long and perhaps half as wide. Inside was something wrapped in plain cloth. Next, he picked up two of the empty teacups and placed them parallel to each other about a foot apart, and then placed a piece of thick paper across their tops. He asked his three guests to sit directly across from him on the low cushions. Then, reaching into the box, he unwrapped one of the most amazing wooden objects that any of them had ever seen, and gently placed it behind the sheet of paper.

The carving must have been created from a jungle

root because it was an eerie depiction of an octopus, but one that was swimming upright and now standing on its tentacles. Each of its tentacles was a masterpiece of detail, with the suction cups fully carved and tapering to different positions on the table. But it was the large bulbous head, and more specifically the deep green eyes that forced one to stare. To be drawn in. To hold the gaze as if it were alive, for surely if there was such a thing as vaite in the wood, this creature possessed it.

"From where you are sitting, please tell me what you see," Grandfather said softly.

"Aside from the sheer power of the carving, Grandfather, this is a very interesting position to observe it. It looks to me that it is standing on its tentacles beneath the water while the head is above the surface," Samantha said.

"That is exactly what I hoped you would deduce! Now, to answer your question, Thomas. If you were to view your higher self, your complete self, as our friend the octopus here, our soul or spiritual center would be as the head above the water. This is the dimension of the non-physical. It is made of the substance of thoughts and emotions, and yes, they do have substance. As in visualizing an object before I begin to carve, the act of creating on the next plane works in the same basic way; intention and thought, reinforced by emotion and love, produce beauty and harmony in the world of spirit. The tentacles represent the various experiences which the soul is having, on the physical plane. Some might say incarnations although not all of those tentacles require a full cycle of birth and life for physical reality to be experienced by the head above the water. So as the true nature of the reality of our soul is understood, each of those tentacles can be seen as a two-way conduit of information and experience back and forth between that which is in physical existence and that which is non-physical."

Tom politely interrupted, "How does that account for you being somewhere you couldn't possibly be?"

"If the communication is sincere enough and the intention is strong enough, new tentacles, in this metaphor, can be projected 'down' into the water anytime it is determined to be helpful to the fulfillment of a worthy goal. Each tentacle is tactile and able to function independently of the others, yet they all retain the same connection to the greater consciousness, which is soul. So, the answer to your question is yes, Thomas, you did observe me in the Honolulu airport because I intended to charge within you a thirst for the quest. That thirst can be stimulated in many ways, a little mystery serving as one of them."

He carefully picked up the astounding octopus and returned it to its wooden lair, which he placed carefully back up on the shelf. He walked over to the opening in the wall of the shop and motioned to his rather dumbfounded pupils. "Now let us meet Kahiko Aukai, one who has, in her day, devoured many a young octopus, I would imagine."

The three followed him down the steps and across the small clearing to where the "shed" was situated at the side of the lagoon. It was no more than a woven cover suspended over a piece of shoreline which had been dug out and deepened. Two panels were leaning together against the support for the roof. Inside was an astounding creature. Grandfather knelt in the sand and whispered in the ear of the nearly twelve-foot-long leatherback, whose ancient shell was covered in barnacles. Slowly she opened her eyes, and then ever so gingerly lifted her head and turned it to look directly at the three young humans who were kneeling together in the sand.

Grandfather moved his lips again, although no perceptible sound came out. Then he said, "She knows you are here. She would like the one with the seaweed hair to prepare himself to receive her message."

Tom who had a head full of curly red hair, got off his knees and sat down cross-legged in the sand beside Grandfather. He closed his eyes and took several very deep, very full breaths, exhaling fully between each one. Then he opened his eyes, but only as slits and looked through them with his pupils upturned. He breathed slowly and began to step aside from his thoughts. As he did so, a most remarkable thing happened. Communication came to him not just in words inside his head as he was well used to, but also in mental images that conveyed emotions and felt almost like physical warmth or radiation on the skin, only inside his being instead.

"i, who was free, am here for moeroa. across oceans unlimited. cold towards the invisible fields which guide us to the north. i rode the currents and explored all that is in this world. i was free to swim and to sing my song of the sea. my garden was everywhere around me. i partook of what I needed. every few cycles, at the special time, i would begin the journey to this place. this warm sand. if too warm all sisters, cooler, and all brothers return to sea. to dive, dive, dive, so deep that nothing can follow. to float in the warmth of the golden ocean above for hours. the white clouds which carried the humans disappeared. long ugly streaks of smoke such as *the mountains belch, now carried them. propelling them faster. many more, until everywhere they were. then to eat the soft white fish that was not a fish but something else. now they are as big as schools of the tiny silver fish. vast, vast schools of death. to dive to capture. to eat and then to starve. what had happened to the world of Kahiko Aukai? what had become of the soft white fish? where did that which never was come from? how will the little flippers find the soft white fish if one such as i, Kahiko Aukai cannot? my kind have roamed these seas since creatures of the land and sea have left for their moeroa. still, we endure. but how to endure with the belly full of soft white fish that never empties? i fear we will soon go to our sleep as the giants of the land and water did before time began. this one who you call grandfather has told me of hope. he has told me the little white fish that do not swim and that do not die will soon die. i hope that is so. my time to dream is coming. i dream that the little flippers will have a chance to be free and to swim and to dive, dive deep and catch little soft fish and to eat and to live. i tire now. this one who you call grandfather has been here, in the silent space between the waves. since the time of the great white clouds did he speak to me. as i now speak to you. each of you must dive, dive, dive. deeper than ever before. you must hunt the little soft fish that never die. you must take them to their moeroa. all that swim. all that fly. all that drink. all that breathe. all that eat. must never again eat the soft white fish that will not die. i sleep now. i wish you safety on your journey. may you swim strong in the currents. and not get lost. and find your way back to this soft warm sand."*

An audible sigh came from deep within the great turtle, and she laid her head back in the wet sand. Tom, who had been verbally relaying the words which had flowed to him for the benefit of the other two, slumped his shoulders forward and put his palm to his eyes. He was visibly upset and emotionally drained. Finally, he spoke in a small voice, "She has told us all we need to know, but I only wish that you could have FELT what she said as I did."

"This is the reason you have come here. There is a task to be fulfilled and a journey to be undertaken. The three of you have known of this task, deep inside your silent mind. You accepted the challenge long before you were born, and now the time is approaching for you to begin. But first there is more I need to show you."

"Grandfather?" Adam asked. "Did Kahiko Aukai say that you were here with her during the great age of sail? That would be at least one hundred years ago. How is that possible?"

"I noticed on your wrist a fine timepiece, a Rolex if I am not mistaken."

"It's the only thing I have left from my father. He was given this watch called a Submariner when he retired from his crew because he had been captain of the lifeboat team for a long time. He passed from us when I was fifteen years old, and I have worn it ever since."

"Does it keep good time being such an old watch?"

"I have it serviced every two or three years and it never fails to keep perfect time. Why do you ask?"

"Oh, nothing important, but what time does it say now?"

"Well, I didn't reset it to the time zone here because I suspected there would be no reason to, but it says two oh five pm and the date says April sixth."

"Good to know. Now let us go back to my sweet little lodge and meet our two elves. We have to discuss a plan I have for tomorrow and see if we are all in agreement."

Together the group turned to walk back to Grandfather's hut, with him in the lead. Tom was lost in thought and turned to follow. Adam and Samantha were last and instinctively reached out for each other's hand motivated by a sense of uncertainty coupled with excitement.

# CHAPTER TWENTY-TWO

The walk back to Mala Surf Camp was surreal for Julia Witherspoon. The man they called Grandfather had done more to shake her concept of reality in the thirty or so minutes she was with him, than she ever could have imagined. And the amazing thing was, that she never did get a chance to ask him what she had gone there to ask. The subject of the big creatures and the diamond mountain never came up.

"He seemed to know I was looking for answers," she said to herself, "but he never allowed me to ask the questions." He told her that guests would be arriving shortly and that he needed time to himself. But he also said that they would meet again soon, and he would show her what she wanted to know.

"Interesting he said show me, not tell me or explain to me," she thought. "And what about him knowing my father? How is this all possible?" Yet, impossibly, he knew about the knife and how Dad got it. "This dude is something else, I have to admit," she mused, "I really have to bring my 'A-game' when I go back."

She was so lost in thought, that the mile went by in a blink. Soon she emerged from the jungle trail that shadowed the lagoon and recognized the clearing that signaled the surf camp was just ahead. Seeing the various huts and lodges snapped Julia back to reality and she wondered what Tony, the cook, had found out. She decided that she would follow through with her promise of helping him with his own place, but it might be offering the owner of the Coconut Crab Café more than he could turn down, rather than something more elaborate.

"After all, that would be plenty for what I need from him. Let's just hope he earns it." she thought as she headed towards the cooking hut.

Tony Perkins was in his usual place at the business end of the fire pit coaxing embers from the previous meal back to life. He may have been in his usual place, but he certainly was not in his usual state of mind. He had done something which, for the first time in many years, disrupted his usual equanimity. There was no way to unbreak an egg, so he just had to live with the consequences, and that was what was eating at him. He looked up, and there she was.

"Hello, Tony, how's your day going?"

"OK, I guess, Julia. I'm feelin' just a bit rooted, I am," he said with a sigh.

"What the hell does that mean, rooted?" Julia demanded.

"Ah, it just means tired, or buggered. Just a bit wiped out, I guess. But no worries, I'll be alright."

Julia kept the pressure on. "You'll be more than

alright, Tony, if you got me what I need to know. So, did you?"

"Yeah, devo."

"Devo?" Julia raised her eyebrows.

"It means definitely. Yeah, I did."

"So, what the hell did you find out? Both of our futures are at stake," she said as the mystery and magic of the previous two hours was fading fast. Julia was again on the hunt.

"I know what the password is, so you can use your lappy in the office lounge."

"I assume you mean laptop. What is it?"

"It's Grandfather, with a capital G." As Tony spoke his name, another wave of emotion rolled over him. "Just Grandfather, that's all to it."

"What about the purchase agreement? Did you get a look at it? What is the status of the sale?" Julia was not distracted or put off by the password a bit. She was her old, focused self.

"Yeah, I took a peek, I did. It's not a sale."

"What do you mean, not a sale?"

"It's a lease agreement, for one hundred years, in exchange for eighteen point five million U.S. dollars."

"A lease? Ummm, was it all signed off on?"

"Deadset, it was. Signed by Grandfather, only he used his real name Kepa Kai, Solicitor."

"So, Grandfather, urrr Kepa Kai is an attorney. I never would have guessed judging by how he looked this morning."

Tony jolted upright. "Looked this morning? Have you met him?"

Julia replied smugly, "Yes, I went for a visit, and we chatted for a while. I just got back."

"Did he have anything to say about your father? That bloke knows more than he lets on and that's no lie."

"He told me that my father had stayed with him when he was here almost sixty years ago, can you believe that? I may be young, but I wasn't born yesterday, and I can do the math. The funny thing was though, that he seems to have seen my knife before. You know, the one I sliced the lemon with? He knew it had my father's initials carved into it. Must be some kind of parlor trick or something, but I was weirded out by it."

"That was no parlor trick, Miss Julia. You may have met him, but you don't know him like I do," Tony said in a subdued voice.

"Well, that may be, but that's not what I came to talk to you about. Were there any conditions or timelines on the contract that haven't been met yet?"

"Just one," Tony whispered.

"What's that? Come on, speak up. This is important, for both of us."

"There appears to be a standard delay before a land contract becomes deadset. I think the word rescission was what was used," Tony explained.

"A right of recission? That makes sense, it's pretty common back in Canada too. How many days did it allow?"

"Seven days, and it was signed yesterday, so there's probably not much you can do, right?" Tony said meekly.

"Not right. There's a lot I can do, and thanks to that password, I'm going to get started right now. Good job, Tony! If all goes like I think it will, you better be thinking where you want your new gig to be, 'cause you'll be on your way! Now I have to get online. See you later."

"Yeah, I guess," was all Tony could say.

# CHAPTER TWENTY-THREE

When the group was seated back at his lodge, Grandfather remarked that Bobby and Arihi were just about back, and it would be best to wait a minute for them to arrive. No sooner had he said those words than the two could be heard approaching. They found a cushion and sat down. The room was quiet. All eyes were on Grandfather.

Grandfather smiled at the young people sitting around him, his honey gold eyes sparkling as he made eye contact with each one in the group. He began in a soft voice, "I was born Kepa Kai many years ago and fished in these waters and lived in a hut with my sister not unlike the one I live in now. I would have remained Kepa Kai and not 'Grandfather' as you now address me, except for an event that happened when I was perhaps fourteen years of age, and yes, Adam, it would have been sometime during the end of the great age of sail. I routinely ventured into the jungle and explored the trails and roamed from the sea up into the mountains in search of the things I needed to eat, like nuts and fruits, or the special woods that I carved into animals to sell in the markets.

"One day I wandered much further into the jungle than usual. Eventually, I climbed to a large clearing and was able to see far out into the ocean beyond the islands surrounding our village. I stayed there basking in the warm sun, drinking from a fresh flowing stream, and gazing out to sea. I must have fallen asleep, but I sensed something and woke up.

"Suddenly they appeared, without a sound. There were three of them and as they walked towards me, I was strangely unafraid, for they were very large, very tall 'people' who had to be the giants that everyone in the village knew of and spoke about freely. They looked more like extremely large and hairy men, rather than monkeys or apes. Their facial features were more what I now know to be Neanderthal-like in appearance. Their long hair was silken and well maintained and varied in color from dark brown to a lighter reddish color, even displaying light streaks of white around the eyes. It covered their bodies completely. There was no hair on the hands and fingers, and their thumbs were just like mine only enormous by comparison. Also, unlike the stories, they had no offensive odor and their hair almost gleamed in the sunshine. Once the shock of their size and the suddenness of their arrival had subsided, I could see that they were intelligent creatures who wished me no harm. I nearly fainted when one of the group spoke to me."

"You who live by the great water. Why travel you here with no others? We are Ramo. Here we live, and up there in the land of sky and light." The creature waved its massive arm vaguely in the direction of the foreboding mountain range which rose into the clouds behind them and became the very spine of the island, unexplored and avoided at all costs by the villagers.

"I am Kepa Kai," I said. "I seek only the fruits and nuts which I need to live. I have heard of you in stories, but I did not know you spoke our language."

"Why are you not afraid little Kepa Kai? When we see those of your kind, always frightened you are, like the ghost of the dead you see and run."

I told him, "When I first saw you, I felt that you were peaceful and meant me no harm. Would I run from the playful fish that stands on its tail, or from the great sea turtle as she lies upon the sand to bury her eggs? All things have a place and if this is your place I will leave and not return if you wish."

"You are wise for being so young. There is much to learn in this world. You may come with us and see what others of your kind have never seen. The choice is yours."

Grandfather stopped, suddenly drained, and leaned back in his chair.

"That for me was the beginning of a new life. It was when I met my 'Grandfather' and was accepted into his family. We trudged high into the mountains that day until we came to a place where water fell from the sky. A cloud of mist hid an opening and through that narrow gorge, we continued."

"What did you see, Grandfather?" Samantha asked.

"Signs of the land being occupied. Instead of barely visible jungle trails, there were well-maintained pathways that were paved with large flat stones. Shelters began to appear, constructed of wood with thatched roofs, but a very different design than those in my village, and of course much bigger. There were gardens with fruits and vegetables and flowers, and off to one side was a place where they prepared food which had huge stone crocks with carved covers that had fires lit next to them. Although exhausted, I was amazed at what I saw."

Grandfather paused for a moment, and Bobby asked, "How large an area was the village, Grandfather? How many...giants lived there?"

"It would be hard to know for sure, Bobby, because the 'village' was spread over a large area in a narrow valley surrounded by very steep mountains. Also, I saw several entrances to a vast cave system where many also lived and which allowed the Ramo, which is what they called themselves, to travel unseen for hundreds of kilometers. It was, and still is, what would better be called an organized society rather than a primitive tribe."

Samantha was excited. "I found all kinds of crazy stuff when I was researching where we were going. Even stories of Japanese soldiers being attacked by giant creatures as they prepared defenses on Guadalcanal, but the Solwata people just accept them as commonplace, like it's no big deal."

Grandfather said, "True, but hundreds of years ago they were a very big deal to the natives. They fed on them. The fact that the native islander population never spread out over the entire islands, and never became more numerous, was for that reason."

Samantha asked, "Does that still go on today? Why weren't you afraid then, Grandfather?"

"The Ramo ceased hunting humans somewhere around four hundred years ago according to their legends, so by the time I was a boy, the memory of hunting parties striking terror in the villages had long since faded. I was told the story of a great Ramo named

'Taka Mikode.' He was both a great chief and what we would call a holy man or sage. It was he who was responsible for changing the behavior of the Ramo from preying on the human population to accepting their right to exist, and he laid out the guidelines by which the Ramo avoided contact with the humans which still exist to this day."

Samantha said, "It is incredible to be able to hear stories through so many generations, Grandfather, when all that remains is the oral tradition of a language which must be primitive compared to ours."

"There are two things wrong with your supposition. First, they do have a written language of sorts which is made of symbols like the hieroglyphics of Egypt. Second, there were not 'so many generations' that the stories were handed down from. I was told of these legends by his son, Luti Mikode, whom I refer to as Grandfather, for it was he that I met in the clearing that morning, and it was he that I lived with for almost two years."

Tom had been listening with rapt attention and couldn't help cutting off Samantha's next question, "Grandfather, that would mean that the Ramo must live up to three hundred years if my calculations are correct. Did they teach you the secret of living longer which you obviously know?"

"They did, or rather I should say Luti did. I became the first human apprentice to a Ramo holy man. Taka Mikode was almost like a god to the Ramo, and he is buried in an extravagant site on the top of Mount Mala, about forty-five kilometers from here, and right in the middle of the parcel of mountains which Liberty just helped the foundation purchase. The site is an archeological treasure, and now we know it will be preserved and guarded forever."

"Thank God for that!" Samantha blurted out.

"Luti followed in his father's footsteps and learned the ancient ways of Ramo spirit work, and I learned and still learn from him. That is the reason for my wanting to meet here together. I would like to take you to Mount Mala and show you some of the artifacts which have now been protected, and perhaps Luti Mikode will grace us with his presence, although I cannot promise. But you will at least be able to see and take pictures to show Liberty just how profoundly important the transaction was that we finalized yesterday. I must pledge all of you to one promise though, and a sacred one at that: you must never reveal any of what you see to the outside world. As it stands now, the legends and rumors of what is there have begun to fade, and for the sake of the beings that I have come to know and love, that needs to continue."

"I would be honored to go to this place, Grandfather!" Tom spoke fervently. "And you say that the Ramo you first met, Luti Mikode, is still alive?"

"Yes, he is still alive, although perhaps for not much longer, relatively speaking. He has a young apprentice that accompanies him now and who has been with him for the last sixty years, so I trust that his ways will not be lost."

"Grandfather, I know we came here on holiday for surfing, but there is nothing I would rather do than go with you to where these people have lived and see what is left to see. So, I vote to go!"

"Me too!" said Samantha.

"And I," echoed Adam.

Arihi, who had been silently observing the exchange said, "Grandfather, I have heard you tell the story of your first meeting with Luti, and the many other wondrous tales of your life with them since I was a little girl. But I never thought that I would go with you back to that place. Thank you for inviting us into that part of your life." As she finished, she rose from her cushion and embraced Grandfather like the granddaughter she had become. Bobby too was moved by what was being offered.

"I had always heard that you spent time out in the bush, Grandfather, not that this whole place isn't outback to a certain extent for sure. It would be dardy to see the place where you were as a boy all those years ago."

"Well, then, it is settled. Bryan and Susie have been with me to the place of Ramo several times and have agreed to stay and watch the camp so that Bobby can drive. This will be a long day for us all, so we had better gather what we need tonight and be ready to go first thing tomorrow morning. You may bring cameras as I said before, but I ask that you do not capture images of Ramo if they should come to see us, only the area and what it holds as physical evidence seen in stone. Dress with protection. We will be in the jungle."

The group rose to leave, with Arihi staying behind to attend to Grandfather. Bobby led them back through the village to where the boat had been beached, and they were soon underway heading back to Mala Surf Camp. They were collectively lost in thought and nervously excited about what the next day was to bring.

# CHAPTER TWENTY-FOUR

Julia walked back to her hut and retrieved her laptop and its battery charger and headed for the office lodge. She was excited and felt like everything she had dreamed of for the last several years was within her grasp. Now, she just needed Alex to come through, but after the last night they spent together, she didn't think that would be a problem.

She climbed the half-dozen steps to the porch and pushed the lodge door open. Brian and Susie were in their office with the door open, so she decided to say hello and make sure she was welcome to stay.

"Hello, Susie. Hello, Bryan. Lovely day it's been! I took a walk up to the next village and it was delightful!"

"Oh, hi, Julia. Yes, that is a wonderful trail to stroll, and the village itself is a gem. We have many friends there," Bryan said.

"I bumped into Samantha Lewis this morning and she seems really sweet."

"That reminds me," Susie spoke up. "I spoke with

Samantha before they left with Bobby for the day, and she would be horrified if we didn't let you stay on account of her."

"It's what we suspected she'd say, but we had to hear it from her." Bryan added, "So, you're welcome to stay as long as you want!"

"Oh, that's great to hear! I must say I would have dreaded going back to Denny's Digs. Not my kind of place!"

"We don't have any issues with them, but then again, I know what you mean," Bryan said.

"I spoke with Tony, the cook, and he said it was alright to access the wi-fi, and he gave me the password. Is it ok if I sit in the other office for a bit? I still have responsibilities back at the ranch."

"Sure, Julia, no worries. Take all the time you need, and you'll be joining us all for dinner, right?" Susie said.

"I sure will! I also bumped into Samantha's boyfriend, Tom. He seems really nice as well."

"From what I gather, Tom McDonald is an old friend of Miss Lewis's, but I wouldn't call him a boyfriend. I think that is a developing tale between her and the other gent, Adam Baines," Bryan said with a wink.

"Oh, that's interesting. I thought he was very nice. There's something about him that's different. Well, thanks for everything. Now I've got to get some work done. Bye!"

"See you at dinner," Susie said.

Julia walked to the other office which was really designed for exactly what she was about to do, touching base with business interests that had to be maintained. Not everyone who visited the surf camp could maintain freedom from responsibilities totally. She booted up her laptop, searched for networks and found "surfmala." So, she hit connect, and entered Grandfather as a password. Immediately she went to her inbox, and there was a message waiting to be read from Alex.

"Hello, Julia. I hope your flight was comfortable and that you're safe and sound in the Solomons. I just wanted you to know that since we last were together (wonderful, wasn't it dear?), I have secured authority from the board that if a major find is discovered, the company will make every effort to secure it. Great news, eh? So let me know as soon as you do, and we can take it from there! Your father's girl all the way!"

Julia Witherspoon hated two things more than anything else. One was to be reminded she was her father's daughter, which she knew and struggled to compete with every day. And the other, was to be patronized by a male, especially someone in a position of authority over her, and that meant Alex. However, until she completed her crowning achievement, which she hoped was close to becoming a reality, she had to play the game. And she knew it.

She started typing. "Alex, are you at your computer?" She waited. No response. She looked at the clock on her computer just to be sure she'd calculated correctly, and she had. It was just before nine in the morning in Toronto.

"Probably sitting in Starbucks, the lazy bastard," she thought to herself. She quickly went to 'Contacts' and found his secretary's email address and sent her a message.

"Lucy, is Alex in the office yet? It's urgent I communicate with him."

This time there was a quick response. "Hello, Julia!

You know him, he shows up when he shows up. Not here yet."

"Lucy, tell him to get on his phone or get back to the office. I expect a reply to the message I sent in ten minutes, no longer."

"Uh, he is my boss, Julia, but I will, umm, make the suggestion."

Julia typed with exasperation, "Ten minutes, Lucy. I also have Peter's contact information and that will be the next message I send if Alex doesn't get his ass in gear. He knows this is important."

"I'll call him now."

Five minutes later Julia received a message from the CFO of Lucarana Mining Company which read: "Julia, my dear, how are you? Enjoying your trip?"

"Good Lord," Julia thought. "Doesn't he have a clue that when I say it's urgent we communicate, that I don't need that crap?"

She typed: "I'm not on vacation, Alex, remember?"

"Of course not. Any luck?"

"I know where my father went, and I know there are lava tubes there. I haven't seen what he saw yet, but I will."

"And what about the big scary apes?" Alex mocked.

"They're real, but I'll deal with that when I go up there. First, you've got to get moving."

"How do you mean?"

"The entire area, and it's huge, has been leased by a land preserve trust run by the surf camp I'm at, for one hundred years."

"One hundred years? That seems to put an end to that. NO?"

"Not yet."

"How so?"

"There is a standard seven-day right of recission in the law governing all land matters here. The lease price was eighteen point five million U.S."

"What are you suggesting?"

"I'm suggesting you get your ass over to legal and make them an offer they can't refuse. And make it ASAP, Alex, there's only six days left," Julia typed furiously.

"That's asking a lot, Julia, in a short amount of time. I'm not sure it will fly."

"Well, if you don't go talk with Peter Allaire, I will email him myself. Soon." Julia knew the CEO, and the thought that a major find would bypass Alex, was a gambit she knew would have an effect on him. And it did.

"Now, now, my dear, there's no need to bother Peter on something as trivial as this. I will run over to legal and have a word with them shortly."

"Trivial? My father saw a mountain of diamonds. You call that trivial?" Julia was fuming.

"No, of course not, Julia. I only meant that I could take care of it. That's all."

"Then do it, Alex. I'll be checking my messages. Goodbye."

Julia sat for a moment, cooling off. "What's wrong with him?" she thought. "Here I am trying to hand the company a major find, and all he can do is call me dear and drag his ass. Unbelievable."

# CHAPTER TWENTY-FIVE

Tom found Bryan and Susie in the lounge looking over what he presumed to be correspondence with a foundation member on a laptop. Bryan closed his computer and asked Tom how the visit to Grandfather's village went.

"I hope I'm not interrupting something important, Bryan, but that's what I wanted to talk to you about if you have a minute."

"Yeah, absolutely, mate, no worries. We try and be as responsive as we can to the folks who have helped build this place, but they all know we're on island time here. So, what can I help you with?"

"I guess I'm coming to understand and accept that what I thought I came here for pales in comparison to what I am experiencing. Three days ago, playing in the waves with Adam and Sam was the extent of what I expected from this vacation, and even though I had a premonition that there might be something more, I had no idea the profound effect that Grandfather was going to have on me. I was wondering if you went through some version of the same process, and how you have come to view your relationship with him if it's not too personal to ask."

"No not at all, and to even ask that question, tells me a lot about what you must be feeling. The answer is yes, we did go through a similar process, I guess you could say 'integrating' Grandfather into our lives together. When we first came here, we could tell right away that this place had the potential to be what we had been searching for. It was remote, beautiful, great surf for an ecological resort and of course, very affordable."

"What made you pull the trigger and commit to this place, which you surely must have known would be a lifetime affair?" Tom asked.

Susie answered, "Grandfather, that's what, or I should say who, although we probably would have done so anyway."

"How's that?"

Bryan explained, "When we first arrived here, it was much like you did. We flew into Honoraria and took the ferry into Auki. When we got off the boat, we hadn't a clue where we were going to go. We were just winging it, I guess you could say. We stopped into a sandwich shop for coffee and a bite to eat, and the only two seats available were opposite a handsome older man with a tattoo across his forehead."

"You mean Grandfather was there waiting for you?" Tom exclaimed.

"That was exactly the first thing he ever said to us. 'Hello, my name is Kepa Kai, and I've been waiting for you. I am most pleased that you have finally come.' I will never forget the chills that went up my spine that day."

Susie added, "That was our first meeting with the man who would become 'Grandfather' to us. I'll never forget it!"

"What happened next? Did he tell you where to go look for property and show you around Mala?"

"No, Tom, he didn't. He told us that our vision for preserving wilderness in a remote place was exactly what our Mother needed. He always refers to the earth as 'Mother.' He also said that he would assist us in any way he could and that if we chose this place and had problems, that he would help. He didn't push us or show us anything, he just quietly encouraged us through his presence, which I'm sure you know, is powerful to be around," Bryan said.

"Especially when you first experience it," Susie added.

"I've done a lot of reading about what people call 'spiritual' subjects like meditation, yoga, and understanding the nature of consciousness. I've been trying to balance that side of myself with the science side, and sometimes it feels like a tug of war, like I'm at odds with myself. Throughout history, the path to understanding has always been passed from master to disciple or student. I guess what I stopped in to ask you is if you feel Grandfather has been that kind of force in your life, since you've known him the longest."

"Funny you should ask that question and again yes, I consider Grandfather to be a spiritual master in every sense of the word. Susie and I have been together since almost the first minute we met. It was not a physical thing, although you can see how lucky I am in that regard. It was because we both were on 'the path' and knew we had found the one who would complete the circle. I had studied Tai Chi for years and Susie was into Kriya Yoga at the time, and we came together in spirit, first and foremost. We look back on it now, and without a doubt believe that Grandfather is a very high being and that he has been guiding us before we ever stepped foot on Malaita."

"What about the tattoos that Bobby and Arihi have? Do you and Susie have something like that? Bobby said it was a sign of devotion or respect, I was just wondering."

"We both do. Here, take a look." Bryan pulled his tee shirt over his head to reveal a beautiful image in ink of three dolphins leaping out of the water together in play. "My dolphins represent the play of spirit in nature, the freedom to be joyful and at complete peace in their environment."

Susie said, "I decided to have a spiral done, somewhat like a nautilus shell, out of respect for Mount Mala, which I hear is where you are all going tomorrow. I think you will observe some things there that will be with you for as long as you live, and maybe help with that tug of war you referred to."

Brian added, "Science has its place in the world, but it's often not humble enough to know what it doesn't know and to accept what it can't prove. Grandfather falls into that category, right, mate?"

Tom said, "Absolutely! And thank you, I think you gave me just what I needed to hear!"

Bryan put his hand on Tom's shoulder and said, "Just told you our story, Tom, but we're glad it resonates with you. We who call Kepa Kai by the name of Grandfather become like family, and there's always room for more!"

"I like the sound of that!"

"One other thing, Tom. I believe that Grandfather is

exactly what I described him to be, but he is also a native shaman, and in that tradition, there are methods of expanding the mind unlike what western religion would accept."

"What kind of methods?"

"We're hosting a celebration in two days in honor of Samantha's birthday, and also what Grandfather calls 'your task.' He asked us to have both the lounge and the office prepared for the celebration for you three."

"Oh, that's nice, sounds like a party!" Tom said.

"There is a vine that grows way up in the mountains, and it is boiled down with other herbs to produce a tonic that has incredible effects on human consciousness. It is not dangerous in any way, and with Grandfather as a guide, it can be a most profound experience, that much I can assure you."

"I see, thanks for the heads-up Bryan, and one other thing. If I wanted to get a tattoo before I left, is there someone who can do it? And will I have enough time?"

"If that is something you wish to have done, it can be arranged. In the old days, the drawing of lines was a test of manhood and took many days. The art is still part of the culture here, but modern methods have been embraced, so yes you would have enough time during your last couple of days, just let me know."

As Tom turned to leave Bryan and Susie, the office door on the other side of the room opened, and there was the girl he had met yesterday morning, gathering some things off the desk.

He walked over to say hello and help her with the door as she fumbled a bit with the cords and her computer.

"Hello, Julia, nice to see you again. Let me get the door for you."

Julia, who was still in business mode, looked up, a bit startled and said, "Oh, hi, Tom. I didn't see you there. Thank you."

"That laptop looks heavy, want a hand with it back to the hut? I'm heading in that direction myself."

Normally, Julia would have dismissed such an offer as demeaning male chauvinism, but something about Tom's .... energy encouraged her to say, "Sure, Tom, that would be nice. Thank you."

He took her computer and shut the door behind her. They both walked to the porch and stood for a moment at the rail looking out at the lagoon. Then Tom said, "I never thought being here would have such an effect on me. I feel like Dorothy. Like I'm in a whirlwind."

"Funny you should say that, Tom. I was feeling the same thing earlier this morning, but I've come back to Earth now."

"What happened?"

Julia paused, parsing her thoughts. Surprisingly, she felt comfortable enough with this man to be candid. "My father was here years ago, and I'm trying to retrace his steps. I was told that a man named Kepa Kai might know something about where he might have been, so I went to see him today."

Tom nearly choked. "Julia, you visited with Grandfather? By yourself? He's the main reason I feel so disoriented. He is far more than he appears to be, that's for sure. What happened?"

"Oh, nothing really, he just played some tricks on me. You know, the way magicians supposedly read your mind? He had me frazzled, but I'm over it now."

Tom stood there on the porch. He turned to look out at the lagoon where the setting sun was just beginning to paint the sky. He drifted into his thoughts until Julia pulled him back.

"Did I say something wrong or offensive, Tom? I didn't mean to."

Tom turned back towards her. He stood there for a moment, only two feet away, and looked deeply into her eyes. She was held captive. Then he said, "Have you ever had the thought that maybe things aren't what they seem to be? We chase around trying to prove ourselves to the world in business, science or to our parents, and in a way, it seems like we end up forgetting who we are. I think I'm beginning to remember. Will you be with us at dinner?"

"Yes, I've been invited to stay as a guest for as long as I want. Speaking of which, it smells like Tony is making something special, want to go see?"

"Sure, let's go."

They walked down the steps and over the crushed shell path to the food hut. Tony looked up and saw them standing together with Tom holding her computer. His heart sank, but there was also a tiny bit of relief. They made a little small talk, then walked together towards her hut. So much for that, Tony thought, but he had to admit they looked good together.

As they were walking Tom asked, "When you were with Grandfather, what did you feel?"

"What do you mean?"

"He is not just an old man in a hut, I'm sure you know that. I'm just curious what you felt. Not what you thought later."

Julia was not used to being asked questions she

didn't readily know the answers to, or which she couldn't finesse as if she did. She was out of her element, and not on the hunt anymore. "Well, I had some dreams my first night here. In fact, I told your friend Samantha about them. There were three steps leading to a hut with a blue door. My father stood before it and it opened just as he went to knock on it. I could barely see who answered, but the man had a tattoo on his forehead that looked like a headband. My father went in. That was it."

"So, what happened when you were there?"

"As I was about to knock on the door, it opened just like in the dream only a girl was there. Her name was Arihi, and she told me Grandfather was expecting me. It kinda freaked me out. Then Grandfather, I mean Kepa Kai, came in the room and said he was glad a Witherspoon – that's my last name, was back in his hut. He had the same headband tattoo, and he said he knew my father. He called him his son. Isn't that weird? It's also impossible, so I figured it was just a trick of some kind."

They were now in front of Julia's hut and Tom turned to look at her again, no more than two feet away. He said nothing for a moment, just looked into her eyes, then raised his right hand and gently put it on the side of her left shoulder, and said, "I don't know you, Julia, but there are some things that I am certain of. What you think was a magician's trick, couldn't be further be from the truth, but you will have to discover that for yourself. Also, I feel that there are two of you inside your being. One I think I know or have known. I'm not sure about the other." He took his hand off her shoulder. "Here's your laptop. We better get ready for dinner. See you there."

As he walked by Sam's hut, he noticed Sam and Adam nestled together on the porch, swaying in the hammock.

Sam called out to him, "Hey, Tom, I have a request! Your guitar is still here. How about you bring it to dinner and play a few songs after we eat?"

"How can I possibly say no? Sure, I'll pick it up on my way back over."

"Hang on, Tom, I'm heading over myself. I'll walk with you."

As they waded over to their lodging, Tom said, "Seems you and Sam have started to hit it off. I couldn't be happier for you both!"

"Well, to tell you straight, mate, I've had a fancy for her for months now, but I never really thought it was mutual. I'm just pinching myself that we are clicking so nice together. It puts a nice spring to your step!"

"As you would say, Adam, rubbish! Sam has been trying to get your attention since the term started. She even asked me if I thought she might have said something to offend you because she couldn't get you to notice her!"

"Well, I guess I can be a bit of a dullard at times, but thankfully we've broken the ice and I can make up for it. She's a wonderful girl!"

"She's my best friend, and I couldn't be happier if the two of you got together, so congratulations for coming out of your coma!"

"Oh, piss off, Tom. Some of us are just a little old-fashioned, that's all, but thanks anyway! What a day this has been. I can't wait to see what gems they've got going on that fire. I'm starving!"

# CHAPTER TWENTY-SIX

Adam waded back over to Samantha's hut and when she stepped out onto the porch Adam whistled. She had put her hair up in a coarsely braided French updo with a beautiful tropical flower placed in the side. It picked up on the color of a stretchy dark blue tank top and a full-length flowery cotton skirt. It was a casual yet elegant look that transformed the surfer girl into a woman who could easily grace the cover of a travel magazine.

"Samantha, you look brilliant! What did you do?"

"Oh nothing, just threw on this resort outfit that I bought for the trip. Do you like it?"

"Like it, I bloody well love it! You look lovely! Come here, let me give you a hug."

"You're a fast learner!"

After a warm embrace, they headed over to the main lodge, where dinner preparations were in full swing. Susie came out of the kitchen, strolled up to Adam and Samantha, and gave Sam a kiss on the cheek.

"Happy birthday, Samantha! You look absolutely radiant! Would either of you like a glass of wine or beer?"

"I'll have a Fosters if you have it. What about you, babe?"

"Ah, babe, is it now? Glad to see you two are making progress! Of course we have Fosters. Do you think we're uncivilized? What can I get for you, Sam? We have a lovely rosé from Australia that I'm sure you'd enjoy."

"No, I think a Fosters would be great too. Thanks, Susie!"

At that moment, Julia, who had been watching the dinner being prepared, wandered into the lodge. Seeing Samantha, she headed over to say hello and meet her new love interest Adam Baines, who Bryan had told her about. She was dressed in a soft crinkled jumpsuit with an all-over floral pattern that she had last worn in Florida at a friend's wedding. Her auburn hair hung just below her shoulder, pulled to one side.

"Hello, Samantha, nice to see you again!" she said. "You certainly look different than last time we met! Very lovely!"

"Right back at you, Julia! That's a beautiful dress, perfect for the island!" Samantha extended her hand in greeting, and Julia warmly took it. "Julia, this is my friend Adam Baines. Adam, Julia Witherspoon. She's staying in the next hut just beyond me, down the trail."

"Brilliant to meet you, Miss Witherspoon. There's lovely!" he said.

Julia and Samantha looked at each other quizzically, and Sam asked, "Okay, Adam, what the blazes does that mean?"

"What, babe?"

"There's lovely. Where's lovely?"

"Oh, that just means something, or someone, looks lovely. Like you do!"

Julia said, "Well, thank you, Adam! I'll try and remember the meaning if I hear it again."

"It will probably mean you're in Wales, Julia. He's got all kinds of sayings that just take a little getting used to," Samantha explained.

"Julia, can I fetch you a beer or something else? The Fosters is just the right temperature, not too cold."

"That would be great, Adam. Thank you!"

While Adam was off, Julia asked, "I met your friend, Tom. He is, umm, he seems like a special guy. How long have you known him?"

Samantha replied, "Tom is my closest friend and has been for years, although I hope Adam will become something more. We'll see. But you're right. Tom is a very dear man. One who has special gifts I might add."

"Like what?" Julia asked.

"Well, for one thing, and don't laugh, he can communicate with animals just like you and I are talking right now. It takes a little getting used to, but he can do it. For another, hear that strange sound outside? That's Tom doing something weird to his guitar. He plays beautifully."

"Wow, a scientist that talks to animals and plays a mean guitar. Does he have a lady in his life?"

"Even that doesn't cover everything. I feel honored he's my friend. But no, there's no one special in his life on that score. I wish there was because he deserves it."

Julia paused before saying, "We only just met an hour ago and talked for a while. I have to admit, there's something about him that, I'm not sure how to say it, that is so genuine and so different."

"Yes, Julia, that's a great word. He is the most genuinely good guy you'll ever meet!" Sam then said, "I hope he finds someone like I think I have. What about you, someone waiting back in Canada?"

"No, not for me. Maybe I've just been too busy or something."

At that moment, Adam returned from the kitchen with a Fosters and gave it to Julia. He held his up to the girls and said, "Cheers!"

"Cheers!" they both echoed.

With beers in hand, Samantha, Adam, and Julia strolled outside to where the cooking fire was once again the center of activity. Tom was busy doing something with the strings, and as they sat down next to him, Samantha said, "Tom, what on Earth are you doing to your guitar? It looks like you're taking the strings off."

"I'm not taking them off, Sam, just altering the way they will sound. I came across this YouTube video a while back, and it was about making a guitar sound somewhat like a Sitar." Then he said, "Hi, Julia, you look beautiful! Nice to see you again."

"Hi, Tom. I'm looking forward to hearing you play."

Samantha asked, "How the heck can a guitar sound like that Indian instrument? It has all those weird notes, and those things are huge. I saw Ravi Shankar on a PBS special a couple of years ago, and it was incredible the music that he creates."

"I think I saw that same special! It was what got me thinking that maybe there was a way to capture just a hint of what he did," Tom said.

"What are you doing to it?" Julia asked.

"A couple of things. First, I loosened the strings so I could take this white piece out of the bridge. It's called the saddle, and normally it's dome-shaped, and slots are filed for the strings to play traditional notes. You can see this one that I'm putting back in is flat across the top, not rounded, and there are no slots for the strings. So, now I'm going to tune the strings back to an open tuning, but one that produces a unique sound. Give me just a minute."

He used the peg winder to tune the Martin to drop E open tuning then said, "Now, the last effect is this plastic handle which I've shaped to fit under the strings. I don't know how anyone came up with this idea but listen now."

He strummed down the strings again, and the effect was amazing. It had that hard to describe warble that one associates with an eastern instrument, and when he did finger the frets, Tom was able to create a simple Sitar sound.

"Wow, that's pretty cool!" Julia said.

"I never heard that before," Samantha agreed.

"I thought I'd play a couple of themes, and if anyone wanted to do some drumming, a kitchen pot or any makeshift percussion piece would work great! It should be fun! Somehow I just don't think Neil Young is what this place is all about."

Adam had checked on the progress of dinner, and when he realized there was still close to an hour before everything would be ready, he grabbed a piece of fruit and let Samantha know that he was going next door to take a peek into his microscope at the now fully prepared sample.

"No need to sit with me, Sam. It will be a bit boring. These guys will be much better company. I'll be sure to be on time."

"Adam, if I may ask, what are you studying under a microscope?" Julia asked.

"I'm researching the level of plastic and microplastic contamination here in this supposedly remote place."

"Have you found much? As a geologist, I am aware that it is a growing worldwide problem," Julia remarked.

"I'm about to begin to find out, but I suspect the answer will bloody well be yes."

Adam left and walked over to the office lodge and sat down at his improvised lab table. He switched on the compact dissecting microscope and prepared a plate with the dried material from the water sample. Focusing on the shelf plate, he could easily see a variety of plastics in view. Different types of polymers leave different-looking remnants after breaking down. He could instantly identify many of the usual suspects found in the oceans everywhere. Bits of fiber material, usually broken off from fishing nets, shards of what were probably water bottles, which broke down into smaller and smaller pieces unless eaten by birds, and tiny pieces of plastic bags dominated the microscope. He removed them one piece at a time and placed them into a vial for further study.

Tom had finished setting up his guitar and put it back in the open case. Julia sat next to him and asked, "How long have you played the guitar, Tom? I enjoy listening to music. Especially in a setting like this. Informal, not a concert or club."

"I've been playing ever since I was a kid. I saw this old guitar at a yard sale in Florida twenty years ago and thought it would be fun to learn. It's actually worth some money, and it's the only guitar I've ever owned."

"You don't hear that much these days," Julia commented.

"I heard you say to Adam you're a geologist. Is that what brought you here?"

"Yes, and no." Julia knew she had to be careful. But for some reason, she didn't want to weave tangled webs around this man. "I came here retracing where my father had been like I told you earlier, but I am also in the business of finding new deposits for the company I work for. So, a little of both, I guess."

"Well, I, for one, hope this place stays just the way it is. Not too many like it left in the world. I do hope you find the answers you're looking for, though."

"What do you mean?" Julia said quietly and sipped her beer.

"I sense an inner struggle in you. I hope it gets resolved, that's all."

"Don't we all have inner struggles, Tom?"

"I think most of us do. It's just a matter of degree and what the issues are. Then, there are the rare ones like Grandfather. I think he's someone who could help anyone with their issues if they sincerely want to resolve them."

"Well, I haven't really given a lot of thought to this stuff. I just have to get up in the morning, compete with all the men at the company, and try and do my best to live up to my dad's reputation as his daughter."

"I sense you just hit it on the nose!" Tom said, looking at Julia intently.

"Hit what on the nose. What are you talking about?" Julia looked puzzled.

"I sense you have issues with men in general, and your father in particular. I'm no psychiatrist and don't want to play one. It's just a feeling I have. I'll bet it's pretty common too."

"I've always thought of it as a competition, trying to prove you're the best, just like athletes do," Julia said with a tinge of defiance.

"Maybe. Like I said it's just a feeling I had, and I didn't mean to offend you. Looks like dinner is about ready, want to get a spot in the lodge?"

"Sure, let's go."

Samantha, who had come over to remind Adam dinner was just about ready, startled him by asking, "So how bad is it here, Adam?"

Adam jumped back from the microscope, obviously spooked.

"Sam, I didn't hear you come in. Bloody hell, you made me jump!"

"Sorry, Adam, I didn't want to disturb you, but dinner is just about ready."

"That's ok, it's always like that when I'm at the scope. It's like I just become microscopic myself and I get immersed in the field of study."

"I know what that's like! What's in there?"

"We've got the same junk I see from California to Wales, and in a fairly surprising concentration. I've only looked at the samples we got from the manta sieve, free-floating stuff, but generally what you find there ends up in the sand as well. So, I expect to see much the same."

"Do you think you can take a break? Wait till you see the whole baked snappers that just came out of the fire!"

"Hell, yes!" Adam turned off the microscope and reached out for Samantha's hand and together they walked over to the dining lodge where everyone was just getting ready to sit down. Samantha noticed that Tom and Julia were sitting next to each other, and guided Adam to the seats directly opposite.

The whole snappers had baked inside banana leaves covered in ginger, shallots, and garlic. When they were unwrapped the steamy aroma was intoxicating, as the flesh just melted off the bones. The meal was devoured in less than five minutes. After some idle banter as the plates were being removed, a large carrot and mango cake with a white icy frosting was placed in the center of the table. The cake held two sets of candles. Three to the left and eight to the right, which formed a circle – 3 0.

Samantha knew it would be her job to blow them out. But before she did, she looked at the group that now was beginning to feel like family and said, "I just want to say that never in my wildest dreams could I have imagined how much I would enjoy being here with all of you! I thought we were going to a rural version of Club Med or something like that, but instead, I feel I've found a new part of my family that I never knew I had!"

Bobby rose from his seat at the table. Being the sentimental type, although it belied his surfer dude image, he held up his pint and offered a toast, "Here's to three Yanks that I'm proud to call my friends! And to Sam on her birthday, the loveliest dardy in bathers this side of the Outback! Happy Birthday, Sam, and many more to ya!"

Everyone raised their glasses and said in almost one voice, "CHEERS! Happy Birthday, Sam!"

Samantha blew out the candles, and the carrot cake was eaten to the last crumb. They all helped clear the table and then settled in the lounge to relax and let things settle in their stomachs. Bryan leaned forward and said to Samantha, "I wanted you to know that Liberty called in on the sat phone earlier today. I told her that you were up at Grandfather's village visiting with him, and she said to say hi to him tomorrow for her. I think she's looking forward to meeting him herself, but she said to give you a big hug for her. And since I'm a man of my word..."

Bryan got up from his chair and took two steps over to Sam with both arms out, and she rose to give him a big hug.

"Happy birthday from your mom! Speaking of her, tell me, how did she come by the name Liberty? I know everyone calls her Lib or Libby, but I just think Liberty is a beautiful name. I always wondered what the story was."

"Well, my grandfather volunteered for World War ll when he was just seventeen, and somehow got in. He was patriotic and wanted more than anything to help defend his country. It was pretty near the end of the war, and he ended up landing at Utah Beach during the Normandy Invasion on D-Day. He never really talked much about it, but when I was a kid in high school, I would hear about how brutal it was."

"Yeah, I've heard stories myself from the Aussies who were there," Bryan said.

"Anyway, he survived the landing, which was a miracle itself, and fought the German Army to the liberation of Paris. You see all those pictures of G.I.'s marching down the streets and being cheered and hugged by the Parisians? He was right there. When the war ended, he came back to Maine and married his childhood sweetheart, my Grammy Rose, and they had a child nine months later. He was still so proud of his country and what they had accomplished in the liberation of France that he wanted everyone in the family to be reminded of it and named his daughter

Liberty. Although it's a bit unusual, I have always thought Liberty is a beautiful name."

"Me too. In fact, it feels like the universe has a poetic sense in that someone named Liberty Lewis could be so instrumental in providing a sanctuary, a kind of liberty you might say, to so much of what makes this island special!"

Overhearing the conversation, Julia seemed to lower her head, although no one noticed except Tom.

"As I said before, I had no idea that there was anything other than a surf trip planned for my thirtieth birthday. I am prouder of Mom than ever! Now, enough about my birthday. Tom, you want to show us how that contraption of yours sounds?"

"Sure." Tom got up and walked over to where his guitar was sitting in the open case.

"Bobby, does anyone here have a gift for banging on a drum or anything? You folks must have had a few guests that get down and jam. Anybody here that can jump in?"

"Yeah, we like to raise it up now and again. That bloke doing all the cooking has a drum set right over there, and I enjoy beatin' on anything that doesn't move, but I'm no good at it like Tony is. Let me get him. I think he's finished up by now."

Ahiri jumped in. "Come on, Bobby, you can hold a beat, you're just being modest. He likes to play hand drum on kitchen pots, and he's good at it!"

Tony came in from the kitchen and walked over to a large chest in the corner of the lounge. He opened it up and pulled out a classic set of bongo drums that had been well used but were of high quality. Tony sat down on the floor and, with a flourish, laid down a roll on the bongos.

It had a calypso rhythm to it, and everyone just listened to what became a short solo.

At the end, he said somewhat apologetically, "Sorry, mates, guess I went a little bonkers on that one. What kind of beat did you have in mind, Tom?"

"If you slowed that down some, maybe I could work off it. Did you ever hear Indian tabla being played? I've been fooling around with some raga-style tunes."

"Actually, mate, I love the tabla. Used to have a set when I was back home. Bobbie, why don't you go get that big aluminum pot back there. That would sound cracker next to these and give us a bass effect."

Bobby came from the kitchen with the large pot and sat down cross-legged on the floor with it in his lap. He gently slapped the outside edge of the pot twice with his left hand, followed by his right hand striking the center. It would have been hard to tell that the pot wasn't made to be used specifically for the purpose it was now being put to. Tony very gently and slowly began a pattern.

"These aren't tabla, that's for sure, but they'll work."

As the pattern began, Bobby mimicked it gently with both hands on the outer edge of the pot and struck the center to join Tony for a bass note. Tom began by fingering the bottom string on his guitar and sliding it to frets in a simple tune he had played before. As he hit the notes, he wove a subtle but piercing lead that played off the percussion. The other five strings all played the droning sound, providing a background to the theme he was developing. The three musicians quickly began to relate to each other through rhythm and beat, and Tom started picking up the tempo with Tony and Bobby intuitively keeping pace.

The sounds they made became hypnotic, and the

percussion made it impossible to sit still. The girls started swaying and clapping their hands but soon rose to their feet and began to move their bodies to the primitive but captivating sound the men were creating. The scene became sensuous and almost mystical as the women danced and weaved together in time with the hypnotic beats emanating from the drums and guitar. Samantha went over to Julia and pulled her out of her seat. Holding hands, they both danced together. Faster and faster the music went. Each player pushed himself to his limit while the women moved with the energy that had taken them over.

Finally, the pace began to slow. There was no verbal communication between them. Tom returned to the simple theme he had started with, and all three players slowly let themselves fade until that last twanging drone of the strings hung in the damp, sweaty air and gently faded.

Both the players and the dancers felt physically drained yet emotionally charged. The event lasted over a half-hour. A contact high with the energies that had been tapped into was felt by all.

Tony broke the silence, "I gotta say, mate, it's been a long time since I got into the zone like that. Simply brilliant! I never heard a guitar sound so good!"

"I hear you! It's the free-form music that gets you there, I think. Maybe its what jazz musicians get into, but I wouldn't know. I just know I don't have to think to play, and the music just comes out. What about you, Bobby, is that how you always play the kitchen pot?"

"No, mate, that was something else altogether. Like Tony said, just got in the zone and stayed there."

"Don't think it wasn't the same for us!" said a now

very sweaty Arihi. "That was how it would be when I was a little girl, and the village festivals lasted till dawn. We would dance until the sun began to rise and never be tired. This was even better, though, because it was with friends I never expected to dance with."

Drained of energy, Bryan suggested they turn in. He said tomorrow they should dress in whatever they had that could provide some protection from the jungle. Although they would be taking the jeep most of the way, there was still a lot of bushwhacking to do on the trail.

Tom walked Julia back to her hut. They both felt something was happening but didn't know quite what. Tom said, "Good night, Julia, I've enjoyed talking to you. I, uhh, I like you. I hope we become friends."

"Same here, Tom. Be careful up on the mountain. See you tomorrow."

# CHAPTER TWENTY-SEVEN

The sun rose over the lagoon and the air was still and heavily laden with the night's moisture. Adam rose and pawed through his rucksack for the pair of all-terrain sneakers which would replace the flip flops he'd had on since he arrived. He put on some cargo shorts, short-sleeve shirt, a bandana, and an extra pair of socks which he put into a small fanny pack. Tom was up as well and dressed in a similar fashion.

"I'll meet you at the dining lodge, Tom. I'm going to drop in on Sam and see if she needs a hand with anything."

"Like getting dressed?" Tom quipped.

"What did I do to deserve this?"

"Just kidding! No problem, but Bobby said he wanted to get an early start since we have to be back here by mid-afternoon, so don't take too long with the chivalry routine!"

"We'll be there in plenty of time. Let's see it must be about ...bloody hell, what happened to my watch?"

"What's the matter, Adam? Did your watch break?"

"I don't think it broke, but it stopped at exactly the time Grandfather asked me what time it was yesterday; April sixth, two oh five pm but that's impossible, this watch was running perfectly up until then!"

"That's interesting. I'll see you at the table. I'm out of here."

Adam waded over to the lodge on stilts by the edge of the lagoon and climbed the stairs.

"Hey, Sam, are you up? We've got to get going early this morning."

Samantha opened the door and walked right up to Adam. She put both arms around his neck and said, "Aren't you going to say happy birthday to me?"

"You bet I am!"

He pulled her close and kissed her for what must have been a full minute. They gently held each other and then pulled apart reluctantly, gathered her things, and headed over to the dining lodge.

Tom wandered back to the cooking hut and looked to see if Julia was about, but there was no sign of her, so he found a seat as his mouth began watering. "She must be sleeping in," he thought to himself. "After last night, who could blame her?"

The kitchen staff had prepared omelets covered with sautéed onions, cherry tomatoes, and avocado, which they served with Dutch oven biscuits and coffee or tea, and the usual complement of fresh fruit. Bobby had eaten a bit earlier and was packing the jeep with some water and snacks and made sure that his favorite machete was in the back as well. When they met him outside the office lodge, he was ready to go.

"Right, there we are, mates, a beaut of a morning she

is. We'll have a choc-a-bloc day, that's for sure. Here, rub some of this over your face and neck, and anywhere else that the bugs can get to. The girls make it up and it works cracker! We'll stop by the village and pick up Grandfather and Arihi, and from there I reckon we'll be about an hour to the trail."

They all piled into the Toyota and Bobby guided it up the trail to the village where Grandfather and Arihi were sitting on the steps of his hut waiting for them. Grandfather placed a beautifully woven pack basket into the rear of the truck and then walked around and got in the front passenger side. There was a slight trail leading back out to the "road" that they had arrived on from the airport, which made it' way south up the island in the general direction of Auki. However, it was not Auki that they were heading for, rather Mt. Mala which was one of the higher peaks along the mountain spine that runs down the center of the island. Once out on the road, which could more accurately be described as a jungle lane, the truck was able to make twenty-five miles an hour on average.

Every so often they would pass trails that veered off in the direction of the sea, and Grandfather would relate to them the name of the villages that were invariably at the end and any interesting details regarding them. In one case, he mentioned that the people of the Lau Lagoon lived at the end of a well-worn jungle road and that they had built their village on a reef by dropping stones gathered from the sea onto it. Over time the artificial island offered protection from the bush people who periodically raided them and who called themselves *wani I tolo* or "people of the bush" as opposed to *wani I asi* which meant "people of the sea." Grandfather himself was born of the Kwaio or mountain people but had unique ease with both cultures. Soon after passing the road to Lau Lagoon Grandfather asked Bobby to slow the truck down and he concentrated on the jungle passing them on their left side. All at once he raised his left hand and pointed.

"There, do you see that boulder? Turn the truck on this trail and drive in until it can't be seen from the road. Past the stone you will find a small clearing. We will get out there."

"Is that the stone you mean, Grandfather?" Bobby asked.

"Yes, why don't you turn the truck around and back up next to it, so we'll be ready to go later."

Once out of the truck Samantha began doing some stretches and Adam and Tom followed suit. Grandfather reached into the back and pulled out his handsome pack basket which had a cloth covering tied over it to protect whatever was in it from falling out or getting debris on it. Bobby also had a backpack which had some water and snacks, a small medical kit, and some hand towels.

"This way, follow me."

Grandfather led the way up the trail single file, occasionally swinging his machete to knock back a vine or shrub that was impeding the way. The trail quickly began gaining altitude as it switched back on the hills

After thirty minutes, the jungle thinned out and another much larger clearing came into view. Grandfather mentioned that this was the first landmark on the hike. The clearing continued up in grade until it finally leveled off close to where the jungle once again took control.

"This clearing is where I first met Luti Mikode all

those years ago, and that was the trail we took when I followed him back to the mountains where he lived."

Bobby said, "This area doesn't look natural, Grandfather, it's so flat and open."

"This clearing was once a place where the Ramo gathered for ceremonies and festivities, and the reason it has remained open is that the entire site is paved with stone just under the surface. At one time there would have been many wooden structures here, but nature shows no trace now. What we can see is the remains of where food was prepared. Come, follow me."

Grandfather struck off to his right through the knee-high vegetation which covered the clearing. He turned and pointed back where they had just come from and said, "There is the very view of the sea that I gazed upon when my grandfather first appeared to me."

The view of the sea was spectacular as the clearing dropped away from them and they could even make out the man-made islands covered with huts out in the lagoon. He continued across the clearing and what they saw next was startling. In an alcove in the side of the rapidly rising hillside, were numerous large circular stone vessels full of green swampy smelling water. Also lying on the ground were large stone lids, some of which had decorative carved tops. Some vessels and lids were broken, but most remained in a condition that was as pristine as when they were being used. The amazing thing though was their unbelievable size. Standing next to a pair of them, Adam, who was about 6'2" tall, could just see over the top of the largest ones.

"These pots were carved from solid stone by the Ramo a thousand years ago. When the tribes gathered for ceremonies, great feasts were made, and foods were prepared much in the same way we would today. They built fires around the outside of the pots, and in many cases, hot stones would be placed inside them as well. Taro root, jungle sweet potatoes, and many other vegetables were prepared here, as well as food which is now forbidden."

No one had to ask what that meant, but they marveled at the skill and craftsmanship required to create the magnificent objects.

"How did they make these so long ago?" Tom asked.

"They are made of limestone which is soft enough to be easily worked with the hard basalt they brought down from the mountains."

"But even so it must have taken years to make each one. Amazing!"

Grandfather reminded them of the size of the Ramo. "You must remember when you look at these artifacts, that they were not created by humans such as us. The ancient race is much taller and much stronger than we. They only abandoned places such as this when the great sailing vessels first began making landfall on these islands. It was foretold that the Ramo would retreat to their mountain sanctuaries in the caves and deep valleys that no humans would discover, and so they have. Come, we are halfway to the spiral stairs."

Grandfather climbed effortlessly up the steep grade followed by Arihi, and the others supported by Bobby in the rear. They continued to climb, and the jungle fauna gave way to an alpine meadow. He stopped and pointed to where the mountain began a vertical rise leading to an unnaturally flat top at the peak.

"That is where Taka Mikode was laid to rest over four hundred years ago. We are not going up there, but there is a large carved crypt with a massive lid over it where he lays, and over there is where the spiral stairway begins."

Grandfather led the way over to where a precise cut had been made directly into the side of the mountain. On one side was a four-foot wall flanking the steps and providing security from the sheer drop-off as the path wound higher. The wall was built of perfectly cut and fitted stones and was an engineering marvel, but it was the mountainside that held the biggest surprise. Carved directly into the polished stone surface were pictographs reminiscent of Egyptian hieroglyphs. They told the story of the life of the great Ramo leader but were unintelligible to anyone except Grandfather.

"This is the written language of the Ramo. You need to understand that this is a civilized race that has culture, although they do not create what is called technology. I wanted you to see this so that you might understand the importance of what was preserved here by Liberty's purchase. These mountains were created from the fire in the belly of Mother, and that fire formed stones that the outside world would dig to the center of the Earth to get. Now, they will be protected, and so is the mountain and the place above."

"I am so happy you showed us this, Grandfather. My mother will be profoundly pleased to have helped save this place. I know that in my heart!"

"And now, let us meet Luti Mikode and his young apprentice."

"Meet him? Where do we go to do that?" Samantha asked.

"We go right over there!"

Grandfather pointed to where two large dark figures were all but invisible until pointed out. One was sitting on a huge flat stone and holding a large carved staff, and the other was standing just behind his right shoulder.

"Come, and each of you do as I do."

Grandfather walked over to the huge, seated figure and stood before him. He raised his right arm and placed it on Luti Mikode's left shoulder and the Ramo did the same with his right arm, placing it on Grandfather's left shoulder. Grandfather stood there for about a minute gazing into the Ramo's eyes and finally said something which no one in the group could understand, but which prompted a response from Luti Mikode. His voice was a deep but gentle baritone, and although the language was unknown, the emotion could be felt by everyone present. It was the universal expression of missing another person. Grandfather then stepped in front of the great Ramo's apprentice and repeated the arm-to-shoulder gesture. When he stepped away, he spoke to the group and told them that the apprentice's name was Lakka and that he had been with Luti Mikode after he had returned to his village many years ago.

One by one starting with Arihi and Bobby, the group of five stepped up to Luti Mikode and Lakka and repeated the formal greeting of the Ramo. Finally, it was Tom's turn. He stepped forward and placed his right hand onto the great Ramo's left shoulder and felt Luti Mikode's huge hand gently alight on his left shoulder. Immediately great pulsing waves of conscious energy flowed into his being immersing him in an embrace of peaceful and loving thought vibrations. The images which flowed to him seemed to take hours but in reality, lasted only seconds. There were scenes of nature in all her splendid glory! Sunrise, sunset. Deep forests. Flowing rivers. Vast grassy planes. Everywhere was life and light emanating from each scene that scrolled through his mind. Then a voice spoke and told him that he was part of Mother just like the Ramo and all living things and that he, Luti Mikode, was honored to meet all of them.

Grandfather walked to where he had taken off his pack basket and untied the string holding the protective cover. He reached in and took out two paper bags and handed the largest to Luti Mikode and the other to Lakka. Luti Mikode placed his huge exquisitely carved wooden staff across his knees and with what could only be described as a twinkle in his deep brown eyes and the slightest hint of a smile on his massive face, he opened the bag. He reached in and to the surprise of everyone pulled out a large jellybean and popped it in his mouth.

"I knew he couldn't wait!" Grandfather chuckled. "He has had a weakness for those things since I first brought him some before the great war. He would have met us here today if for no other reason than jellybeans! However, he knows what happened this week and that his people will have far more protection from the outside world than ever before. He especially came to honor you and your mother, Samantha."

Hearing that, Luti Mikode stood up. He was an imposing creature. His facial features were more human than what one might have imagined, and the long hair which covered his body was auburn with touches of white and gray around the face where no hair grew. He almost gave the impression of a grand old two-legged gentle lion, slightly stooped under the weight of old age.

The great Ramo turned to Lakka his apprentice and said something which only Grandfather understood, and waited while Lakka picked up a basket, intricately woven from fine, supple vines similar to Grandfather's pack basket. Something was inside the basket, but Grandfather did not reveal the nature of the gift, rather he simply placed it inside his pack where the jellybeans had been.

Grandfather then said something to Luti Mikode and Lakka, and the young apprentice nodded his head and pointed his long arm up towards the mountain peaks which were now half covered in clouds. Luti Mikode motioned to Lakka who reached into a small pouch that he wore on a thong across his shoulder and gave something to his master.

Luti Mikode turned to the group and said in near-perfect English, "Time it is for us to return to our home. This token of our people's thanks, for your mother Liberty it is. Although we will not meet again on this island, know that I, like my son here, will be with you on your journey. And you, Thomas, know that you may reach me in spirit if need you have. Like your Grandfather, if the call is given, answer I will. And now we leave. May Mother guide you and love you. Long life and open hearts to all of you."

Luti Mikode reached out his hand to Samantha and she opened hers to receive a large yellow stone which even though uncut, still sparkled in the mountain sunshine. In a mere five paces, the two Ramo had melted into the jungle so quietly and completely that one could almost wonder if the whole event had been imagined. But each of the group knew it was real and would be remembered for a lifetime.

Grandfather turned toward the trail they had hiked in on and asked, "What time is it now Adam?"

Surprised, Adam looked at his watch and said, "Bloody hell, its twelve twenty-five, April seventh."

"Time to go back."

# CHAPTER TWENTY-EIGHT

Since Julia hadn't been invited to make the climb up Mt. Mala that morning she took a relaxed stroll through the lagoon, walking in knee-high clear warm water. The sand was soft yet firm beneath her feet, and the sounds of fish breaking the surface and the jungle waking up nurtured her still, inner self. She couldn't remember the last time she felt so at peace, although she rarely took the time to consider such things. But something seemed different. "What is it?" she thought to herself.

Then she thought of Tom, and she remembered him saying he wanted to be her friend. All her life it seemed, men wanted something from her, but never just to be her friend. She had deliberately avoided going to the cooking hut mainly because she didn't want to seem like a third wheel as they got ready to go. But there was a little tug. How did he look, ready to climb the mountain that she desperately wanted to climb herself? "Get a grip, Julia!

You've got work to do!" she thought to herself and turned to get something to eat.

Tony was still at the camp stove cleaning up, and she smiled at him and said, "Hi, Tony, anything left to eat? I didn't want to bother the gang as they were getting ready to go."

"I don't think they would have been bothered, Miss Julia, especially after last night. You seemed to belong like you've been here for years, just like them. I saved some of the omelet for you. Here you go," he said, handing a plate to her.

"Thanks, Tony!" She sat on a log and took a bite and then realized she was famished. "I can't ever remember music that made you want to move the way you guys played last night. It was great, and you, Tony, were great on the drums!"

"Oh, thank you, Miss Julia, but it was really Tom who held that one together. He has a knack on that guitar! Crikey he was good!" Tony said.

"You all were, it was fun."

"It was crackers seeing you let yourself go. If you don't mind me saying, I didn't think you bloody had it in ya!"

"Oh, I like to get down to music now and then, Tony. I'm not made of stone, you know." She said this, but in truth, she almost never danced to music, any kind of music. Maybe that was part of the reason she felt different this morning. Not only did she dance with abandon, once Samantha dragged her to her feet, but she loved it. Something she'd never experienced before, letting herself go.

"Well, I've played the beat with lots of folks, but Tom set us up with something I never played before. It was brilliant. If I hadn't been beating on the drums, I would have been up there flinging myself about with you ladies. That's deadset, it is!"

"Tom seems different from anyone I've ever met. Samantha told me he can talk to animals just like we're talking now. He also has a way of almost knowing what you feel, even if you don't see it in yourself. Hard to explain."

"There's only one other person I've ever met like that, Julia. Someone you already know."

"Grandf...Kepa Kai?"

"Deadset. He's a real cobber, that one. There seems to be a bit of him in your friend, Tom, devo."

Tony waxed Australian, and Julia looked at him quizzically. "Uh?"

"I mean he's a real friend, and Tom definitely seems a bit like him. That's all to it, Miss Julia. But you should know, 'cause seems like there's a spark between ya." Tony smiled and finished what he was doing.

"Well, I'm not sure about that. I've got see if the company has any news for me, so I guess I'll go get my laptop and find out. Thanks for saving me breakfast, it was delish!"

"No worries."

Julia walked back to her hut, thinking to herself. Tony was right. Tom did give her some of the same vibes as Kepa Kai did, only it was different. But how? He was thoughtful and attentive when they talked, and very perceptive, just like Kepa, but what was it? She walked over to the one dressing mirror each hut had and stood before it. She reached up and messed her hair, then shook her head back and forth. She looked different to herself. More relaxed. More comfortable in her own skin than she'd felt in a long time. Then she realized why Tom was different.

"It's because he's so sensual, that's it," she said aloud. Sexy, yes, but that wasn't it, lots of men were. It was that Tom had a way of being so genuine, like Samantha said, that he was totally disarming. That allows me to feel what I usually push away. "Interesting," she thought.

Back in the business lodge, Julia booted her laptop and checked her company email account. There were several messages. One from Alex, of course, so she opened that first.

*"Julia, how are you my dear? Our legal department is digging into the laws down there and I think they'll have answers for us later today. Hopefully we'll be digging down there in the future as well. Have fun. Miss you!"*

Julia typed, "Thanks, Alex." and that was all. She was beginning to detest the man.

The next message was from her department, International Explorations. She opened the message and began reading.

*Dear Miss Witherspoon,*

*We received coordinates from Legal, relative to a large tract of land located on the island of Malaita, in the Solomon Islands. We were advised that you are responsible for our interest in the acquisition of the tract.*

*Initial satellite surveys indicate favorable magnetic anomalies which, as you know, may indicate the presence of kimberlite. Also, arial surveys show the presence of Pandanus candelabrum, a small stubby palm that thrives in soil containing kimberlite minerals.*

*So, initial results indicate the possibility of diamond transport through the stability zone, and a substantial deposit of E-type diamond.*

*Congratulations on your discovery.*
*Jonathon Tuley, Director of Explorations.*

Julia reread the message three times, letting the significance set in. It was what she'd been hoping for, and now it appeared to be real, no longer a dream. Her heart raced as she opened the next message. This one was from Peter Allaire, CEO of the company.

*Dear Julia,*

*It is with great pleasure and great admiration that I write you on behalf of Lucarana Mining Company. It seems that you may have changed how history will regard your father going forward, and also, you may have changed your future as well. Explorations tell me that there is a very good chance that we may have a new discovery on our hands, and that has not happened in a very long time.*

*The company is in the position to acquire the lease on the tract of land which you alerted us to, and Legal has begun researching the law there, and drawing up an offer. We realize that time is of the essence. One quirky thing turned up, but which should not present a problem. They found that Solomon law requires a wet signature on all land purchase or land lease documents. No faxing or docu-sign on this one. So, you've been promoted! You are now Assistant Director of Explorations, and as such are very much able to represent the company with your signature. Congratulations!*

*Also, in the seemingly likely event that we do decide to explore and ultimately mine there, you will remain as Director of Ground Operations, Malaita. Again, congratulations are in order!*

*On a personal note, I never knew your father, but I can say that having a Witherspoon return to a prominent role in the company seems fitting to me.*
*Very Truly Yours,*
*Peter Allaire, President and CEO*
*Lucarana Mining Company*

Julia shut down her computer and just sat at the desk, staring at the blank screen. Her heart was racing as she digested the two messages from the company. The message from Alex she had deleted. She wasn't too surprised that Explorations had found evidence of kimberlite, although it was rarely found in a mountainous environment, because her dad had seen it with his own eyes. Aerial prospecting had come a long way since his time. It was the speed at which the company was moving that surprised her. And unsettled her at the same time.

"Oh, Julia, I didn't know you were here! Sorry to disturb you. I saw the door was open and was just making sure everything was secure," Susie said, as she pushed the door back to inspect.

"Good morning, Susie. You're not disturbing anything. I was just expecting a message from my company, so I stopped in to see if it was in."

"Everything okay?" Susie asked.

"Yes, everything is fine. In fact, I received a small promotion."

"I guess absence does make the heart grow fonder, even in business! Congratulations!"

"Well, I'm not sure my new position is one that I'll

relish, but it's always good to be recognized for what you do."

"Any plans for today? The gang won't be back till later in the afternoon. Want to go for a walk with me? Bryan and I usually walk the entrance trail together, but he's busy catching up on communications with patrons. A little company would be nice."

"Sure, Susie, that would be great. When do you want to go?"

"Give me about an hour to finish my chores, then I'll be free," Susie said.

"See you back here in an hour!"

# CHAPTER TWENTY-NINE

The walk back to the truck was uneventful and understandably quicker than the trek up, and soon they were back at the clearing and loading their gear in the Toyota. Bobby distributed some snacks he had brought, and everyone relaxed at the back of the truck before the bumpy ride back to the camp. There was a hushed conversation that was focused on the amazing meeting with the Ramo and all that had happened that morning. Adam spoke up and asked Grandfather a question.

"Grandfather, Luti Mikode's staff looked familiar, like some of the pieces you showed us at your workshop. By any chance was it something you made?" Adam inquired.

"You have a good eye for the craft, Adam, and although my techniques have changed over the many years since that piece was made, the answer is yes, it was a gift from me to my grandfather."

"It was brilliant. That wood looked like oak we have back home."

"A typhoon wrecked a sailing vessel on the beach near our village shortly after I returned from the mountains. I salvaged the bowsprit which was made of a hardwood I had never seen. The wood was good to carve and the whole piece was straight and true. It took me almost two years to express my gratitude to Luti Mikode for taking me in and sharing the mysteries of his knowledge with a young boy from the village. I remember walking back up the trail, this very trail that we are standing on right now, carrying that staff which must have weighed half as much as me at the time. When I arrived at the meadow, he was there waiting for me. I almost collapsed from having carried it up. It meant the world to him to tell me how much my gift pleased him and that it would be passed down to those who held the spirit of the Ramo."

Tom said, "It was beautiful, Grandfather!"

"I still consider that staff my finest artistic creation, and Luti Mikode has always had it with him all the many years since that day. Someday, it will pass to Lakka."

The trip back to the surf camp seemed to pass much quicker than the ride out. Each one of the group was lost in thought, especially Bobby, who drove almost automatically. When they were almost there, Grandfather asked Bobby to pull over at the trail that led down to the lagoon.

"I will see you all later this evening. There is something I must do right now, but I will be back around dinner time. Each of you may have a 'birth-day' as well. I suggest you get some rest. We have shared much with Mother so far today. Until later then," he said, as he turned and walked down the trail he once carried the great staff up so long ago.

Julia met with Susie at the camp office and together they began the stroll down the trail to the camp entrance. Susie pointed out the various tropical flowers that she and Bryan had planted over twenty years earlier and which now had spread and were blooming in the filtered sunlight beneath giant banyan trees. The jungle floor was open and relatively sunny where they had been maintaining it for years. Susie told Julia the story of how they struggled with so many things in the beginning. Finding natives they could trust and who could trust them, building the huts and lodges, and all the trials and tribulations that launching an enterprise in a remote location like Malaita implied.

Julia was fascinated and asked questions, as the journey that Susie and Bryan had taken was described in detail. Then she asked a question that caused Susie to pause.

"The thing I can't quite get my head around, Susie, is that you still look just about my age. But you're talking about what must have been back-breaking work, done for over twenty years. What's your secret? I want some of that!"

Susie remained silent for a few moments, thinking how to answer her. They strolled slowly until she stopped and turned to Julia and asked, "When you went to visit Grandfather, how did he address you when you met him?"

"What do mean?"

"I mean did he call you Julia, Miss Witherspoon, or what?" Susie asked again.

"Well, it was actually nothing like that at all, and I thought it was weird at the time. He called me, 'my child.'

And he referred to my father, who visited him almost sixty years ago, as his son. Why do you ask?"

"I ask, because it's part of the reason we let you stay with us the first night. Grandfather has taught Bryan and me that very often things happen which seem like a coincidence, but they aren't," Susie explained, and then added, "When he has a relationship with someone, he rarely calls them by their given name. The only one I've heard him call by name is Tom, but he calls him Thomas for some reason. He never calls me Susie, he calls me 'my child' or Bryan 'his son.' It's his way of identifying his flock, I guess you could say."

"But I had never met him before. Why did he do that?"

"You may not be consciously aware of it, but I am sure you've had a relationship with him before ever coming here. I know it. Now, to answer your question, how old would you guess Grandfather is?" Susie asked.

Julia thought for a moment and said, "That's a tough one. I would guess he's around sixty, but he acts a lot older, or maybe wiser might be a better word. Wisdom always comes with age, right?"

"Hopefully one gets wiser with age, yes. But if I were to tell you that Grandfather is well over one hundred years old, what would you say?"

"Impossible, he's so fit, so vital."

"We are having a ceremony to celebrate Samantha's birthday tonight. Part of that ceremony will be the taking of an herbal beverage that he makes. If he asks you to participate, you will have your first question answered personally. If he doesn't, let's just say that our minds don't know everything when it comes to what is and isn't impossible."

They continued their stroll back to the lodge, which was now in sight, in silence.

Arihi stayed with Bobby and within minutes the group arrived back at the camp. Samantha and Adam went inside the office lodge while Tom hung out with Bobby and Arihi for a few minutes in the lounge. Adam wanted to take a quick peek at the plastic contamination in the sand sample before putting his travel lab away. He was beginning to feel it had been left in place longer than it should have, although no one would ever say anything.

Samantha stopped by Bryan's office and said, "Hey, Bryan, we just got back from the trip up Mount Mala with Grandfather. I must say it was one of the most amazing days of my life!"

"I imagine it must have been. Did you get to meet Luti Mikode and his apprentice Lakka?"

"Yes, we did. It was amazing! How blessed we are to be able to know them from firsthand experience! When Luti Mikode spoke in English after speaking with Grandfather in that other language, I almost fainted. He seems to be so wise, and so gentle. I can see why Grandfather became devoted to him."

"Susie and I have been there with Grandfather several times while those two just sat together silently. We always feel so privileged to be allowed to share what they have, even if from a distance. I know that both Grandfather and the Ramo appreciate what we have been doing here for the last twenty years, and especially since your mother became involved in such a big way."

"Luti Mikode gave me a gift which he said was from all his people. It's a very pretty yellow stone."

"A yellow stone? Do you have it with you?"

"Sure, it's right here in my pocket. It's pretty heavy actually."

Samantha reached into her pocket and withdrew the gift that the Ramo people had given her family. She opened her hand and gave it to him. Bryan didn't say a word for a long time, but finally, he took a deep breath.

"Samantha, do you have any idea what this is?"

"Not really, but it's a very pretty color yellow and the shape is amazing."

"Yes, very pretty indeed. This stone is a perfectly formed octahedral diamond which if I had to guess, must weigh close to one hundred carats. Not only would that make this one of the rarest and most valuable diamonds in the world, but it is also a significant artifact in Ramo culture."

"I think closer to one hundred and twenty-five carats!" Julia said as she and Susie came within earshot. "May I see it?" she asked.

Bryan hesitated for just a moment, and Samantha noticed and said, "It's alright, Bryan. After last night we're like newfound sisters, right Julia?"

"Yes, Samantha, what a night!" she said, reaching for the yellow stone Bryan held out. "This came from the mountain where the Ramo live?" Julia held the stone up to the light, inspecting the clarity of the diamond as much as the naked eye would allow. Then she handed it back to Bryan.

"According to Grandfather, there is a cave that is sacred to the Ramo, and which contains a tremendous statue that was carved from stone eons ago by their ancestors. The statue is of a primal being, meant to represent the archetype of 'Being' itself. He told me that the statue had a brilliant yellow stone placed in the center of the forehead which represented the third eye. I believe that this may well be that very stone. A most remarkable gift, indeed."

"Oh my God, Bryan. I can't accept this. You've got to speak to Grandfather and see if we can return this stone. Will you do that for me?"

"I'm not so sure that would be a good idea. I don't know if the Ramo would take that as an insult or not, but I will ask Grandfather if you wish me to. Do you think that you should consult with Liberty first?"

"No, I don't. I know my family would never want to possess something of such tremendous importance to the very people we are helping to preserve. Please tell Grandfather that I wish to return it with the greatest respect and honor possible."

"Samantha, I think it would be best if you told him that yourself. After all, I would say that there are at least three new members of his family, and who better to ask than one of his children?"

"You're right, and I think I know just how to do it."

Bryan said, "Just don't be disappointed if he says no, Sam. Let's see what Adam is up to. I see you two are becoming much closer than I noticed when you first arrived!"

"Yes, how can anyone not fall in love with such a wonderful person in such a wonderful place like this? I have so much to be thankful for!"

They walked out of Bryan's office and over to the table where Adam was putting his equipment back into the travel case. He had examined the sample which was derived from beach sand, and it had told him what he already knew, that the level of plastic contamination was as bad even in this remote place as elsewhere in the world. Bryan mentioned that even in the relatively short time he had been in Mala, it was obvious that more junk was washing up on the island than when he'd first arrived.

"It's like there's an endless supply of this crap, Adam, and it breaks our heart when we think of all the birds and fish that are being killed by it, like Grandfather's big turtle. Isn't there anything being done by science to get a handle on it?"

Adam said, "You'd think it would be a top priority in the scientific community, and although the subject is gaining awareness, it just doesn't have the political clout that global warming does, which is a shame."

"Right now, my priority is having a nap. I'm whipped!" Samantha said.

"I think that would be a good idea you two. There is something special planned for you tonight, and Grandfather would be disappointed if you couldn't keep your eyes open!"

"Sounds good to me, babe. That was one jammed-packed morning we had, and I'm a bit knackered myself!"

Adam and Samantha left the office lodge and stopped by the outdoor cooking hut to scavenge a few pieces of fruit before heading over to her hut, on the side of the lagoon. They stood for a moment with their hands on the railing looking out to sea, fully aware of the fact that this was as romantic a place as either could imagine, anywhere in the world. Adam put his arm around Sam's shoulder and drew her close.

"In some ways, I envy Bobby and Arihi. I couldn't think of anything more appealing at this moment than just staying here with you and living in this paradise!"

"You are learning fast! What a nice thing to say! I feel

the same way, but I doubt we'll be so lucky as to fall into a gig like this. Come on, let's get some rest before dinner."

They turned and walked into the hut and flopped down next to each other in the sumptuous bed with the fabulous view of the lagoon and immediately drifted off to sleep, arms entwined around each other.

Julia left Susie and Bryan at the office and walked over to the cooking hut. She could just see the back of Tom's head of red hair walking towards the lagoon and started to shout to him, but didn't. She wasn't sure why, but she was disappointed in herself for pulling back, when he was right there. "Oh well, later," she thought.

# CHAPTER THIRTY

Julia was a bit tired, but there was no way she could take a nap. Not after seeing that unbelievable yellow diamond only a few minutes ago. It wasn't just that the diamond was huge that excited her. It was the intense canary yellow color, which is extremely desirable in the market. And the fact that even with the naked eye, she could see it was probably flawless. "If there is one up in those mountains, there must be more," she thought. "Dad was right, now I've got the proof. I just need to tell them."

Julia put her laptop in her daypack and headed back to the office lodge. She needed to send a message back to the company, but who should she send it to? "Not Alex," she thought. "I've had about enough of that weasel." So, should she send her report to Explorations? Or directly to the company CEO, Peter Allaire? She decided to send it to Peter, and carbon copy it to the Exploration team. After all, if that yellow beauty didn't cement in stone that Lacarana Mining had a site worth exploring, nothing would. And she, Julia Witherspoon, would be the Director of Operations, Malaita, according to Peter. Her lifelong dream was about to unfold, yet for some reason, she wasn't feeling the thrill she'd expected she'd feel. "I wonder why?" she thought as she approached the cooking hut.

She turned when a voice said, "Hi, Julia. I looked for you when we got back." Tom was sitting on a log munching on some fruit, and she didn't notice him at first.

"Oh, hi Tom. I looked for you too. I was in the office with Bryan and Susie when you guys got back. Samantha showed them the gift she received from the Ramo. I must say, it was a very impressive stone. It's a shame Samantha is going to return it. The world would love to admire it," Julia said casually.

"Actually, I was hoping that she would make that decision. I'm proud of her." Tom spoke in a somber tone.

"Why is that?" she asked.

"Why do you think, Julia?"

Julia had to stop and ponder Tom's question for a moment. "I have no idea. Like great works of art, the public has always appreciated being able to enjoy objects of rare beauty. That stone certainly qualifies as rare and beautiful!"

"I noticed you didn't say 'diamond,' but that is what it is, right?" Tom asked.

"Yes, it is a magnificent canary yellow diamond of extraordinary clarity. The world would love to see it." Julia spoke with the passion of a geologist.

"What about the Ramo?" Tom asked quietly.

"What about them?"

"Grandfather said that they placed that stone as the

third eye in a sacred statue that has been a major part of their culture, over a thousand years ago. I think Sam is doing the right thing, don't you?" Tom said, issuing a subtle challenge.

"Well, maybe. Apparently, her family already has enough wealth that something that valuable can be given away without a thought. Me, I don't think I could do it. Just think what it must be worth." Julia spoke a bit defiantly.

"Yesterday, when we visited Grandfather, I met a friend of his, who is dying. I'd like to introduce her to you. Assuming we have time tomorrow if you'd like."

"That would be nice. I'd love to go with you. She probably could use the support."

"Okay. It's a date!" Tom said with a smile. "You'll be impressed with the old gal, I guarantee it! Right now, though, I'm going to go back to my cabin and get a little rest. They've got something special planned tonight in honor of Samantha's birthday, and I'd like all the energy I can get. You might want to do the same."

Julia was strangely excited by Tom using the word "date" but said, "I'll probably lie down for a bit, but there's something I have to do first. Have a nice nap. I'll see you in a bit.."

Tom got up and walked back to his hut, and Julia watched as he left. She admired the way he moved and carried himself. "Relaxed, yet confident," she thought. Then she got up and headed for the office to file her report.

Closing the door behind her, she sent an email to Peter Allaire that read:

"Dear Peter,

I have seen and held a diamond that came from the

area under consideration. It is magnificent! If you are at your desk, please acknowledge.

Julia Witherspoon"

She sat at the desk waiting anxiously for a reply. It came quickly.

"Julia, exciting news! Tell me about it. -Peter"

"It was a monster stone, at least 125 carats. No inclusions to the naked eye. Canary yellow, deep color."

"Good Lord, Julia. That is fabulous news! I think the company can afford a small finder's fee, say, 2 percent of the purchase price in company stock. Good job!"

"Is Legal ready to go?"

"Almost. Offer being prepared for courier delivery now. Will advise when your signature is required. Three days at most. Stay in touch." - Peter.

Julia quickly did the math on the bonus Peter just offered her. Lucarana Mining was trading on the Toronto Stock Exchange, in a range between $10 and $12 Canadian. So, she calculated that roughly 250,000 shares of company stock would be added to her retirement fund.

She smiled as she thought how proud her dad would have been.

# CHAPTER THIRTY-ONE

Adam woke up and splashed some water on his face. He bent over and kissed Samantha and let her know he was heading over to the island to change his clothes and would see her over at the main lodge after a bit. Samantha said that she needed to freshen up as well. He waded over to the island and stopped on the porch and stood for a few moments reflecting on the incredible events the last four days had unveiled. Mostly he was amazed at the shift in his thoughts, or as Tom would say, his consciousness, that being on the island had affected. Much of that of course was due to this man they had come to know as Grandfather. So much of what he accepted as normal reality had been turned upside down, that he just did not feel as "grounded" as he was used to. The idea of communicating with a sea turtle was somewhat foreshadowed by Tom's story of helping people understand their horses, but still, the idea took a little getting used to. And if that wasn't enough, meeting individuals from an unknown race of hominids and then hearing one speak in English! That and the trick Grandfather pulled, stopping and starting his watch, was having the effect of making him feel surreal, like he was in a dream.

Then there was Samantha. He had been mildly aware that she might have been trying to catch his attention back on campus a few times, and he found her incredibly attractive, and not just physically. He just wasn't prepared for the onrush of emotion he now felt about her. His Welch demeanor was rugged both physically and psychologically. He always prided himself on being like his father, who was tough as nails, and fearless in a storm saving lives in a twenty-foot lifeboat pounded by waves as big as houses. Now, for the first time in his life, he felt a palpable softening taking place deep in his being. Sure, he had run around with the girls in high school and had his fun, but this was different, and he wasn't sure where it would lead him. But it felt rather brilliant, he had to admit.

"Hey, Sam, are you ready to head over to the lodge?"

"Not quite, Adam. You go on and I'll catch up with you in a little bit."

"Right, and don't be afraid to wear that same outfit you had on last night. You looked bloody beautiful, babe."

"I appreciate you saying that, but I think it's getting time to think of another way of saying it, without the 'bloody' part. Somehow it detracts from the compliment which I would otherwise be delighted with."

"Ummm, I guess I never thought of it like that. I'll see what I can do but forgive me if it slips out now and again. Old habit, that one."

"What, calling women bloody beautiful? And here I was thinking you were different from other guys!"

"No, I didn't mean it that way, honest! I just meant that saying 'bloody this or bloody that' is something I've done since a kid."

"I know, I'm just teasing you, and if you can't help yourself then I'll just have to get used to it! See you over at the lodge."

When Adam wandered into the cooking area, he noticed something was different from how the other meals had been set up, but he couldn't quite put his finger on what it was. He looked around to find Tom, and not seeing him, walked over to the lounge where he found him sitting in a low club chair.

"Hey, Tom, what are you doing here all by yourself? You look rather pensive, is anything wrong?"

"I'm just thinking how rich life has been since we've been here, and how much I'm not sure I look forward to going back to the real world of science and school. As far as being here by myself, something's going on over in the other lodge, and I was asked to stay here till dinner is ready, which suits my mood just fine. I was hoping to see Julia. We've been talking a bit."

"I've noticed you have. She's a looker for sure, but there seems to be an edge on her. Wound a bit tight I'd say."

"I agree, she is. But there's a soft side as well. Anyway, this should be an interesting evening."

"Well, I've got to say that since we've been here, it's been one bloody bombshell after another! It's both brilliant and disruptive at the same time. Talk about having your preconceptions rattled! I like it here, but I don't think I'd want to stay forever. At some point it might get a bit boring," Adam mused.

"You might be right but think about how much you could learn and take back with you. I think if we spent enough time with Grandfather, we would see how profoundly changed we'd become. I can see that happening already."

"This shift in perception isn't a bad thing, it's just that it challenges so much of what I had thought I knew about everything. Turned it bloody well upside down, really!"

"Well, I have a feeling that Grandfather has a little more of that in store for us tonight."

"What are you talking about? What's going on?"

"When you and Sam were working on the samples in your travel lab yesterday, I stopped and had a few words with Bryan. He told me that when Grandfather accepts new apprentices, you might say, he guides them on a journey. The journey entails the use of a mixture of jungle plants and roots which he said have a profound effect upon our consciousness in a very uplifting and spiritual way. Not that we have to take the journey, we don't. It's just that Grandfather sees it as a great gift to give people he cares about and is committed to, and that apparently includes us," Tom explained.

"Wow, I had no idea this was in store. Where does he get it from? Does he make it himself? How do we know it's safe?"

"Do you remember when the Ramo gave Grandfather a basket which he put where the bags of jellybeans were? I think that was it. Bryan said that the ingredients used to make the mixture are only found in the high valleys up in the mountains and that the Ramo have used them for a thousand years. Grandfather is intimately familiar with how to administer the substance, and Bryan said it causes no harm. He and Susie have taken it themselves many times. He said it opens your heart and allows you to communicate directly with Mother."

"That would be the spirit of Mother Earth, I would imagine. Once again, I seem to be facing the idea of the Gaia theory. I will have to ponder this. I've smoked a little pot now and again, but never anything more than that. This is something to consider."

"The reason that dinner is not the feast we've become accustomed to here, is that sometimes there is a reaction in your stomach when you drink the liquid, and you need to purge. So, a light meal is preferable, but again, Bryan said there is no pressure whatsoever, just an offering."

"I'll be curious how Sam reacts to what you just told me."

"Well, you won't have long to wait. Here she is now, with Julia. Why don't you fill her in? I'm going to play my guitar for a bit before we eat. Hi, Sam, you look lovely as usual. You too, Julia. Did you get a chance to catch some rest?"

"I laid down and rested. I don't think I slept, but I feel good. What's going on? Things seem different tonight," Julia said.

"I'm going over to the lounge to play a few tunes. If you'd like to join me, I'll explain what I know, and I've been known to take requests!"

"Sure, I'd love to," she said to Tom and followed him towards the lounge. "See you in a few," she said to Samantha and Adam.

Samantha sat down in the chair Tom had just gotten up from and Adam filled her in on what Tom had told him. As she absorbed the information Adam could see in her face two sides of her being digesting the data.

"Wow, I didn't see this coming!" she said.

"Nor me. I'm uncertain what to do."

"Do you think we'll be alright? Is it safe?"

"Tom said that Bryan and Susie have taken it many times, and they seem fine."

She knew that she would not be able to decide which way to go until the last moment, and she suspected that it would be an intuitive decision when she did. She turned to Adam with a question. "Well, Adam, you're the strait-laced one in the bunch, what are you going to do?"

"I'm not sure. I think I'll just play it by ear and see what happens. This isn't something I have considered, but Bryan told Tom that it's a life-changing experience in a very positive way, and I have all the respect in the world for Bryan and Susie, so we'll see."

"That's exactly my approach. I don't want to be reckless, but I also don't want fear to stop me from understanding more about myself and nature. I certainly trust Grandfather. He would never do anything to cause us harm. So, like you, I'll just see what happens."

Tom told Julia what he knew about the events planned for the evening, but he wasn't sure if she would be invited by Grandfather to participate, so he didn't dwell on the subject. Instead, he asked her, "What kind of music do you enjoy listening to?"

"Oh, you're gonna laugh if I tell you."

"No, I won't, it's all good. I'm intrigued, tell me."

"Well, I remember as a little girl the music my father listened to, and I've always liked it since. You know that rock and roll from the fifties? Before the Beatles came?"

"You mean like this? Tom asked, as he began the

classic chord progression which so many songs from that era used. Then he began to sing a song written in 1956 by The Five Satins, 'In the still...'"

"I love that one!" Julia said.

Tom was just finishing the song when Susie poked her head in the door to say they would be eating in the open hut next to the cooking pit. They walked outside to find palm thatch bundles tied together in rolls and spread to form low benches in front of the banana leaves which presented the meal. Bobby and Arihi were already there, and Bryan was speaking softly with Tony and Susie who were just sitting down. As they found their places, one more person stepped onto the raised platform and took a seat next to Bryan. It was Grandfather, and he was dressed in a way they had not seen before, looking both impressive and, a bit intimidating. Light shimmered off his body which was draped with shells and feathers, and every move he made was announced by the sound of the shells ringing. He wore a headdress made of brightly colored feathers which formed almost a halo around his head and gave him a regal look. His lower body wore a knee-length skirt that looked like hemp and was dyed with the same iconic geometric lines used in tattoos. Shells tinkled on his ankles with each step he took. He was quite a sight. He still looked like himself, but as if he were from a different century than the man who had signed papers with the government three days earlier.

Once seated, Grandfather invoked thanks to Mother for providing the nourishment they were about to receive. The food placed in front of them consisted of only raw fruits and vegetables. They ate quietly, and the silence only enhanced the sense of anticipation that they felt.

Finally, Grandfather, who had not eaten anything, stood up and addressed the group.

"Thirty years ago, this being we refer to as Samantha, left the security of her mother's womb and a world which was familiar to her, the world of spirit, and entered forth into the world of substance. This is what we acknowledge when we celebrate someone's birthday. Upon taking the final breath, we leave this world and are reborn back into the form of spirit. In a sense, we then have completed one cycle of life. I ask you, if it were possible to be reborn back into the world of spirit, for a limited time and without physical pain or suffering, would it not be a precious gift to know what to expect when the cycle does complete itself? Most people live their lives ignorant of that aspect of themselves, which provides the foundation for the total cycle of their existence. Why is this?"

Grandfather raised his arms and placed his hands on both sides of his head and turned to look at each person in the room individually. Then he released his hands from that position and arched them both upwards until they met and formed a circle over his head.

"The reason for this is that people are held prisoner by their minds. When we are born into the world of substance, we have no choice but to accept the camouflage by which it exists. This world is constructed by the totality of the thought forms of all the beings that live in it. Including, but not limited, to us. Creatures like my sister Kahiko Aukai who has traveled to every corner of it never once questioned her place in it. She knows that she is spirit in the form of a great sea explorer and will soon return to her true identity. But at no time in all those years of swimming did she ever separate herself from the knowledge of her true being. It seems that we, mankind, are uniquely talented in the art of forgetting ourselves."

Julia turned and looked at Tom as Grandfather mentioned the name of the "woman" Tom and her would visit tomorrow.

Again, Grandfather remained silent for several minutes and gazed across the room.

"Although I entered this world with more clarity of my true nature than most, somewhat like our friend Thomas here, it was not until I went to live with Luti Mikode that the veil of camouflage was lifted for good. He offered me a gift of immense value. The gift of realizing my true nature, and tonight I offer that gift to you. I do not consider Luti Mikode a holy being or shaman or any other term one might wish to use. To me, he has been a wise teacher, a dear friend, and in all ways a part of my family. The only way I can describe him is as a grandfather to me, and that is the way I have been honored to accept whatever recognition those of you wish to use when you address me. We are family in spirit. The great gift which Luti Mikode bestowed on me was made possible by an ancient spirit medicine which the Ramo have used to remember themselves for over a thousand years. It is the pulp from a vine that grows in the high mountain valleys, mixed with bark and leaves. It allows the active, thinking mind to step aside for a time, and enables a direct perception of both the inner world and the outer world to be possible. This is what I refer to as the second birth-day."

Grandfather walked a few steps toward the trail leading to the office lodge, then turned around and gazed again at the group.

"In the lodge, you will see cups of two sizes, one twice that of the other. All of you except for our four new friends know about these cups. In them, I will pour that which I have received from the Ramo, according to each of your wishes. I can promise you two things, and I am certain that your friends will agree. First, you will not be physically hurt in any way. Second, you will not be mentally the same in many ways. The gift is there. Anyone who wishes, may receive it. If not, there is no shame. You too, my child," he said looking at Julia.

One by one the group got to their feet and followed Grandfather to the lodge. As they entered the lodge, they were surprised at how the main room had been changed. All the furniture had been removed and was stored in the office next to Bryan's. In the center of the room, nine yoga mats had been rolled out and arranged to form a semicircle of rays leading out from a center that contained a small low stand on which were flowers and a wrapped bundle of herbs. Next to each mat, on the inside of the circle, were small wooden buckets with metal bails.

On the table where Adam had recently broken down his travel lab, was a vessel made from a large, dried gourd that had been scraped and painted in the ubiquitous geometrical designs seen everywhere on the island and carved with animals and sea creatures. The neck of the gourd had been hollowed out and cut open near the end, serving as a pouring spout. Lined up on the table were two rows of nine cups, made from small gourds. Finally, placed on a carved root which created a perfect stand, was a drum constructed from a large piece of jungle vine. The outer ring of the vine was extremely tough and had been used to make the hoop for the drum after the soft inner pith had been removed. The drumhead was pigskin, as was the beater, and it was carved and beautifully decorated.

Grandfather asked the group to choose their places, and they followed the lead of the others and walked to the outer end of the remaining yoga mats left vacant by them. Grandfather then said in a low but powerful voice, "We have come, Spirit Mother, to seek wisdom in the Vine of Soul. Our hearts are open. Our intention is pure. We ask that you take each of these children into your womb. Dissolve the illusion which keeps them blind. Let them remember that they dwell in spirit. Guide and protect them on this journey of rebirth. We ask this in love and respect for all that lives."

Grandfather motioned to the person standing immediately to his right, who happened to be Bryan. Bryan walked from the end of his mat to stand in front of the table. After a moment, he reached for one of the smaller cups and held it out to Grandfather, who poured the brownish-orange liquid from the large gourd into the cup, filling it about three-quarters full. Next, Susie walked to the table and repeated the same choice made by Bryan, who had returned to the end of his mat. When Bobbie took his turn at the table, he reached for the larger cup and gave it to Grandfather for filling, followed by Arihi, who did the same. Tony was next to walk to the table. He stood there much longer than the others, and turned to look at Grandfather, and then back at the table, before turning to his right and walking back to his mat. He knelt and rolled his mat back up and carried it over to where it had been stored, then he left the room. Next, it was Samantha's turn. She walked to the table and stood there contemplating her choice. She too turned to look at

Grandfather and then reached for a small cup. Grandfather filled the cup, then raised it to his forehead and held it out to her. She took it and slightly raised it, looking into Grandfather's eyes, and then returned to the end of her mat. Adam also chose a small cup, and Grandfather honored him also by raising it to his forehead, before handing it to him.

Julia walked to the table and stood there looking at the two sizes of gourds. She was tempted to follow Tony out of the room, but something made her stay. She reached for a small gourd and held it out to Grandfather, her hands shaking just a little. Grandfather did not pour the Vine of Soul right away. He stood there in front of her, then reached out and held her hands, circling them around the cup. She was mesmerized by his warm honey eyes and relaxed noticeably. Grandfather poured the liquid into the cup, and after holding it to his forehead, he extended it to her. Not sure what to do, Julia raised it slightly and returned to her mat.

Last was Tom. He walked around the circle of mats following in the steps of the others and stood before the table. Grandfather, however, lifted his hand. He looked at Tom for a moment and then reached for a large cup and filled it for him, slowly raising it to his forehead, then holding it out to him. Tom took a step towards Grandfather and reached out both hands to receive the gourd full of the Vine of Soul. When he was back at the end of his mat, Grandfather spoke.

"Walk to the front of your mats and place your cups on the ground next to the purge buckets." They all did as he asked. "Now please lower yourself to your knees." As they were all rearranging themselves Grandfather struck a match and walked to the center of the ray of mats and lit the herb bundle on fire. He let it burn for a few seconds and then waved it back and forth extinguishing the fire, but the bundle continued to glow, and smoke wafted through the room. It was not exactly like sage, but it wasn't like incense either. Rather, somewhere in between. It had the effect of creating a sense of the sacred in the room.

"You may now give yourselves to the Vine of Soul."

Each of the participants reached for his or her cup and raised them to their lips and drank. Tom, taking longer, was the last to put his cup down.

"Lie back. Relax into the Vine."

# CHAPTER THIRTY-TWO

By this time, the sun had dropped far beneath the horizon and Grandfather lit numerous candles that were on the table. He then picked up his drum. The sound it made was deep and resonant and it coupled with the entrancing scent of the herb bundle, allowing an anchor for the senses.

Julia was apprehensive as she swallowed the viscous liquid. She had never taken anything of a psychedelic nature, so she wasn't sure how she would react. Fortunately, her stomach didn't either. She drifted off and soon realized that she was back in the home she grew up in as a little girl. There was the green vinyl hassock she used to balance on, and there was the worn leather Chesterfield sofa that her dad cherished. Why was she here, she wondered, and why am I alone? She remembered vaguely when her mother died. She was around four years old, and from then on, her dad, Ross, was her only connection to the adult world. But then he left. Where is he? And again, she asked, why am I alone? She felt a sense of panic rising. It felt like her body, from her head to her feet, was being squeezed tightly, as if a giant python had her in its coil. Then she noticed something was different. She was no longer in the empty flat in Toronto. She was in another room, and she could hear voices. She followed the sound and drifted through a passageway. The light was dim, and the surroundings were strange but vaguely familiar. Then she saw her father, wearing his favorite plaid lumberjack shirt, facing another man whose back was turned to her. It was the image she always kept in her mind of how he looked as he embarked on his great adventure. Young, handsome, and vibrant. And then he left her with a nanny for nearly four years. She said to him, "Daddy, I found it. I found where you went. I found your mountain that shines. Aren't you proud of me?"

A voice replied, although her father's face remained impassive.

"I have always been proud of you, pumpkin. It is me who I am ashamed of."

"Daddy, why do you say that? You are a great man. You are my hero."

"And I left you, alone. For four years. Then I left you for good when you were still so young. I failed you. Yet I found something of great value."

"You found the diamond mountain!"

"No, my precious daughter. I found myself. With his help."

When he said this, the man whom she could not see rose, and turned to face her. He was surrounded in a pale white light which formed an oval around his form. His eyes were radiant and faintly golden in hue.

There was just the suggestion of markings across his forehead, and Julia realized who she was looking at.

"My child, I told you that my son Ross is dear to me. As are you. But you must decide which treasure you will pursue."

Julia felt energy flowing around and through her as she silently voiced her reply. "I just want to prove that my father didn't fail. That he found the treasure he left me to discover."

"I found my treasure, my daughter. I hope you do too."

"That is why I came here, Father," she said mentally.

"But there is another treasure which you may seek, child. One which demands a much greater mountain to climb, but which is infinitely more valuable." The words flowed into her being from the man she knew was Grandfather.

"Seek the treasure, pumpkin. Find it. Find it. Find the treasure within."

The room faded. Julia fell asleep. She was exhausted, her energy drained.


Adam realized quickly that something was happening. As he lay on his back looking at the poles in the structure supporting the ceiling, he noticed that the poles were moving, reconfiguring themselves into a new form that allowed him to look up into the night sky. As he observed the stars through the opening, he began to realize that he was no longer in the lodge but was ascending into the sky himself. He continued to hear the rhythm of the drum, but he became aware of a large bird gliding slowly towards him. As it came closer, he could make out that it was much larger than he was and pure white, and in fact, it was a giant Albatross, which held stationary in the night sky next to him. Adam examined the great sea bird closely and then thought to ask it a question. "Great bird of the sea, how is it that you are here, and that I am in the air with you?"

The white Albatross turned its head to look directly into Adam's eyes and said, "My son, I am that which represents freedom of spirit. Hold out your arms and come with me." Adam held his arms out from his side and was amazed to see that they were covered in white feathers like the Albatross. Together they soared out over the ocean where time and distance melted beneath them. "Look below, son, do you see the river of death?"

Adam craned his neck down and immediately saw a vast river flowing across a low plain towards the sea. He looked closely, and what he saw shocked and saddened him; it was so full of human waste that it was impossible for anything living to exist at all. "Great one, how is this possible? Nothing can live in the waters below."

He turned to look at the Great Free Spirit who said simply, "Come, see more." From the height of their soaring, Adam could see nothing but open ocean. Then they were lower off the water and again the spirit bird told him to look down and observe. "See below you the continent of death. No creature of the air or swimmer in the sea may visit this place without death."

Adam knew from somewhere back in his

conscious brain that what he was looking at must be the Sargasso Sea, a vast floating landmass of debris the size of many small countries. As he looked closely, he could see all manner of creatures from sharks and whales to birds and turtles entangled in nets and lines, dead or dying on the surface of the artificial island. He wept at the sight of it. Then they soared off again. This time there was something familiar about what was coming into view. He saw below him the unmistakable pattern of waves breaking on beaches, and tall cliffs rising out of the sea. He knew instinctively that they were soaring along the western coastline of Wales.

"My child, even here it exists. Below you is the best of what has been left, but the death is still everywhere, in the bellies of the hard bodies living in the sand, and in the flesh of the swimmers feeding upon them. This is the legacy of your kind. This is what you have given your life to, and you now must act. For the love for all living things, you must now choose your path. I, the Spirit of the Free, will be with you. I am you, and you are a part of all that is. Remember, you are a part of all that is, creation below and creation here. Now you will return, but do not forget."

Adam again was able to smell the herb bundle and hear the drumbeat Grandfather was still creating. He gazed upward at the underside of the thatched roof and then turned his head to look at Samantha. When he did, a tremendous feeling of warmth which he could feel throughout his entire body flowed through him, and when he closed his eyes that warmth was visible as a violet cloud saturating his inner vision. He knew then what the tangible feeling of love was.

Samantha did as Grandfather requested and relaxed on her mat. She had trepidations about what was to happen since the only altered state she had ever experienced was from one glass of wine too many. She felt a mild sense of unrest in her tummy, but not enough to reach for the bucket. The liquid was viscous and had a not unpleasant citrus tone to the taste, and she had no problem getting it all down. What she first noticed was that the room began to vibrate. It was like looking into a pan of water placed on a stereo speaker; everything was shimmering.

Next, she saw the room fade and everything began to turn green, and she had the distinct sensation she was in deep vegetation or a jungle. She could still feel the pulse of the drumbeat in her being, but all sounds had faded, and she was immersed in a surreal world of plants and flowers which seemed to be consciously aware of her presence. As she drifted deeper into the lushness, she became aware of something in motion high in the canopy of the dense jungle growth. It was something that seemed to move by itself, and as she focused on it, she could tell that it was some kind of flying thing, because there was the unmistakable movement of wings. As it drew closer, she realized that she was looking at the most beautiful butterfly she had ever seen. It shimmered in an iridescence of colors that constantly changed as it slowly descended towards her. Behind the magnificent creature shown a golden orb of light which it seemed to ride down on as it came to a rest in front of Samantha.

The great wings of the huge butterfly folded gently against its body, which Samantha now realized was that of the most beautiful female she could ever imagine. While in flight and backlit by the golden orb, Samantha couldn't see the details of the creature that were now apparent. It had a silky, white feathery body, which was that of a female, but it was the face that was so utterly captivating. It was the face of all women everywhere, indescribably beautiful, but without a hint of ethnicity. Samantha could only stare, but she also realized that there was no threat and nothing to fear, and therefore finally asked, "I do not know where I am, and I do not know who you are, but I would like to learn."

There was a radiance surrounding the creature which glowed with an aura that pulsed with energy. "I am Gaia, the Mother of all that lives in this world. You are in the place of becoming, my child, where anything that can be imagined can be brought to life. I wanted to show you this so that you would know that creation allows for any possibility. Think, my child, of a flower that you have loved in your life."

Samantha's thoughts moved back to when she was a child growing up on the coast of Maine, and she immediately thought of her favorite flower, the lupine. She remembered the whites and blues and purples all sharing the sunlight on a small hillside that ran down to the rocks and the sea. As she thought of this, great multi-colored lupine began to grow, unlike any she had ever seen in Maine. They were pink, they were candy-striped, they were every combination of color and texture imaginable. Samantha stood entranced by what she was seeing.

"You see, my child, everything is possible in this

place of becoming. Now I want to show you the secret of life in your world. Look deeply at the plants you see. Feel them. Be with them. Merge with them." And Samantha did just that; she willed herself to become one in spirit with the plant world which completely engulfed her. Everywhere there was green, but as she concentrated on the images she was seeing, she realized that her consciousness was inside the plant life itself. Then she saw tiny particles of light falling from the golden orb above. Each particle pulsed with energy, and as it touched the surface of the vegetation, that plant pulsed slightly as well and absorbed the photon of light. The whole of her surroundings was pulsing as it absorbed the photons of light entering its cellular structure. Samantha realized she was witnessing the process of photosynthesis which indeed was the secret of life in her world. Mesmerized by the sight, she could have stayed in that state of being far longer but for the gentle voice of Gaia calling her.

"Now you know, child, that everything in creation lives on the light. As above, so below. The light you see before you, is but a poor imposter of the light which you will breathe when your dance here is over. That light will nurture you for eternity and will take you into itself and you will know it for what it is, the light of love. Remember this. The answer to that which you will seek lies in the smallest of things. The smallest of things. Do not forget what you have learned here, my child, and may you always, always seek the light!"

Samantha felt herself returning. The butterfly being had faded, and the dense greenery slowly succumbed as well. She could still hear the beat of the drum and smell the herbs smoldering an earthy fragrance into the air. She was thirsty but did not get up right away. She opened her eyes and turned to her left and saw Adam lying on his side watching her. He reached out his hand and she reached out hers and together they rested, looking into each other's eyes.

When Tom lay back on his mat, he knew immediately that he would need the bucket, and he waited with apprehension. It did not come right away. The feeling was not like having a stomach bug which everyone experiences at times, and as unpleasant as that is, this feeling was of a different order. It felt as though his whole being was about to purge itself of anything dark or negative. When he did finally reach for the bucket, he did so with a feeling of relief, just wanting the horrible anticipation to be over. He emptied his stomach of a not great amount of liquid and then lay back down on his mat.

At once he knew he was no longer in this world, but where he was, he had no idea. He was fully aware of who he was, but there was no basis for understanding his existence, no guideposts to point him in a direction he needed to go. Through his eyes, everything around him was gray, like looking into an intensely dense fog. There was no definition or orientation possible. It was unnerving, and he felt the rumbling of what he knew could be panic growing inside his being. As he strained to discern anything which might give him bearings, he noticed movement in front of him.

Yes, there was a figure approaching him, and the grayness was diminishing. He could make out that the figure was humanlike and was moving directly towards him. It stopped a few feet away and stood motionless. Words flowed into Tom's mind though no lips moved on the figure standing in front of him. "Do you know who I am?" The question was phrased in his mind.

"No, should I know you? Where am I?"

The figure answered, "Yes, I would think you would know me, and as to where you are, we will get to that shortly. Look closer, do you recognize me?" Tom strained to see the features in the face of the strange figure in front of him. All of a sudden, a shocking realization came upon him, and his face revealed what he now knew. "I see that you do know who I am. Once again, who am I?"

Tom looked away from the figure standing there, and then turned back and said, "You are myself."

The entity replied, "That is correct, or more exactly, I am the composite of all of your selves, for you have many. You have managed to remove the veil, although it will only be for a short while. There are some truths that I want you, who I am also, to understand in mind, and to know in being. The totality of this universe in which we exist is far, far greater than anything you can now imagine. You, we, are multi-dimensional, although at this time you experience only an infinitesimal aspect of the totality. Look!"

As the entity said that word, the grayness surrounding them burst forth into a cacophony of color and shapes. Images appeared such as what might be seen by photographs taken through the Hubble telescope. Galaxies coming into being and descending into oblivion, life evolving from nothing and then being extinguished back to nothing. The ebb and flow of existence were laid bare both in the physical realm as well as in the subtle planes. It was a breathtaking presentation of images, bold in color and texture that portrayed the rising and falling of life. Energy was congealed into matter. Form was created out of nothingness, and yet one aspect remained constant. The light.

"Do you not see and feel the light of creation?" the entity which was Tom asked. "It is the light of the creator himself. It is what we are, as well as all that exists. Come, let us go into the light together."

The entity and Tom moved together towards the light in a gentle yet purposeful way. As they traveled closer, the light became more and more piercing, all-pervading and a part of everything, until Tom looked down at his arms and lower body to see that it too was light which had condensed into the matter, he called his body.

"Be not afraid. This is the light of creation. We are of the same essence as that of everything that exists, we are all one being, and we experience existence as surrogates of the creator. That is the great truth, which all seek to know. You have journeyed far and are now beginning the path of return. Remember what you have seen and understand what you have heard. Know that you will never be alone, and that the totality of your being awaits you."

Tom awoke to find himself alone on the mat. How long he had been there he did not know. Everyone had left the lodge except for Grandfather, who sat quietly beside him. It was very late, and he sat up and tried to reorient himself. He began to recall where he was. He looked to the center of the ray of mats at the now extinguished herb bundle, and then he turned to look at Grandfather. He was still uncertain of what he had experienced. Was it a vision?...Or a dream? No, it had to be more than that. It was real, he knew it was. Grandfather sat next to him and extended his right arm and placed it on Tom's left shoulder, in the manner of the Ramo.

"It will take you many months, even years, to understand what you have learned tonight. I can only say that the Vine of Soul creates that which only that exact individual can use and learn from. Whatever you experienced was meant for you, and you alone, but it is absolutely a truth lesson. Use the information wisely. I honor your journey. Now, it is time to go rest. I will see you in the morning."

# CHAPTER THIRTY-THREE

Adam and Samantha walked together back to her hut after leaving Grandfather and the others. There was no question in either of their minds that they would spend the night together. Nor would the heretofore platonic relationship continue. They both wanted to share the energy they had felt in their Soul Vine journey with the other, and it would be physical lovemaking that would provide the deepest and most complete way to do so. Neither one had ever been "in love" before and now that they both felt it, they were overwhelmed by its power. As the sun rose, they lay together listening to each other's breathing and the jungle birds, which were just beginning to stir. Samantha got up and returned with two bottles of water.

"So many new things we've experienced being here, and now this. So much to take back with us, and so much to be thankful for."

"Yeah, you can say that again! I want to tell you

something, and it's hard for me to say. I really, uh, I'm uh..."

"For God's sake, Adam, just spit it out, and in case you're wondering, I love you too!"

"Brilliant! That's just what I was going to get out, eventually! When I came back to reality last night, I looked at you and this feeling I can't describe just washed over me, and I knew that it was love. It was love for all living things, to be sure, but most of all for you, and I needed to tell you."

"Well, believe me when I tell you that I had a similar experience. My guide, I guess you can call her, emanated the purest love I could ever imagine. I can still feel it now within me, and I want to share it with you. She also showed me what she called the secret of life. It was amazing! Adam, it was the actual working of photosynthesis within all living plants, and we were inside the plants themselves. It was a profound insight, but more than that, she has given me a clue or a hint about something, but I'm not exactly sure what. I just know that something profoundly important was shown to me. There is something I must do. Some kind of task or a mission. I know it in my being, but I'm not sure what it is."

"What do mean, Sam?" Adam asked quietly.

"Gaia told me that the answers I will seek will be found in the smallest of things. She said to be sure to remember. But I don't know what it is I will be seeking. What did you experience? What were you shown?"

Adam paused before answering as he gathered his thoughts. "My guide was a giant spirit bird. An albatross to be exact. We flew together over the seas, even to the coast of Wales. I was shown that the entire Earth was being poisoned. All living things were suffering. It was very powerful, and something I will never forget."

Samantha looked off into the distance, right past Adam. She stared at nothing as she entered a place inside her where answers have always flowed on their own. Adam, having never seen her do this, was mildly alarmed, thinking she might have a medical condition. Then she snapped out of it and said softly, "Adam, do you have any doubt that we are bonding through love?"

"No doubt, babe. It's brilliant, it is. Don't you?"

"Yes, of course. We're combining our energies together and becoming more as one," she said.

"That's a bloody nice way to say it, Sam. Oh, there I go with the bloody again. Sorry!"

"That's alright. But think if we combined our journeys with the Vine into one as well. What would the combined message be?" she asked.

Adam pondered for a minute, then said, "That's an interesting question. My albatross showed me that what I do in science is what we need to do to stop the killing in the oceans as well as on land. What you do in science - genetic engineering, is certainly all about, what did you call it? The smallest of things? Maybe that's the answer you seek. I think if we combine the two, the message is pretty bloody brilliant."

"Yes, that was what struck me. Find the smallest of things, which to me are microbes like bacteria or viruses, and use them to help heal Gaia. Remember when we first met Grandfather? Remember what he said before we ate our meal with him?" Samantha asked.

"Didn't he say something like, for those who have been chosen, there is no surprise? No turning back."

"And he mentioned pain and healing. I think he was

talking about us. About something we are about to do. Something we must do, but what is it?" Samantha said anxiously.

"Well, from what I see, there is a correlation."

"What do you mean, Adam?" Sam asked.

"Grandfather has a dear friend dying from ingesting plastic, right? And he must see what we saw with all the birds dead on the island. Even Bryan said its one of his main concerns."

"Yes, he did. Go on."

"Follow me on this. You mentioned microbes, including bacteria. Did you know that the oil industry uses microbes to clean up oil spills, like at Deep Water Horizon?"

"I think I've heard that, but why is that important?"

"What is plastic made from?" Adam asked softly.

"Oil," Sam replied.

"And if you could..."

Adam was cut off as Samantha blurted, "If I can genetically modify a microbe that already has the capacity to metabolize oil into one that can consume plastic, it would—"

Adam finished her thought. "It would bloody well be the exact thing that might help Gaia! A game-changer for sure, and there's nobody more qualified to do it than you!"

"Then us, Adam. And that includes Tom."

"He'll be a huge help trying to figure out where and how to use the microbes if we get to that point. That's deadest, as Bobby would say."

"More than just that, Adam."

"What do you mean?" Adam asked.

"I mean it feels...it's like he has a connection to the

mysteries we've been sharing. He may be a link, that's all."

"Speaking of Tom, I think I'll wade on over and change my clothes. I'll see how he's doing. Pretty interesting thoughts. I wonder what he'll think? I'll see you in the kitchen in a bit."

Adam walked up the steps to the porch of the island cabin, just as Tom was beginning to sit up in bed. He walked over to the little kitchenette and grabbed a bottle of water and brought it back for him.

"I think you might find this as good as a Creamflow. I was bloody thirsty when I woke up just now."

"You can say that again, thanks!"

"How long did your journey last? Sam and I left while you, Bobby, and Arihi were still with Grandfather."

"It's hard to say exactly. I think I got back here maybe four hours ago, but I'm not sure. I don't know about you, but once I left my body, time was irrelevant. As far as I was concerned, I might have been gone a month. There just wasn't anything left to associate with, but obviously, I'm here, so it was hours at most."

"In all my life, I never experienced anything even close to what that drink did. It was so fantastical, yet it all bloody-well made sense. I can remember every detail of the experience even now, so I know I wasn't dreaming."

"No, that's for sure, it wasn't dreaming. I'd say, for me at least, it was a guided out-of-body experience of the most profound kind imaginable."

"That's a brilliant way of putting it, Tom! I have heard of so-called out-of-body adventures people say they experience, but I always thought it was rubbish. Until last night, that is."

"Well, I'd say we chalk it up to another first that this amazing place has given us! Hey man, are you starving, or is it just me?" Tom asked.

"Hell no, it's not just you! Let me throw on some fresh clothes and we'll get our butts over to the kitchen!"

They waded across the lagoon, and both shared a new sense of awe of everything around them. Everything seemed more vibrant in color and texture. Sounds were more intriguing. Smells were poignant and there was simply a heightened sense of awareness that they both were consciously observing in themselves.

As they reached the shore, Tom said, "I'm going to check on Julia. We're going to walk up to the village later. I'll catch up to you in a minute."

"Brilliant, but remember, first to the mill grinds!"

"What the heck is that supposed to mean?"

"First to the kitchen eats! That's what!"

"We'll be right along."

Tom walked down the little trail that led to the next hut where Julia was staying. He was awash with emotions, and his heightened sense of perception magnified everything. The truth was, that he was feeling a little overwhelmed by all he had experienced since getting into Samantha's car and heading to the airport only five days ago. But at the same time, he felt more alive than he ever had before, and that was exciting.

He climbed the steps to the porch and knocked gently on the door to Julia's hut and said softly, "Julia, are you up? Everything okay?" There was silence, and he waited. As he was about to knock on the door with a little more urgency, he heard a creak from inside and the door opened.

Julia stood in the threshold. She had just woken up

and was wearing her light cotton gym pants and a tee shirt. Her feet were bare, and her auburn hair looked like it belonged to a wild woman. It occurred to her that no man had ever seen her look this way, and under normal circumstances she would never have opened the door. But this was not the norm, and she said in a low, soft voice, "Good morning, Tom. I guess I was out like a light. Good thing you thought to get me up."

Tom just stood there. He could say nothing, but he felt something weird in his chest. Then realized it was his heart pounding.

"Are you alright, Tom? I'm sorry I look like this, but it won't take me long to get ready."

Tom was roused from his stupor by her voice and realized that he was staring at her. He said in almost a whisper, "You are the most beautiful woman I have ever seen. Especially just the way you are right at this moment. I hope you're not offended. I guess I was just in a daze."

Julia stood there processing what this man had just said. The only thing she could think to do was to step forward and give Tom a kiss on the cheek and say, "That was one of the nicest things anyone has ever said to me. Thank you. Come on in, I'll be ready in a jiff." She turned her head so Tom wouldn't notice as she wiped a tear from her eye that threatened to roll down her cheek.

"I'll just sit here on the porch. Everything seems so much more alive. I guess it's the after-effect of the vine. Can you feel it too?"

"I feel something different, that's for sure."

"I meant what I said. Vine or no vine," Tom said as he sat down and looked up at her.

"I'll be out in a minute."

Julia closed the door gently behind her and just stood for a moment behind it. She felt flushed, as if she had just taken a hot shower. "How could he say that when I look like this?" She thought to herself. She walked to the dressing mirror to see herself as Tom had seen her. She almost didn't recognize the face staring back. "No make-up, hair a mess and a tee shirt and gym pants. And he says I'm beautiful. Wow. Well, if he likes the natural look, I guess I can oblige."

Three minutes later she was back on the porch in sandals, a knee-length capri, and a plaid cotton short-sleeve shirt. She had given her hair only the most cursory attention, but she had to admit she felt good, like being a little girl again. When Tom looked up as she stepped through the door he stood up and gave her a return kiss on the cheek. "This is the Julia I spoke of before. Let's get something to eat. I'm starving!"

"Me too," she replied. "Let's go."

# CHAPTER THIRTY-FOUR

"Samantha and Adam walked together sharing a new sense of awareness of everything around them. Things seemed more vibrant in color and texture. Sounds were more intriguing. Smells were poignant and there was simply a heightened sense of awareness that they both were consciously observing in themselves.

Once they arrived at the cooking hut, they realized that they were ravenous. Tony had created a masterpiece of coconut crab omelets draped with avocado and a delicious island salsa. For once Adam eschewed his usual decaf coffee in favor of the real thing as Samantha walked in with a perceptible glow to her. She smiled cheerfully and said good morning to Tony, and then helped herself to a man-sized portion of the omelet.

In between bites Sam said, "I don't know how you do it, Tony, but everything I've had to eat here rivals the best food I've ever eaten anywhere! What's your secret?"

Tony replied, "Well, Miss Lewis, that's a right dardy thing to say, thank you! I don't know, I just put things together from a sense of what I feel they want to be. Like this brekky here, the coconut crabs get the sweet flavor from what they eat, and eggs get the same from the chickens all around, so I just slam it all together and hope for the best! Usually works out though, I think."

"You think? I know!" Samantha laughed.

Adam, who was grinding at the mill, looked up to see Julia and Tom walking together into the cooking arena. He nudged Samantha, who looked up and was delighted by how nicely her old friend and new friend seemed to fit. She said, "Good morning, guys. We forced ourselves to leave some omelet for you! I love your new look, Julia!"

"Thank you, Samantha! It makes getting ready for the day a breeze, that's for sure."

Tom asked, "Say, Tony, do you know if Grandfather is still here, or did he go back to the village?"

"I think he's still here, Tom. He usually stays around the next morning after the ceremony just in case anybody had issues with anything they saw or experienced. I know I did my first time with the vine, but I guess he knew everyone would be fine."

"I didn't realize that you had a personal relationship with Grandfather, Tony. If you don't mind me asking, how come you changed your mind last night?"

"Yeah, mate, Grandfather has been a real cobber to me. Uh that means friend in Australia. Anyway, I was a bit of a mess when I first came here to work, and Grandfather has helped straighten me out. That was about three years ago I reckon. Anyway, I've taken the vine a number of times, even full cup twice, but for some reason, I just didn't feel it last night." Tony unconsciously glanced at Julia, but no one noticed, and he continued, "Grandfather told me to listen to my inner voice and be sure it feels right before I do it. I think maybe he knows more about me than I do about myself! Anyway, I just thought it was better to sit that one out."

"Out of curiosity, do Susie and Bryan always take the vine?" Samantha asked.

"Well to tell you the truth, it's been a while since we've all gathered to take the Vine of Soul, but yeah, they usually join in with the group. I think it mainly has to do with Grandfather kicking back more lately. He keeps hinting that his business is almost finished. I don't know what that means exactly, and I don't like the sound of it. Did Bryan say anything about the properties of the drink?"

"Not really, other than it is a profound experience, it's different for each person, and that it won't harm you," Tom answered.

"Yeah, mate, that part about not harming you is a bit of an understatement. The Vine of Soul is the reason why Grandfather, who I reckon must be close to a hundred fifty years old, looks the way he does. Same with Bryan and Susie. You'd never guess they're in their fifties, would ya?"

Julia joined the conversation, "Susie told me that the vine has that effect, but she didn't say how it worked."

"One time Grandfather said something about that. He said it was the opposite of what happens when someone goes up into space. You know what they say about if you travel to Mars and back you age slower than the people who stayed on Earth? Well, he said that the vine slows down how you perceive everything around you, and when that happens you don't create a future for yourself as fast as everyone else around you. It's a bit bonkers to me really, but that's the gist of what he said."

"So that must be part of the reason why it was so important for the mountain valleys to be protected from the outside world. Could you imagine what would happen if it ever got out that there was a fountain of youth up there?" Samantha said.

"You're right about that. Grandfather doesn't give anyone multiple tastes of the vine unless they are special to him. There is a lot of trust involved. Of course, it's easy for him to know who he can trust because he kinda knows everything already, I'd say." Tony's voice dropped a tone, and he wrapped his arms around his knees as a feeling of shame washed over him.

"Are you alright, Tony? You sounded sad when you said that." Samantha asked.

"Oh, I'm okay. I was just thinking how much that old boy means to me, that's all there is to it."

"I hope he's in the lodge because there's something I need to talk to him about. Thanks for sharing with us, Tony! It's amazing how much everyone in this place feels like family to me already!"

"I'll take that as a compliment, Miss Lewis, and the feeling is mutual!"

Tom and Julia continued with their breakfast as Samantha and Adam walked over to the office lodge, and just as they got there the door opened and Bobby and Arihi walked out. They were holding hands and had silly smiles all over their faces. Samantha held the door for them and then asked, "You two look like a cat that just caught a mouse! Would you mind telling us what's going on?"

"We'll let Grandfather tell you. We've gotta bloody well run. Bye for now!" Bobby was smirking as he and Arihi walked toward the trail leading back to the village.

Sam and Adam went inside, and it looked for all the world that Grandfather was sitting there waiting for them, which indeed he was.

"Hello, my children, did you rest well after meeting the Vine of Soul?"

Adam said, "Definitely, Grandfather, I slept like a baby! I feel more alive now than I have in a long time."

"The vine has properties that enable you to access your energy at a level not often experienced, and it provides a very positive charge that will stay with you for quite a while."

"Grandfather, Tony told us that the vine has, I guess you would say anti-aging properties. Does that affect start with just one cup of the liquid?" Samantha asked.

"Yes and no. The vine acts to slow down the process of creating one's reality, and I think you will all feel the effects of that for some time, although you will inevitably get used to it. The feeling of heightened awareness, for example, being more attuned to the world around you and not so obsessed with the conversation going on inside your head. That is the beginning of the process, but it must be reinforced before it becomes a permanent feature in your being. Then it must be taken every so often to maintain the physical effect, say once or twice a year. That is what Bryan and Susie were doing last night."

"And what happens if you decide to stop taking the vine for whatever reason? Do you age fast and die right away?" Adam asked.

"No, Adam, it doesn't work like that. You do continue to age even if you take the vine, just not as fast. Once you stop taking it, however, in about a year your normal aging begins again. Luti Mikode stopped taking the vine five years ago. He felt that he had achieved what his life mission required of him and that it was time to let the natural process take its course. His young apprentice is more than worthy to serve the Ramo in his stead, that I can assure you."

"Well, I am even more pleased that my family was able to help keep the lands of the Ramo safe from the world. I can only imagine what would happen if the vine was even suspected of existing. Speaking of being safe, Grandfather, there is something I need to ask of you."

"What would that be, my child? Anything you ask, I will give, if it is within my power."

"I would like you to return the yellow stone to the Ramo for me."

Grandfather sat still, and closed his eyes briefly before saying, "Samantha, that would be difficult, even for me. The Ramo culture does not take back that which is once given. It would be an insult to them if I were to bring it back up the mountain. The gift was the most important thing they could give, for the most important thing they could receive, their continued freedom."

"I suspected that, Grandfather, so this is what I would like you to do. Please take it with you back to the Ramo and tell them that it is the greatest gift my family could ever receive and that we will cherish it forever. But tell them that in the world of men, it is priceless beyond measure and that there is no place we could keep it where it would remain safe. Tell them that I ask of them the honor of safekeeping my family's greatest treasure because the only truly safe place we can think of, is with them. Maybe someday that will change, and I will return for it, but until then it needs guardians, and I ask that they do that for us."

"Samantha, you are wise beyond your years. I will

take the stone of the third eye and ask my friends to guard it with their lives for you and believe me they will."

Just then, the door to the office opened, and Tom and Julia walked in. Grandfather looked up and smiled. "Hello, my children, my heart has joy seeing you together. Come, join us."

They sat down on a couch next to each other, and Tom asked, "Grandfather, just now we passed Bobby and Arihi looking like two children with a big surprise. Can you tell us what's going on?"

"They have changed their minds about waiting ninety days for marriage. They want to be wed while all their family is here, meaning all of you. So, the ceremony will take place tomorrow afternoon. However, they will have to be patient for the gift I will now start on."

"How sweet that they want to bind their lives together while we are here. It makes me feel that we do have a second family here on this island."

"Thomas, you would be surprised to know just how true what you said is. This is but one act of a very long play, and the actors change roles many times."

"Grandfather, I asked Bryan about the possibility of getting a tattoo before I left, and he said that it would not be difficult and that there is a man in the village who practices the art. Would you know who he is?" Tom asked.

"Yes, of course. His name is Seth Luwi, and you can find him easily. Everyone in the village knows him. Just walk over and ask where he might be. He does beautiful art, drawing the lines."

"Thank you. Julia and I are going to visit Kahiko Aukai later. Maybe I can find the time to have it done. Will the dollar be accepted in payment?"

"Just mention that I told you to go to him, Thomas. Seth is as a son to me."

Adam said, "We're going to do a little exploring and maybe some snorkeling. I can't get over how bloody brilliant everything seems. I can't wait to see how the underwater world looks. Ready, Sam?"

"Ready as I can be! See you guys later. Grandfather, here is the stone of the third eye," she said reaching into her small day pack. "Thank you for honoring my request!"

"The honor is mine, my child. Until tomorrow."

Adam and Samantha wandered down to the boathouse, while Tom and Julia sat for a minute with Grandfather. He looked at the two of them and smiled. "I am most pleased that all my children are finally together with me. Perhaps you will stop to visit me while Thomas is with Seth Luwi," he said looking at Julia. "There is something I would like to discuss with you."

Julia was instantly on guard, having become convinced in spite of herself that the man sitting in front of her did, indeed, have ways that were hard to fathom, but replied calmly, "Thank you, Grandfather, that would be lovely."

"Then it is done. I must leave now. I am old, and a nap is refreshing, especially after being with the Vine of Soul. Until later." Grandfather stood up and as he began to walk out of the room, he paused behind the couch that Tom and Julia still sat on and reached out both of his hands. He placed them on their shoulders and said, "My dear friend, the ancient one, will be pleased that you both will visit her. For this, I thank you!" Then he continued on his way, shutting the door gently behind him.

Tom said, "I noticed you called him Grandfather. That makes me happy. Why the change?"

"I don't know. I guess because everyone else does, and it does just seem right," Julia replied.

"Hard to imagine calling him anything else! I think I'll have a little rest before we walk up to the village. I can walk you back to your cabin if you're ready."

"No, you go on. Just stop by when you're ready to go. I left my laptop in the office, and I need to check on my messages."

"No problem, see you in forty minutes or so," Tom said, as he got up and left the lodge.

Julia sat for what seemed much longer than it probably was. Her thoughts rippled through her being like waves on a beach, carrying her emotions up and down. Then she got up, went into the office, and with a deep breath, turned her computer on. There were three messages waiting her reply.

She briefly read a typically banal note from Alex, which at this point was just plain annoying, so she deleted it without an answer. The next two, however, were a bit different.

Opening the email, which was sent from The Legal Department, Lucarana Mining, she quickly read the message.

*Dear Miss Witherspoon,*

*Please be advised that an appointment has been set for you to sign all documents (see attachments) as per law, required by The Jurisdiction Governing Land Acquisition, Solomon Islands. As we have previously discussed, the seven-day right of recission expires three days hence, and the appointment is at their office in Honiara at 1:00 pm of that day. Address and directions attached.*

*Our courier will meet you with all the necessary original documents one hour prior to the closing, so please factor that in on your scheduling. You may review the attachments, but in short, it is merely your signature that is required, and we have been assured that the closing should take no more than one hour. The courier will wait to return with the signed copies, and once in his possession, transfer of funds will commence.*

*Again, The Company congratulates you on this momentous acquisition, and Legal stands ready to offer any assistance as may be required!*

*Very Truly Yours,*

*Victor Gates,*

*Senior Legal Counsel,*

*Lucarana Mining Company*

Julia sat quietly. Her rollercoaster of emotions did not stop, and she felt confused. But she was excited also, and she opened the next message from the C.E.O. - Peter Allaire.

*My Dearest Julia,*

*I am so pleased to inform you that all arrangements have been completed for the signing of the one-hundred-year lease on your discovery. Legal has done a stellar job, and in three days your first official act as the Director of Operations, Malaita, will commence. We couldn't be prouder of you, and I know your father would be as well!*

*One other tidbit of interest, which should please you, is that we have entered into initial discussions with Oceana Hardwoods, which is the largest forestry and logging operation in the entire South Pacific. The surveys show that the diamond-bearing tubes are located in a tiny fraction of the entire lease holding, and the value of the timber, as determined by the aerial surveys, is off the charts. The company deems it only fair to reward you for this windfall as well, to the tune of 5 percent gross revenues. It would seem congratulations are again in order! You will soon be a rather wealthy young lady, and I couldn't be more pleased!*

*Yours,*

*Peter*

Slowly, Julia rose from the desk, and closed her computer. Thoughts of where she would buy a home, what kind of car and where she could travel washed through her. The prospect of being in charge of what the company must now be sure will be a massive operation, kindled desires she had only dreamed of her entire professional life. She stood on the threshold of greater success than she ever could have imagined, greater even than her father's fabulous career. As she walked to her cabin, however, her thoughts yielded to her senses. The birds seemed to serenade her. The flowers smelled as perfume wafting in the tropical air, and the gentle breeze blowing in from the sea caressed her face.

Mother was calling.

# CHAPTER THIRTY-FIVE

Tom allowed himself to slowly drift back into waking consciousness. He was sitting cross-legged on the porch and with the continuing influence of the vine, had found it easy to access his inner energies through meditation. After a minute of stretching the stiffness out of his body, he went into the hut for some water. He felt refreshed and energized. His thoughts turned to Julia and the "date" with the ancient one they were about to go visit. For some reason, he never believed that he would ever find what people call a "soul mate." He always saw himself being alone when he thought of the future, which he seldom did. However, the vision of Julia, standing there in the doorway, was something he knew would stay with him for the rest of his life, and it sparked a thought that maybe being alone wasn't inevitable. He looked out towards the open ocean before wading back to shore. The sea was like life, he thought. A blank horizon fraught with possibilities and endless opportunities. But where will the voyage take him? He stepped off the porch and into the lukewarm crystal-clear water and turned towards the shoreline.

Julia rested deeply for twenty minutes, then took a shower. She felt excited, but also like she was being split in half. She pondered the fact that miraculously, two of her greatest desires seemed to be realizing themselves in this remote place, and so quickly. At thirty-four years of age, she had all but given up on the hope of finding a man who cared more for her than her looks, and most just cared about themselves most of all. She remembered the warmth and gentleness of her father, even though she was so young, and he had so little time for her. In Tom, she sensed a possibility that for the first time since then, there was someone worth getting to know. "Someone who might just...no..." she thought to herself. "Someone who could, make me happy." But what about her career? It was a now a foregone conclusion that her life was about to change and provide all the rewards anyone could possibly imagine.

Tom knocked gently on the cabin door, and Julia said, "Be right out, Tom. I'm all ready to go."

Tom turned to look back out into the lagoon. He stepped to the edge of the porch, resting both hands on the wooden railing, leaning forward. He heard the door open and close quietly and sensed Julia standing next to him at the railing. He turned his head slightly to acknowledge her and said, "Whenever I look out to sea, I always feel so small. It's teeming with life, but you don't see another human out there. Kind of like life itself. Makes me feel lonely sometimes."

"I think I know what you mean, Tom."

"All set? Let's go."

As they turned towards the jungle, Tom instinctively held his hand out slightly behind him for her to use for support on the stairs. Julia looked down, and in that moment, she felt something for nearly the first time in her life. She felt she was safe and secure with a man. Something she hadn't felt since she was a child. She took his hand and held it until the narrow path forced them to walk single file.

They made their way up the trail that ran along the edge of the lagoon, stopping often to look at the little details of life all around them that are usually missed when passed by too quickly. A coconut crab, nearly two feet across, was systematically prying open a small coconut with its massive claws. An osprey dove into the water with a terrific splash, and then fought to regain the air with a silvery fish wiggling in its talons. And there, just next to the mangroves was a dugong, a close relative to what was common in the waterways of Florida.

Tom pointed it out and said, "Where I'm from in Florida, I see manatees all the time. They're one of my favorite animals. So peaceful and harmonious with each other, but for some reason I've never tried to communicate with one.'

"Maybe you're just respecting their space. I get that."

Everything seemed slowed down. Each frame of the movie they were watching was a scene unto itself, and it was astounding how vibrant and alive the world was. The Vine of Soul did indeed have a residual effect, and it was pleasantly profound.

At last, they came to the outskirts of the village, as the trail wound through the jungle along the shore and branched over to Grandfather's hut. Julia had not seen the back of his abode when she visited him before, so she didn't recognize the place.

"What are those structures, Tom? They're funky, but cool!"

"The larger one, under the Banyan tree, is Grandfather's workshop. He is a true artist the way he carves things from wood! The other one that looks like a shed is where we're going. Follow me," he said, holding out his hand. There was no hesitation as Julia took it, and hand in hand they walked to the final resting place of the great sea creature, Kahiko Aukai.

When they rounded the closed side of the shed Julia gasped when she saw the colossal size of the ancient one. Her eyes were closed, and she did not move, prompting Julia to ask, "Are we too late, Tom? Is she dead?"

As Tom was about to answer, Kahiko Aukai opened her eyes, staring up at them, then lifted her head. Tom said, "Sit here next to me, Julia. I will need a few seconds." Tom and Julia sat alongside the ancient mariner, and Tom rolled his head on his shoulders, centering himself. Then he closed his eyes into small slits and became quiet within.

He formed the words in his mind, "Ancient one, I have returned with a friend. We come to honor you. I will leave soon and wanted to see you again."

As before, words flowed into his consciousness, and emotions too.

"*i who was free, have always come to this warm place in the sand. many journeys did i make, at the special time. once, many cycles ago, here, did i lay and sit with me he did, as you do now. with him was another, as you have now. little flipper she is, to the one called ross.'*

As Tom spoke her words, Julia was stunned to hear her father's name spoken in such a strange way. She leaned closer to the great creature as a tsunami of emotions crested over her.

*"he came to this warm sand, as you have. seeking that which cannot be held, feasting not on little white fish, but on desire. i returned at the next cycle, to this warm sand, and lay here i did. they both sat with me, as you do now, many times. you, little flipper, you are as he was, but not as he became. journey he did, never to return, a little flipper to guide. you are that little one. the one called ross, see him again i will, soon. and you, with seaweed hair, a journey you must make, to help little flippers everywhere. you, little flipper, like ross seek that which cannot be held, like ross find it within, find it with seaweed. i bid you farewell now."*

Exhausted, the great sea turtle lowered her head, and her eyes shut tightly. Tom too, was spent, and he slumped forward and leaned into Julia. Not knowing what to do, she put her arm around him and lowered her head to his shoulder. They stayed like that for a few minutes, but it could have been hours. Tom finally regained his composure and sat up as Julia removed her arm.

Tom wiped the back of his hand across his eyes, where tears had watered them. He looked at Julia and said, "She won't be with us much longer. She knew you were here, and now that she has given you that message, I think her journey will be over."

He reached out his hand and laid it on the head of the ancient one, and with a gentle pat said, "We will never forget you Kahiko Aukai, swim in peace." Then he said to Julia, "Let's go on to the village, there's someone I'd like to meet."

They both rose, and this time it was Julia who reached out her hand.

Tom held it as they walked.

# CHAPTER THIRTY-SIX

Tom and Julia left Kahiko Aukai with heavy hearts and walked past Grandfather's workshop and living hut, and into the village. There were two boys unloading fish from a dugout canoe and Tom walked up to them and asked if they knew a man named Seth.

"Ya, ya, Seth is there." They pointed towards a lane that wound between two of the larger structures in the village. "Go down to there. All the way to hut with yellow door. That is house of Seth. He artist Seth. Make pictures. Draw lines in skin." With that, the boy who was giving him directions turned sideways so that Tom could see his right arm which was beautifully tattooed in geometric forms common to the Solomon Islands.

"See? This Seth!" The boy proudly slapped his arm to reinforce the point that Seth was a great artist.

Tom thanked them and they headed for the narrow lanc. It wasn't long before they were standing in front of a well-kept hut that had many artistic embellishments tastefully enhancing its rustic appearance. The door was indeed yellow, but lower down, there was a beautiful image painted of an island in the lagoon, and the yellow was the sun rising in mid-morning bathing the water with golden light. Tom walked up the steps and knocked on the bright yellow door.

After a few moments the door opened, and Seth Luwi stood in the doorway smiling the biggest smile with the whitest teeth Tom had ever seen.

"Hello, mate, I've been expecting you. I got word from Grandfather that you might want a bit of art to take back to the States with ya, and I'd be happy to oblige!"

"My name is Tom, although Grandfather calls me Thomas. He's the only one who calls me that, not sure why, but nice to meet you! This is my friend Julia."

"Well, if you're getting to know Grandfather, then you probably get it that he does everything with a purpose, so he probably knows you from before. Nice to see you again, Miss Julia!" Seth said, extending his hand.

"Before what, Seth?" Tom asked.

"Just from before, Tom. Another life, another dimension, who knows? But if he calls you Thomas, you can be sure there's a reason."

"I like Thomas, it feels more like you than just Tom," Julia said.

"See! There it is, mate! You and the lady here probably both knew the old cobber from before. That's what I reckon. I heard there was a Vine of Soul ceremony last night. Did you both attend?"

Julia answered first, "Yes, we both did. It was...I'm not sure how to describe it, very profound. Something I will remember for a long time."

Tom agreed. "I had an amazing journey as well and it's a big part of why I'd like to get a tattoo. I want to remember this place and honor Grandfather. When I first arrived here, amazing that it was only five days ago, Bobby showed me a tattoo he had and told me it was something he had done out of dedication to Grandfather. I guess I know what he means now."

"Yeah, he has the same one that Grandfather has on his forehead. Did that one almost ten years ago, I did. Any idea what you might want it to look like, mate?"

"I think so, but first I need to know what it will cost, and how long it takes. Even though I'm from the States, I'm still on a tight budget. Luckily there's been nothing to spend even a nickel on since we've been here."

"I've got you covered, Tom, no matter what it is," Julia said.

"Didn't Grandfather tell you no worries? I wouldn't take a penny for lines made for Grandfather, nor one of his own. So, what were you thinking?"

"I know that Grandfather is really upset with all the damage being done by the garbage we let go into the ocean, and we saw the dead birds on the little island next to Charles Right. Also, I have a gift, you might say. I can communicate with animals, just like speaking with you. It breaks my heart to listen to Kahiko Aukai tell me of the 'soft white fish that cause death.' So, I thought if you could do it, I would like two seabirds on the shoulders with Kahiko Aukai in between on my neck. Would that be possible?"

"That would not only be possible, but brilliant as well! I can shade the ink to light gray for the birds and do a real cracker job in colors for the ancient one."

"Out of curiosity, did you grow up in Australia too?"

"Naw, mate, but I played for the Solomon Sevens

national rugby team, and the accent just rubs off, I reckon."

"So how long will it take? I'm sure you must have heard that Bobby and Arihi are tying the knot tomorrow afternoon."

"Well, the seabirds I do all the time, and turtles are pretty common as well, but I'd like to do something special for the old girl, so I'll need to work that out on paper. Once I've got it, I can ink it in probably three hours. I do it the modern way now with a horse, but I can still use the rake and hammer, although you wouldn't like that trust me. It takes a long time, and it hurts like hell. I can have you up and about before dinner."

"Well, I guess I'll walk back to Grandfather's place. He said there was something he wanted to talk to me about. I'll see you later, Thomas. I mean, Tom. Nice to meet you, Seth!" Julia said.

"Same here, Miss Julia! I'll see ya tomorrow at the wedding, I will! Say hi to the ole man for me!" Seth replied cheerfully.

Julia smiled warmly and left to stroll through the village, once again feeling slightly out of sync with her normal self. She thought it was weird that she called Tom by the other name, and wondered what Grandfather wanted to see her about. Thinking of her commitment to the company, she began feeling trepidation as she once again approached the hut with the blue door.

As before, Arihi answered her gentle knock, only this time she was greeted with a warm hug as she entered the charming main room of the hut.

"Wonderful to see you again, Julia! How are you feeling?"

"I feel fine, Arihi! In some ways better than fine. More alive, I guess you could say."

"Yes, I know what you mean. The vine stays with you for a few days in subtle ways. It's always my favorite part of the experience. There's something I need to do in a little while and after you have a word with Grandfather, maybe you'd like to come with me. I have to see a patient in the next village over. If you're not busy, I'd love the company," Arihi said.

"No, I don't have anything planned. I came with Thomas – err there I said it again. I mean, Tom, but he's getting a tattoo done by Seth so I'm free and would love to have something to do."

"Tom is a special person, and I think of him as Thomas too. I guess we could call that the Grandfather effect! Speaking of which, let me take you out to his workshop. He's been expecting you."

She led the way through the hut and out to a structure that seemed to have merged itself into the giant Banyan tree it was surrounded by. The roots, which grew down from the branches and gave them support, thickened with age, had been woven with palm thatches to form walls. The massive trunk had shelves carved into it where Grandfather stored his tools. Bamboo rafters were tied together to form a roof that was covered with palm leaves that were layered and woven to keep things dry even in a downpour. Grandfather was sitting on his low chair, working with a chisel, but he put it down when he heard their footsteps.

Arihi said, "I'll leave you too alone. I'll be in the cooking hut when you get done, and we can leave then. See you!"

"It is nearly her time. We won't be long. Here child, sit

down," Grandfather said motioning to Julia to sit on a cushion.

Julia did as she was instructed as Arihi left. Grandfather stood up and walked the dozen steps over to the trunk of the banyan tree. He dropped to his knees and removed several tools from one of the lower shelves. Then, he reached in and slid a board that looked like part of the tree itself forward, to reveal a secret hiding compartment deep within the tree. When he returned to his chair, he held something that was wrapped in cloth. He removed the covering and held the yellow diamond of the third eye in front of Julia. It sparkled even in the shade of the workshop.

"I have promised my child, Samantha, that I would return this most magnificent gift back to the Ramo for safekeeping. I will fulfill this promise in two days, after my children leave our island. I would like you to accompany me," he said, handing her the stone. "As you can see, it is quite heavy, and I am quite old. Someone to share the burden would be helpful."

Although Grandfather could have walked up and down the mountain a dozen times with the diamond, Julia had no choice but to agree. "If you need help, Grandfather, I would be happy to go with you. You said in two days, not three. Just to be sure?"

"Yes, child, we will return the gift the day after our friends leave for America. You will be able to keep your appointment."

Julia was startled by what the old man just said, but kept her composure and said vaguely, "I just have something I need to do, that's all."

Grandfather took the diamond back from Julia, and

returned it to its lair, carefully replacing the items in front of the door. He returned and sat back down.

"When my son, Ross, first came to me, he had come down from the mountain that we will soon climb. He went there looking for the very thing which you will carry back. Over the years, he and I made that climb many times. I know that he would want you to see what he saw and hear what he heard. It will help you decide, my child."

"Decide what, Grandfather?" Julia asked in a meek voice.

"Life offers many roads to travel, and many directions to take. My son, Thomas, will soon leave this island, to fulfill his destiny with his friends, but I suspect it will not be for long. You have many possibilities ahead, but right now, you need to journey to the next village with Arihi, because she may need help as well. Go now, I will see you at her wedding tomorrow."

Julia stood and was going to say something, but didn't, and left Grandfather to his work.

# CHAPTER THIRTY-SEVEN

Julia left Grandfather and again found herself out of sorts with her normal demeanor. There was just something about that man, she thought, that throws me for a loop. "But why?" she wondered. "He is as sweet as can be, so why do I always feel...threatened?" she almost said aloud.

Arihi had just finished baking cookies for the next day made with sweet jungle fruit that was everyone's favorite. As she was putting them in a paper bag, she broke one in half and shared it with Julia. "Umm, delish!" Julia said. "Bobby is a lucky man!"

"Thank you, Julia! I hope you make someone feel the same way someday."

"I guess I've never really allowed for that possibility," Julia mused.

"Let's get going, there is another kind of fruit that is ripe and needs our help!"

"What do you mean?"

"You'll see. Here, would you mind carrying this?" Arihi said handing Julia a heavy canvas bag.

Together, they left the cabin and walked to the center of the village where an old Volvo 122 from the 1960s was parked. It sat behind a line of logs set in the sand next to a variety of other vehicles of various makes and condition. It was rough, but started right up, and soon they were on the road heading back to the village Julia had first visited and was glad she didn't have to stay at.

Julia had the canvas bag in her lap and peeked inside to see what was so heavy. "Wow," she said, "what a beautiful carving!"

"Grandfather always creates a gift for someone getting married or in this case, having a baby."

Seeing an Osprey with a fish in its talons, Julia remarked, "A baby? I hope it's a boy because this is one realistic looking bird!"

"He always knows," Arihi replied.

When they arrived at the village and parked, Arihi led them in the opposite direction from Denny's Digs and soon they came to a small hut built on poles standing at the water's edge. A group of islanders, mostly women, were standing outside and making low, nervous conversation. Seeing Arihi, they parted a path for her to the steps and their voices rose a notch.

The girl was all of nineteen years old and had a head of bright blonde hair. She was sitting in a chair sweating, and in discomfort. There was concern in the air. A young man who stood alone off to the side was visibly relieved when he saw Arihi enter the hut. He followed the others out the door after giving his wife's hand a squeeze and her forehead a kiss.

"Hello, Suri. Are you ready to meet your son?" Arihi

asked as she stroked the young girl's sweaty forehead.

All the girl could muster was a tight-lipped attempt at a smile and a nod of her head.

Arihi took Julia aside and said to her quietly, "The little one is in the breech position. Suri will need all the help we can give to bring him safely into this world."

Julia whispered, "I've heard the term, but what does it mean?"

"It means that instead of arriving headfirst, he is feetfirst. It is a much more difficult delivery," Julia whispered back.

"What do you want me to do? I've never even seen a birth."

"I want you to sit with Suri. Rub her head. Talk to her. Help her with the pain."

At that moment a strong contraction caused the native girl to arch her back and cry out. Julia looked bewildered at Arihi, who nodded towards Suri in a gesture to go to her. Then she opened her travel bag and took out something that had been made by tightly twisting very fine jungle vines into a small stick-like bundle, which was tied off with thread at each end. Handing it to Julia she said, "Here, give Suri this to bite on, the juice of the vines will help her with the pain."

Another contraction came quickly and when it was over Arihi spread a sheet on the floor and asked Julia to help her move Suri into a hands and knees position on the ground. Once there, she placed a small pillow in front of the girl's head. Another contraction. Another cry of discomfort. Julia was bewildered and concerned. "Why do you have her like this?"

"The little one must present his butt to the canal on his own. Fortunately, that is the case. I didn't want to see his feet. Now we can wait and allow for natural dilation to occur. It is important to be patient and let Mother and Suri prepare the path for the little one, but it won't be long."

Another intense contraction caused Suri to bite down on the root bundle, but her anguish was still heard through clenched jaws. Julia knelt next to her and instinctively put her arm around the young girl, who looked up and leaned slightly into her.

"A couple more and I will ask you to push, Suri, but not yet. Almost there, honey."

Ten minutes, and three more intense contractions later, Arihi told her patient, "Now, Suri! Push now! Bring him home!"

The young girl bit down on the root and finally was able to give the urge all the strength she had. Arihi carefully guided the buttocks and then, finally, the head of the little one through the birth canal and into the world. When the first cry was heard, a subdued cheer spontaneously arose outside, and Suri slumped her head to the pillow as Julia held her and rubbed her shoulders. "Good job, Suri! Way to go. You did it! He's beautiful!" Julia said triumphantly.

Exhausted, she turned over to rest her back against the chair she had been on and smiled at Julia and said, "Thank ya, Miss Julia. Thank ya."

Arihi dried and wrapped the baby, gently handed him to Suri, and said, "Well done, little sister, meet your baby boy." Then she said to Julia, "Go to the door and tell them he is perfectly fine and ask Jimmy to come in and meet his son."

"Me? I don't know these people."

"You do now, Julia."

# CHAPTER THIRTY-EIGHT

The drive back to Grandfather's village was a happy one. Julia was in awe of what she had just experienced, and the two girls chatted like old friends. Soon the village was in sight and as they walked from the car to Grandfather's hut Julia said, "Tom said he's getting a tattoo done, so I think I'll check in at Seth's and see how it's coming along."

Arihi gave Julia a hug and said, "Thanks for your help, it really made a difference. You're one of Suri's family now. That's just the way it is. I'll see you tomorrow. It's a big day for me and Bobby and I'm glad you'll be there!"

As Julia walked towards Seth Luwi's hut she felt strangely satisfied, and at peace. It occurred to her that for the first time in her life she felt like she had friends. Not just business acquaintances, but actual friends. Susie and Bryan were like the aunt and uncle she never knew. Samantha and Adam were like high school best friends she never had, being the loner that she had been. And Arihi was becoming like a sister. Then there was

Tom. How did she feel about him? She thought maybe he's the big brother I never had growing up, someone I could have confided everything in. How great would that have been! Then she thought, "No, that's not it. It's something different, although that would have been grand."

Her thoughts were interrupted as she found herself in front of the beautiful yellow door of Seth's hut. She climbed the stairs and knocked gently, then opened the door in case Seth was concentrating on his work, which he was.

He noticed her out of the corner of his eye and said, "Does Suri have her son?"

"Yes, she does Seth, and he's beautiful. What an experience. How brave was that girl!"

"I don't know what they would do without Arihi. Suri has her son, and Tom almost has his art. I'll be done in ten minutes. Want to have a look?"

"Sure, but that was fast. I thought you said it would take four or five hours," Julia remarked.

"It has, Miss Julia. You must have wandered off," Seth said.

"Wandered off, what do you mean by that?"

Tom, hearing the conversation, answered for Seth. "I think Seth means wandered off from your thoughts. Time has a way of flying by when you're not focused on thinking."

"Right, mate, that's it exactly. Drawing lines does the same for me. What do you think, Miss Julia, like it?"

Julia walked up to where Tom was leaning forward into a cushioned support which gave Seth the perfect angle to work on his neck and shoulders. She looked down and said, "It's beautiful, Seth! Tom, you'll have something special with you for the rest of your life! I can definitely tell it's Grandfather's friend."

"That's what I wanted. I'm glad you like it!"

Seth said, "All that's left is a little cleaning up. You guys need to be on your way, or you'll miss dinner, and with Tony's cooking that would be a crime!"

In short order they were again on the trail walking the mile back to the surf camp. Tom was told to keep his shirt off just to be sure it wouldn't get stained and to let his skin breathe. Julia noticed how the figures rippled as she followed Tom down the path single file. She fought the desire to reach out and run her hand across Kahiko Aukai's broad and colorful shell. Then they could smell the garlic and spices wafting in a gentle dusk breeze, and realized they were famished.

As they came into view of the cooking hut, Bryan looked up and smiled and said, "There they are, finally! Let's have a go at it!"

Adam said, "Hey, mate, we were getting worried, about to send out the posse, we were!"

Tom showed his friends the art of Seth Luwi, and they marveled at how realistic it looked. Julia held them captive with her description of the birth but didn't mention her meeting with Grandfather. Satisfied with their meal, the group decided to retire to the lounge to relax with a glass of wine or tea and enjoy each other's company before calling it a night. There was a bittersweet feeling in the air. Happiness for the wedding of Bobby and Arihi, tinged with sadness that their time together would soon come to an end.

Samantha said, "Let's do something fun tomorrow. I know you don't know how to surf, Julia, but that doesn't mean we can't get in the waves! They have body boards, and anyone can do that. What do you say, guys?"

"Sounds brilliant to me, babe. We've got most of the day to kill before the ceremony, and Bobby sure isn't going to ferry us around. I can drive a boat though, no problem. If that's ok with you, Bryan."

"Sure, Adam, we'll be heapin' busy getting the place ready. There's a great spot up island where the waves break just off the beach. You can't miss it."

"What do you say, Julia? Sounds like a plan to me," Tom said.

"That would be great, but there's something I was planning to do tomorrow. I need to touch base with work. Let me see if I can do it now. I think the time difference is still good," Julia said as she pushed herself up from the couch where she was sitting next to Tom.

"Well, then, it's settled," Samantha said. "I'm going to go sit on my porch and watch the stars come out. You coming with me, Adam?"

"Bloody right I am!"

"Alright, good night, everyone. See you tomorrow," Sam said as they both left.

Julia looked down at Tom and said, "I may be a while. Don't wait for me if you want to get back to your cabin."

"Actually, I feel like playing my guitar for a bit. It always helps me relax, and besides, there's something I want to ask you. Take your time."

"Alright, I'll try not to be too long."

Julia, walked out of the lounge and over to the office where a small LED candle lamp provided just enough light to see. She pushed open the door and sat down at the desk where she had left her laptop. It didn't take long to boot up and soon she was looking at what she knew

would be there, emails from Lucarana Mining. The first
was from Alex and after reading it she just hit the delete
button without replying. Next, there was information
from the legal department with attachments containing
copies of the lease documents and instructions on what
to expect and how she should handle various aspects of
the closing, which was now just three days away. After
that, she reviewed a message from the Explorations
Division requesting a detailed report of any aspects of the
terrain, the wildlife, and the people of the area, that
might be useful to them logistically.

Finally, there was the email from Peter Allaire that
she knew she would find in her inbox, and which she
knew would have the most substance. She gave it her full
attention.

*Dear Julia,*

*I hope these last couple of days have found you in good
health and anxious to get to work! As you know Legal has you
scheduled to represent the company in three days, and I know
that you have received instructions from them in a recent
email.*

*What you don't know, is that we have arranged for a
television crew to film the event and interview you after the
proceedings have concluded. You are making history, and we
want the shareholders of Lucarana Mining to be able to
celebrate with us. It will be taped, and we are hoping to air it
nationally, over the coming weekend.*

*So far, we couldn't have asked for a more cooperative
government than what we have discovered in Honiara, and
they have assured us that we may begin operations as soon as
our project report is available for their review. Fortunately,
their environmental concerns are minimal, although they do
require that our labor force be at least 75 percent native. At*

*the current average wage in the Solomons, we are hardly going to bring workers from Toronto down there anyway!*

*Make sure you look your best for the cameras, which for you, shouldn't be too hard to do! If you feel you must come back to Canada to wrap things up, don't delay because we anticipate beginning preliminary operations within sixty days, and we'll need you there twenty-four/seven. Who knows? Maybe you'll never want to leave!*

*Please advise if anything is required. Otherwise, have fun with the cameras! The courier has been given a satellite phone which will be yours to keep. Please call me after the TV shoot! @ 416-766-4664*

*Sincerely*

*Peter Allaire, CEO, Lucarana Mining*

Julia sat for several minutes, reading, and rereading the emails. She acknowledged her instructions from the legal department in a short note of affirmation, then returned to Peter's letter. Cameras? TV interview? "Holy crap," she thought to herself. "They're going full-on rock star on this one!" Then she remembered that one of the reasons Peter Allaire had remained at the helm of the company was his uncanny ability to keep its stock price up. The dog and pony show he cooked up was right out of his playbook. She just wished she wasn't the pony on this one. Tentatively, she began to write her response to the CEO of her company.

*Dear Peter,*

*Thank you for the trust you have shown in me! It is my intention to reward that trust in every way possible. I will...*

She was stuck, not knowing what to say or how to say it. She put her head into both palms, rubbing her eyes and trying to focus. Then she continued writing.

*I will do my utmost to represent Lucarana Mining in a manner commensurate with the responsibilities you have entrusted me with, and my father would have been proud of!*

*I see no reason to return to Toronto at this time if the company can move the contents of my small apartment to one of your storage facilities and notify my landlord of the new developments.*

*A new chapter in the history of our company will commence in three days, and a new beginning in my life as well.*

*I am honored to be representing the company, and I will do my best!*

*Very Truly Yours,*
*Julia Witherspoon*


She reviewed what she had written, started to make changes, and then called it good. "Brief and to the point," she said out loud and hit the send button. She closed her laptop and sat in the dark as a kaleidoscope of images flashed through her mind. Images of diamonds being dug from the earth, and images of a little baby boy coming into the world, all mixed together. She pushed back from the desk and got up to go back to the lounge, curious what Tom wanted to ask her.

Tom was sitting on a small, upholstered bench, opposite one of the couches in the room, his guitar across his knee, still shirtless. He looked up at Julia as she walked in and sat down on the couch. There was a moment of awkward silence. Then Julia said, "Play me something you like, Tom, one of your favorites."

"Have you ever heard of Tommy Emanuel?"

"No, who is he?"

"He's a guitarist I like to listen to from Australia. An amazing musician and seems like a great person. I've been trying to work out how he plays one of my all-time favorites."

"What is it?" Julia asked.

"You'll know.'

Tom began to gently fingerpick an intricate version of a sweet melody which was familiar to almost everyone. He only used his voice to highlight the melody, not to sing the song, letting the chords and runs carry the tune, but sang the song Dorothy sang in the Wizard of Oz, "Somewhere,.... then continued fingerpicking. Then he sang, " is where.... you'll..."

It was a lovely version of a lovely song, and Julia's eyes were moist when he finished.

"That was beautiful, Tom. I love that song!"

"Me too, ever since I was a kid," he said putting his guitar back in the case.

"You said there was something you wanted to ask me?" Julia said softly.

"Yeah, and I've been thinking how to ask it."

"Go for it."

"Well, I was just curious if you have someone back in Canada waiting for you to get back. I mean I know someone as nice and as pretty as you must, but I just wanted to know for sure," Tom said as he latched his guitar case, and then turned to look at her.

"Why do you want to know? And the answer is no, just to answer your question."

Tom looked down at the floor, then gazed up at Julia and said, "We're leaving the day after tomorrow. I can't believe how fast it went. I was just thinking maybe we could find a way to visit each other when we get back. California is nice, and I've never been to Toronto. I'll miss you. I guess that's all I wanted to say.'

Julia didn't know how to react. The images of cameras were still fresh in her mind, and the words she wrote to Peter about her life having a new beginning flooded back to her. Instead of answering him directly she asked, "What about you, Tom? Is there anyone special in your life?"

"I guess that's what I'm trying to find out. I have the sense that things are going to change. That we are all in for a very different life than we thought we had coming."

Julia leaned forward and said, "What do mean? That sounds scary!"

"I've had the sense that a tidal wave of change is about to break for a long time. This trip, meeting Grandfather, the Vine of Soul...it's all connected somehow. I just don't see the whole puzzle yet. I think it would be a great gift to have someone in your life you can count on, and lean on if necessary, and somehow, I don't think we met by chance." He said this looking intensely into Julia's eyes.

Julia flushed, and turned away from his gaze and said, "I have a lot of responsibilities with my new promotion, Tom. It's going to demand all of my time."

"Oh, I see. Well, forget I asked the question. I hope I didn't make you uncomfortable."

"Don't say it like that! I will miss you too!" Julia slid off the couch and onto her knees in front of where Tom was sitting. She reached up, put her arms around his neck, and gently pulled him towards her for a warm hug and then a gentle kiss on the lips. "There, does that answer your question?"

Tom took both of his hands and put them on either side of Julia's face, holding her cheeks. He returned the kiss in the gentlest of ways and said, "I guess it does."

# CHAPTER THIRTY-NINE

The next morning Tom woke early and sat by himself on the edge of the steps leading up from the lagoon. Adam had stayed at Samantha's hut so there wasn't the usual rustling in the cabin of someone getting up. The sun was beginning to brighten the horizon, but still had a half-hour climb to get above it. The birds in the jungle were just beginning to stir.

He closed his eyes. His breathing slowed as he inhaled and exhaled each breath fully, holding at the top and bottom for five seconds, before continuing the cycle. Instead of drifting into the familiar state of meditation and no thought which this practice usually produced, this time something different was happening.

His inner sight became flooded with a cacophony of images that were disjointed and wildly unfamiliar. His heartrate began to rise, and his breathing was no longer the gentle cycle of control he had established just seconds before. It was like getting on an inner rollercoaster. Once started, there was no way to get off until the ride was over. Parts of it were thrilling and some were terrifying.

Visions of a changing world flashed through his mind. A world that was full of flames and chaos. Fear and destruction. Everywhere, people were running. They were scared for their lives. Buildings were on fire. People jumped from windows. Cars and trucks stopped in the middle of streets. There were endless lines of abandoned vehicles. Planes crashed into the middle of cities. Ships drifted aimlessly with the current, floating steel islands of survival of the fittest.

Then there was an image of Samantha. She was looking into something. A large microscope. She looked up at him. But she didn't see him. She continued her work.

Adam was there. With another man, someone he could not see. They were hunched over a flat table. Studying maps. Surrounded by charts. They never looked up. Something seemed familiar about the other fellow, but then they were gone.

He was now in a dark, humid place. It had an earthy, organic smell that penetrated his being. Strange bags hung from the walls. A dim light reflected off them. Exotic shapes clung to the bags. Rows upon rows of them.

Then he saw a group of people. It was night. A campfire blazed. There were six. They stood in a semi-circle at the edge of a great river. Something was thrown into the river. A figure stood alone by the water's edge. Arms held high. The campfire crackled with sparks. The figure turned to face him. The fire danced in Grandfather's golden eyes. Another figure stood just beyond the light of the fire. It - was it a she? - seemed to be waiting for something. Lastly, he saw himself. He didn't know where he was, but he knew it was somewhere on this very island.

Tom gradually drifted up into waking consciousness, his heart still racing. He felt bewildered. He knew he had just experienced the most profound vision he had ever known, but it was like dumping five hundred pieces of a jigsaw puzzle on a table for the first time. Some pieces stuck together, and some were upside down. The straight lines and corners provided clues, but the whole thing was a confusing mess until he could begin to piece it together.

Then he heard Adam call from Samantha's hut. He waved acknowledgement and went into the cabin to splash some water on his face. His back felt a little itchy where his new friends were getting settled in, so he threw on a tee shirt and jammed his feet into flipflops and began the fifty-yard wade to shore. He realized he was starving. He looked up to see Julia was waiting for him on the edge of the sand. Without a word, he took her hand and together they strolled over to the cooking hut. The folks there did not fail to notice the outward sign of affection the simple act announced, but no one made a comment.

Instead, Susie said, "We knew this day was coming, but just not so soon! Bryan and I couldn't be more pleased to have you three, uh, you four," she said, looking at Julia, "here to share the wedding of our daughter."

Bryan added, "Yeah, that's deadest, Suze! It'll be bangin' later, but right now we're just happy to have our family extend to you all. Speaking of the wedding, we'd better get to it, Suze. A lot to get done we have!"

"Can we stay and help?" Samantha asked.

"Heavens no! This is what we do. You guys go and

have fun. We have plenty of help coming from the village," Susie said.

"You know where the boat and boards are, and Edu Break is just down there," Bryan said pointing north up the island. "The boat almost drives itself. Just keep an eye out for the dugongs and have fun!"

The four walked down to the boatshed and Adam hopped on the boat and began to study the Yamaha outboard's controls. He had watched Bobby, but just wanted to be familiar with the boat himself. Tom and the girls stowed the bottles of water and snacks they had brought and were picking out body boards and skimmers for some fun on the beach. They put the small boards in the rack, untied the lines and were off. The quiet engine pushed the boat smoothly, with barely a wake, as Adam took the time to sightsee on the way. Tom and Julia sat together in the bow, while Samantha stood next to Adam at the helm.

She turned to Adam and whispered in his ear, "I'm so happy Tom seems to have finally found someone. She's great with him."

Adam glanced at Sam and said, "I hope so, babe."

Samantha gave him a quizzical look, and asked, "What do you mean by that?"

"I just sense that there's more to Julia than we know. It all happened in a blink, but it would be brilliant if it does work out. That's all to it."

"It happened pretty quick with us too, Adam, once you got your head out of the sand!" Samantha teased.

"I can be a dull bastard at times, I admit. But I make up for it in the long run!"

"Look, there's the beach!" Samantha pointed to a

beautiful crescent of white sand as they rounded a point covered in mangrove.

Adam drove the boat towards the sandy shoreline, lifted the motor up and let it glide in gently. Tom grabbed the bow line, hopped over the side, and pulled the aluminum hull a few feet onto the sand, tying it to a coconut palm that had fallen over.

"Can you believe this place?" Julia exclaimed as she handed the boards down to Adam and Tom. "It's like paradise, and we're the only ones here. Amazing!"

"Yeah, that's what we all said down at Charles Right. Perfect waves and no one there but us. It was heavenly!" Samantha answered. "Do you know how to use a skimmer board?"

"I've seen kids do it, but not really."

Samantha and Julia practiced until they were both off gliding across the shallow beach like two school kids in the summer, having fun and enjoying each other's company. Taking a break, they laid beach towels under a coconut palm that grew towards the beach at an impossible angle and sat down. Samantha asked, "Is something bothering Tom? He seems out of sorts today."

"I was just about to ask you the same thing. We had a really nice time after you guys left. He played his guitar and we got to know each other better. But this morning he's hardly said a word. I don't think it's anything I did, but who knows?"

Samantha took a moment before replying, "I've known Tom a long time, and he's my best friend, with the exception now of Adam, but that's different. He's... oh, how can I say it, he is someone that's solid as stone, and doesn't play games of any kind. With him, it's not about ego or control, it's about connecting with him on a deeper level. It can be difficult, but if you're willing to do that, I think the rewards will be profound. In some ways I envy you."

"That seems strange to say, considering how close you and Adam seem," Julia said quietly.

Samantha continued, "I don't mean it the way you think. I mean that I envy you becoming the one he shares with because it used to be me. He's like the brother I never had. If something is bothering him, he will let you know, but it could also be one of his visions, or something completely unrelated to your relationship. It's just the way he is. He's also brutally honest, so you'll know after he processes it."

Julia recalled something Tom had said. "He did say something last night. He wanted to know if I had a boyfriend back in Toronto, and I said no. But then he said he sensed something was coming. How did he say it? A tidal wave of change, that was it, and he said having someone to count on will be important. He wanted to know if it could be me. He said there were no coincidences, or something like that."

"Yes, that sounds like Tom. And he has mentioned that before. Something coming, but not sure what." Samantha paused, then reached out and squeezed Julia's hand. "With Tom, it's either all or nothing."

"What do you mean by that?"

"I mean, there's no superficial bullshit. He demands you be real, and if you're not, he'll know. I think at some point, anyone would have to make a choice, but you're the first woman I've ever seen in that position."

At that moment, Adam and Tom arrived where the girls had set up with the canvas totes from the boat containing bottles of water and snacks. Tom turned to jam his boogie board in the sand and the art of Seth Luwi shone in the sun as his muscles rippled the seabird's wings. They all shared the food quietly, just taking in the magnificent scene they were a small part of.

Then, true to form, Tom spoke, "I guess I've been a little to myself this morning. I hope you guys aren't annoyed."

Julia spoke first, "I was afraid I said something that put you off, Thomas,...err, I mean, Tom."

Tom reached to his right and squeezed Julia's hand. "No, nothing like that. I'm sorry to make you feel that way."

"What happened, Tom?" Samantha asked.

"Well, as you know, I try and meditate in the morning when I can. This morning it was a doozy, but not in a good way," Tom replied solemnly.

"A vision? What happened?" Samantha leaned forward, concern in her voice.

"That's what I've been wrestling with. You were there, Sam, working at your electron microscope. You were doing something intense, very absorbed, and hardly looked up."

"That's me at the scope, for sure," she agreed.

"And Adam and I were doing something together, and other people were there who I don't know, and in a weird place. Then we were all there, at the edge of a great river, and we threw something in. Grandfather was with us. Then I saw the world on fire with destruction everywhere. It really upset me. I couldn't get it out of my head."

"Was I there, Tom?" Julia asked in a whisper.

"I think so. I think you were there, but in the shadows."

Adam had been listening closely to everything Tom said, his analytical mind working through possibilities of meaning. "Sam and I were talking about things the other day, and we both bloody well felt that something was meant to be. I mean look, here we are, and the first we hear is that Grandfather has been expecting us."

"Same thing he said to Bryan and Susie!"

"Right, babe. And what is it that really gets him hoppin'? It's all the crap we leave everywhere that kills everything, including his old friend Kahiko Aukai, right, Tom?" he said, pointing to Tom's back.

"For sure, Adam. And he also said something when we first met at dinner...what was it? For those who are chosen, that was it. Like we're all on a mission, but we just don't know we've been recruited yet."

Samantha spoke up, "And Gaia showed me the whole process of photosynthesis and then told me to seek answers in the smallest of things!"

"Right, babe, and what are the smallest things?"

"Microbes, that's what. The smallest living things are microbes," she answered.

"We use microbes to clean up oil spills at Lucarana!" Julia said excitedly.

"I didn't know you mined in the ocean," Samantha said.

"We don't, but we're based in Canada, and you can't knock over a drum of diesel and not file a report, and that happens all the time. Clean up always uses a mixture of microbes mixed in sand."

"Maybe that's what I saw when they, uh we, were standing by the edge of a river. Something was thrown in, but I couldn't see what."

"All I bloody know is that something needs to be

done. I've lugged enough of that crap off the beach to last a lifetime, but there's always more," Adam vented.

"Isn't plastic made from oil?" Julia asked.

"It bloody well is!"

"The microbes eat the oil. Why can't they eat plastic too?"

Samantha said excitedly, "That's just what Adam and I were talking about yesterday! If I could modify a microbe, let's say a bacterium, that already has the capacity to metabolize oil, into one that can consume plastic..."

Julia finished her thought, "Then maybe it could be used to clean up plastic like we do for oil spills!"

"Exactly!" Samantha exclaimed.

Tom said, "Maybe the vision wasn't so bad, but there was a lot going on. Speaking of which, we'd better be getting back 'cause I'll bet there's a lot going on back at the camp!"

# CHAPTER FORTY

They arrived back at the main lodge to a scene of much greater activity than when they left. Everyone associated with the camp was there and a large number of villagers as well. The two main lodges were adorned with hundreds of flowers, and the fragrance was as if fine perfume had been splashed around with abandon. Out in the cooking hut, a veritable feast was in the making, with fish and crabs roasting over the coals and a suckling pig slowly turning on a spit. Fruits and vegetables were stacked in large woven serving baskets and many of the native villagers had brought sweet and savory dishes which they were known for.

In a way, it was a formal uniting of what had been a very amicable relationship between the surf camp and the village for years. One of the village's favorite girls who had been adopted by the owners of the camp was marrying their righthand man, and this drew the two peoples together even closer. The expression "love is in the air" couldn't have been more real that afternoon.

Tom saw Seth off in a corner with his ukulele and joined him with his Martin. It turns out that Seth was nearly as accomplished a musician as he was an artist, and the two explored what tunes they both knew. Julia wandered with Samantha and Adam meeting new people and just enjoying the festivity.

"What a change from this morning! It's hard to believe they got all this done while we were at the beach!" she said.

Adam agreed, "I guess Susie knew what she was saying about having all the help she needed. This place looks brilliant!"

At last, the moment came when everyone was called over to the main lodge and a hush settled in amongst the guests. Grandfather was dressed all in white, from a white headband tied around his forehead, a billowed shirt, and white dress slacks. He almost gleamed in the afternoon sun. He stood in front of a small table that held flowers. A bowl of herbs had been lit and gave off a scent similar to nutmeg. The guests all stood back in the room, and some were even out on the wrap-around porch looking in through the windows. It was standing room only.

Tom and Seth walked up to the left and behind Grandfather and Tom began to fingerpick the chords to a song which Seth complimented with tasty leads on his ukulele. After going through the chord progression once, Tom began to sing, and Seth immediately followed in harmony. Together they performed an emotional version of a very popular song often sung at occasions like this as if they had played together for years. It was The Wedding

Song, by Paul Stookey. When the last line, "There is love" faded, Grandfather began to speak.

"I am an old man now, and I have seen many things. It is a privilege for me to call so many of you my children, and an honor to be called Grandfather by you. In the great cycle of life, one must be prepared for many changes. However, one thing that will never change is the purity of love between a man and a woman when it is founded and held in spirit. When love is spiritual love, it rises above all others. It is accessing the very force that creation itself was wrought from, and which holds it together even now. It has been said that love conquers all. I would say that love creates all. It creates all the goodness we see in nature. It creates the bonds which bring out the highest and most noble aspects of our human selves. And ultimately, it allows us to use it as a source of energy that can bring us all the way home to our creator."

"My two dear friends and children, Robert and Arihi, have been sharing this love for some time, and I am delighted that they now wish to bind their lives together, although it is ninety-one days before we all thought! However, their decision to marry in the presence of our newest family friends is a wise and loving choice."

He paused, then said, "So let them now come forward."

Arihi walked up to the table escorted by Bryan, who left her in front of Grandfather, and returned to Susie's side. Bobby was accompanied by Seth, who acted as his best man. He too, stopped just behind Bobby, so that Arihi and Bobby stood together, in front of Grandfather.

"Is it true, Arihi, that you choose to walk through life in Spirit with this man Robert Berry?

"Yes, Grandfather, it is true."

"And will you always strive to help him express the highest and most noble aspect of himself that he can be, in sickness and in health?"

"I will, Grandfather."

"And you, Robert, is it true that you choose to walk through life in Spirit with this woman Arihi Mathews?"

"Deadset I do. Uh, yes, Grandfather, it is true."

"And will you always strive to help her express the highest and most noble aspect of herself that she can be, in sickness and in health?"

"I will, Grandfather."

"Robert, this ring is your pledge of eternal love to this woman, Arihi. Please put it on her finger."

Bobby did as he was instructed.

"Arihi, this ring is *your* pledge of eternal love for this man, Robert. Please put it on his finger."

Arihi did as she was instructed.

"Now, please hold your two hands together in front of me."

They both clasped their hands together and held them out to Grandfather, who took a piece of soft twine and wrapped it around their two wrists, binding them together.

"It is with utmost love and affection that I use the authority given to me by Spirit and law to declare you Arihi, wife of Robert, and you Robert, husband of Arihi. May you both live long loving lives together, knowing your two energies have merged as one."

"I believe it is customary to kiss the bride, Bobby," Grandfather teased.

And Bobby did just that.

The room erupted in cheers and clapping with

hugging and pats on the back offered and received by everyone. The sound of a ukulele began furiously strumming the chords to a familiar song quickly followed by the bright, resonant sound, of the old Martin strumming to a rock rhythm as Tom and Seth broke into the famous Beatles tune "Eight Days a Week." The party was in full force and quickly spread over to the lounge and the food waiting there.

It was a wonderful evening of fun, laughter, and even some comical stories told by the master of ceremonies himself, Grandfather, who could tell the funniest tales about the simplest of things. But eventually, the guests thinned out, and lights were lowered, leaving only Grandfather and his family, minus Bobby and Arihi, who had retired to spend their first night together as husband and wife. Mixed emotions hung in the air, as everyone knew, that with the new members leaving the next day, a magical time at the surf camp would be closing. Bryan was the first to break the silence.

"Well, mates, I know the old saying goes, 'All things come to an end,' but that's not the case the way I look at it. All things change, and in the changing, new opportunities come forward. That's one of the many things we've learned from Grandfather, right, Suse?"

"Yeah Bry, that's deadset as Bobby would say! We sure will miss you three, though. It seems impossible that you've only been here a week. Feels more like we've known you all our lives. And thank goodness you didn't go back to Denny's Digs, Julia. That would have been dreadful!"

"You can say that again!" Julia agreed.

Grandfather, who had been sitting quietly, got up and walked over to a corner of the lodge where he had placed his woven pack basket earlier and returned with it and sat back down with the group. He began working on the cords that held the top secure. When he finished untying it, he opened the cloth cover, and he reached in and took out three bundles. They were delicately crafted of the finest of fibers such as silk but were surely some jungle plant known only to him. Each bundle was about the size of a large cantaloupe and was pliable in Grandfather's hands.

"The Ramo have created a special gift for the three of you, one that even I have not known about until yesterday. They have ways of 'seeing' possibilities for the future, and I have learned some of these ways, but not to the degree of Luti Mikode. He is a master in every sense of the word. He knows the journey that you will now embark on may have many challenges and perhaps even danger." Grandfather handed each of his three new family members a bundle, one at a time with an air of ceremony, touching each bundle to his forehead before extending arms straight out to each of them.

"The gift you hold in your hands is a unique combination of plants and herbs mixed with a special preparation of the Vine of Soul. You will like this part, Adam. Your instructions are to prepare a beverage exactly as you would prepare a cup of tea and sip it as you would any hot drink. However, only take the tea when you are in good spirits, not fearful or anxious."

Tom asked the question that they were all thinking, "What will the effect of this tea have on us, Grandfather? Will it be like what we experienced with you?"

"No, it will not be as what each of you experienced in the ceremony. This tea will have a mild psychological effect, but a profound physical one. You will feel a bit

THE CLEANSE – MALA

perhaps like the after-effect of the ceremony, like how you felt when you woke up the next day. Things may seem in a sharper focus. Smells and sounds may be more intensely sensed, but that's all. I am only relaying what Luti Mikode has told me. I have never known of this tea much less taken it."

"So, the mental effect is mild, but what about the physical effects, Grandfather?"

"Thomas, this tea will give you the same physical slowing of life as the half cup of the Vine of Soul does which we have used for years in the ceremony. The effects of the tea will be very subtle, but over time it will become obvious. For this reason, each of you must be sure to adopt a lifestyle in the years to come which enables you a certain invisibility in the world. If you cannot do this effectively and joyfully, you should stop taking the tea, and destroy what you have left. These are the words of Luti Mikode."

"Grandfather, this is a most profound gift indeed, but can you tell us how often and how much of the tea we need to take to maintain the slowing effect?" Tom asked.

"As far as the amount, Thomas, just imagine taking apart a bag of Earl Grey. As they say, a little bit goes a long way. And as far as how often goes, listen to your inner voice, and let that be your guide, but you have enough here for years, and if you return to this island, more will be waiting for you if you so desire."

Samantha had been silent but now spoke up, "Grandfather, I don't know if it is possible to receive a more profound gift, I can only hope that we can live up to the expectations which it implies, and I worry we might not.'

"My child, there are no expectations. There are no

demands, and there is no possibility to 'fail.' There is only life. When it is lived with intention, and with integrity, and with love, all things are possible. Remember the ancient swimmer. She who lived so long and has traveled so far never had to try to find her way, she just lived it. She lived the nature of her being. And so too will you three. Just live the nature of who each of you are, and let your paths unfold. All will be as it should. And as for them, so for you, my child," he said turning to Julia.

"Grandfather, may I ask you one thing?"

"Of course, Adam, anything. There are no secrets here."

"Well, about the tea...will drinking the tea prevent someone from dying like from an accident, for instance?"

"Adam, you are surely a warrior and a noble one at that, but I can assure you that if you fall off a cliff, you had better land in the water because the tea will not protect you in the least."

"Okay, brilliant! I just wanted to know, not that I'm thinking of doing crazy things. I'm just processing what this gift implies."

"As Bryan and Susie I'm sure can tell you, it does take some adjustment to the realization that the timeframe one has to achieve one's goals is much greater, but that does not diminish the importance of living life moment by moment, right here, right now."

"That is true, Grandfather," Susie affirmed. "It has been many years now that our cup of the vine has been slowing our speed through life, Adam, and I can say with certainty that the gift has allowed us a better appreciation of life and living, not something we take for granted. I could certainly see how it might be abused, but that's why the secret is safeguarded like it is. I, for one, know that you four dear friends will grow wiser and more loving as years go by and will touch all who come into your presence."

"Now, my children, I must leave. Whether or not we meet again in this life or this world, know that each of you are in my heart and thoughts, no matter where you go or what you do. I promise each of you that if you seek me, you will find me. And you, will find me in my hut, tomorrow, my daughter," he said looking at Julia, who nodded.

Grandfather stood up, completely at ease and relaxed, yet a solemn air hung in the room, a kind of formality that everyone sensed.

"Now, my children, come here and embrace me. Let us share the energy of love and let that love be a guiding light which shines a path between us."

One by one, Adam, Samantha, and finally Tom stood up and hugged Grandfather in an embrace of loving energy. Then he stood in front of them and smiled the biggest smile they had seen and said, "Ciao, look after yourselves!"

And with that, Grandfather turned and walked out the door.

The rest of the group just stood there, watching him leave. Bryan and Susie suggested if they wanted a beer or glass of wine to help themselves, but they decided to call it a day and headed for their hut. The four friends walked over to the lounge and Sam and Julia poured some wine and served the men, who were talking quietly. They made small talk until Samantha announced that she was ready to turn in, and she and Adam retired for their last night on the island.

Julia sat with Tom. There was an awkward silence

between them. Each was lost in thought, but sharply aware of the poignancy of the moment.

Finally, Tom broke the ice. "There was one last piece to the vision I had this morning that I didn't mention."

Julia was surprised and said, "What was that?"

"The last thing I remember was being back here. I don't know where I was exactly, but I know for certain it was on this island. Then it all faded out."

Julia's thoughts flashed through her mind. Possibilities opened and closed in rapid succession. Then she said, "I'm tired and I'm going to have a long day tomorrow. I think it's time to go to bed." She paused, then said, "But I don't want to be alone tonight, Tom. Not with you leaving in the morning. Will you come with me?"

# CHAPTER FORTY-ONE

The next morning was a sad one. Tony had breakfast ready just after sunrise and let the group know that they had forty-five minutes before they needed to meet at the jeep, which he had moved next to the office lodge. He would be driving the three friends to the airstrip for the flight to Honiara and said he wanted to allow plenty of time for ruts and the unexpected. Tom and Adam had both met at their Crusoe hut, and had their gear already packed and waiting outside. Samantha said she would be ready in a jiff and Adam walked her back to help with her bags.

The night had been intimate between Tom and Julia, but not consummated completely. Tom felt that they should leave something to look forward to, something that would draw them back together, if it was meant to be. In some ways it already had the effect of deepening what they were feeling.

Julia looked at Tom and said, "Turn around, Tom. Let me see your tattoo in the sunlight. I want to remember it." Tom did as he was asked and lifted his loose cotton shirt. Julia put one hand on each of his shoulders and rubbed the two seabirds, making their wings move as if they were flying. Then she brought them together at his neck where the ancient one swam.

"There. I will keep that image in my mind until I see you again. Now, can I ask for one more favor?"

"Of course. What is it?"

"Would you play me another song? I think we have time."

Tom unlatched his guitar case and gently pulled out his old friend. He strummed a couple of chords, trying to let the right song find itself. Then he began a song he hadn't played in a long time. It was an old standard. He fingerpicked it and hummed the melody as he played, then he sang, "See the pyramids", then he continued with just the notes and chords. He sang, just enough to highlight the melody and hummed as he continued instrumentally to the end.

Julia was captivated by a song she had heard but couldn't recognize, played in a manner that was sensuous and jazz-like. She reached out and put her hand on his arm which rested on his guitar and said, "That was so beautiful. What was it?

Tom replied, "Oh it's just an old tune I learned a long time ago, but I don't think I've played it in years," he said putting the guitar back in the case. "It's by Patsy Cline, it's called—"

Just then Tony walked abruptly into the lounge and said, "There you are! Let's go, mate, shake a leg. We've got to hit the road!"

"Ok, Tony, I'm coming."

Tom carried his guitar out to the Toyota and carefully

stowed it in the back. Adam and Samantha were already sitting in the truck. Bryan and Susie were waiting together for a last goodbye. Tom walked over to Susie who was teary. She gave him a warm hug and said, "We will miss you all so much! Please come back when you can!"

Bryan stuck out his hand and said gruffly as Tom took it, "Right then, off with you, mate. Don't want to miss the plane." Then he pulled Tom's hand toward him and gave him a one-arm hug around the shoulder, to which Tom responded in kind, and said, "I'll miss you both, but someday I'll be back. I promise."

Finally, he turned to Julia. Bryan and Susie stepped away to give them some privacy. He walked to her and took her in his arms saying, "I love you. I'll find you." He gave her a warm kiss, and then turned and hopped in the jeep. The three stood together as other three vanished down the trail in the old truck. The emptiness was profound, but things had to get done.

They walked up the stairs to the office and stood for a moment in the main room.

Susie said, "Well that was a week like we've never had here before. There was so much happiness and joy! I'm sad it's over."

Bryan added, "Yeah, Suze, that's deadest! I guess I'll ring up Libby and let her know they're off." And he turned and opened the door to the office.

Julia said, "I wouldn't have missed this week for the world! Thank you both again for allowing me to stay!"

Susie replied, "You're part of the family now, Julia, and are always welcome here no matter what! I've got to get this place organized. Believe it or not we've got a small group from New Zealand coming in a few days, so it's back to work!"

"Speaking of work, I've got to hop over to Honiara tomorrow for business, but I'll be right back. I think I'll drive back to Auki this afternoon after I visit with Grandfather. Should I leave my things where they are, or would you want me somewhere else?"

"You're fine where you are, no worries! Just drive safely. You can't help but end up in Auki if you take a right at the entrance."

"Is there anything you need there? Just give me a list!"

"No, but thanks for the thought. Tony will make another supply run in a day or two," Susie replied, and then she said quietly, "Julia, it's none of my business, but I couldn't help but notice that you and Tom seem to have a...connection happening. I just want to say I think he's one of the most, umm, let's say, interesting men I've met. In fact, it feels like we've known each other forever, and I am so happy for both of you!"

Julia looked off for a second, then said, "Yes there is definitely a spark there, and a bright one at that. I don't know if life will allow it to keep burning though. And I agree, I've never met anyone like him either. Thank you for saying that."

The two women embraced warmly, then Susie left for the lounge, while Julia walked six steps to check her messages in the other office.

She sat down at the makeshift desk and opened her laptop. She was surprised that there was only one message in her inbox, which wasn't from Alex whom she hoped was finally giving up. Nor from Peter. It was from The Explorations Department, and she opened it.

*Subject: Logistics*

*Dear Director Witherspoon,*

*As you are aware, Explorations has been tasked with fast-tracking the commencement of mining operations in Malaita. You are now the Operations Director of Mala Mining, our new subsidiary, and since you are already on site, are ideally positioned to expedite the discovery and acquisition of necessary elements we will need in terms of infrastructure.*

*Below, please find a list (in no particular order), of some of the requirements we will need filled in the coming weeks and months. Any contributions you might make towards that end will only speed our journey towards profitability. All departments stand ready to assist. Time to get to work, Julia!*

1. *Secure site for operations center on Honaria. Please see contact list below. Honaria Commercial R.E. LLC*
2. *Establish banking relations (personal and company) with ANZ Bank. Contact: David Walsh, CEO.*
3. *Investigate possible locations for shoreline infrastructure to be built on eastern side of Malaita.*
4. *Conduct job interviews with native islanders.*
5. *Identify possible terrain suitable for mine-worker housing.*
6. *Meet regularly with political affiliates we are now establishing.*

*For the time being, Miss Witherspoon, you are our sole representative and "boots on the ground," so you will indeed have your plate full. This is the beginning of a career that has been notable, but which is about to skyrocket! Please know that you have the complete and utter support of all departments of the company, and in particular, my office.*

*Congratulations on a job well done, and another about to be!*

*Very Truly Yours,*
*Jonathon Tuley*


Julia closed her laptop, unplugged it, and put it into her leather carrying case. She went to her hut and changed into clothes suitable for a hike in the jungle.

She packed her business attire as well.

She was beginning to feel the hunt again.

# CHAPTER FORTY-TWO

Julia turned her rental truck down the road towards Grandfather's village well ahead of the schedule they had agreed on just to be sure she'd have enough time to go wherever he wanted to take her, and still get to Auki before sunset. She was slightly annoyed with herself for agreeing to hike up a mountain with him, because there was so much on her plate now. But she realized that she couldn't have predicted how much things would change in so short a time. The haunting melody of the Patsy Cline song looped in her head over and over as she drove.

She turned down the rough road leading to the village and drove carefully around the potholes and up to the parking area. Locking the doors, she headed down the little trail that would eventually end at Grandfather's porch. Surprisingly, the door was left open, and she took it as an invitation to come in, which it was. Grandfather was not to be seen in the hut, so she wandered out to his banyan tree workshop, but still no sign of him.

Then she heard his voice say softly, "Here, my child," and she walked towards the lean-to he had made for the old sea turtle. He was sitting in the sand next to his old friend, and when he looked up, she could see a hint of sadness in his golden eyes.

"The ancient one has gone to her moeroa. Her long sleep. Her time here is over."

"I'm so sorry, Grandfather," Julia said solemnly.

"For what, my child? She lived a life of integrity, as the creature she was born to be till her last breath, never wishing for more."

"Yes, but it must be sad for you. I'm sure you'll miss her."

"I will not miss seeing her waiting in the sand for this day. More importantly, my child, is she believed that the curse of the white fish that never die is nearly over. In this, she found joy at the end."

"I'm not sure I know what you mean, Grandfather," Julia said quizzically.

"That's not important right now. Just remember what was spoken of here in the days ahead. It won't be long now."

"What won't?"

"A great cleanse, but never mind that now. We have a task to fulfill. Are you ready?" he asked.

"Yes, my truck is in the village." She answered.

"Here, take this. It is your burden now," Grandfather said handing Julia a small but heavy bundle lying in a basket, which she knew could be only one thing. "Let us begin our journey together."

The ride up to the trailhead was mostly silent, except for the haunting melody which refused to leave Julia's mind, but at one point she asked, "Thomas, I mean Tom, told me about a vision he had yesterday. It sounded horrible. He said it was about changes that may be coming. Is that what you were referring to back with the ancient one?"

"My son Thomas, and that is his name, as you also know, possesses many gifts. Who will receive them is not yet known. But they will be shared. There, see that boulder?" Grandfather pointed to the large stone just off in the jungle. "Pull into the clearing just there and drive carefully past it."

Julia drove in and turned the truck around as Grandfather had instructed, so it was ready to go when they returned.

"Now, my child, let us return a gift I never would have thought possible to return. It is your destiny. Come," he said, leading the way up the trail to Mt. Mala.

The jungle began to thin as they climbed higher. Grandfather made sure to stop just enough to give Julia time to recover and hydrate, then pressed on.

Julia had the yellow stone in her day pack slung over her shoulder, and it was, in fact, beginning to feel quite heavy. Then, as she looked up, she could see that the jungle was opening just beyond Grandfather, letting sunlight in for the first time in an hour.

"Grandfather, why is this area so open? Why isn't the jungle canopy overhead?"

"Look closely, my child." Grandfather picked up a fallen branch and dug into the floor of the clearing until the sound of stone could be heard. "This is the place where I first met MY grandfather, Luti Mikode. Same with your father. It was a place of celebration for a thousand years and is paved with stone."

"My father? He was attacked by large apes and never came back. That was what he wrote in his diary."

"That may be what he wrote after his first journey here, but when he came to live with me, he stopped writing in his book, and put it away. He and I came to this place, and others, many times. He was never attacked, just frightened."

"What actually frightened him?"

"They did!" Grandfather said, pointing up the plateau.

"What? I don't see anything," Julia said bewildered.

"You will, my child. Come, follow me and do as I do."

They continued walking towards what Julia had thought were dead tree trunks near the side of the rapidly rising mountain. When the tree trunks moved towards them, she felt panic rising in her being. Grandfather reached behind him and squeezed her hand and whispered, "They come in peace and love, my child. Fear not."

The two groups of beings met near a jumble of large carved stone vessels which Julia looked at with amazement. They stood opposite each other, then Grandfather raised his right arm and placed his hand on the left shoulder of the creature which held a large, magnificently carved staff. The creature returned the gesture of greeting, and Grandfather stepped to his left and motioned Julia to take his place. The great Ramo raised his arm, and in the most careful way possible, slowly lowered it onto Julia's shoulder, giving it a gentle squeeze, and smiling a Ramo smile, with a twinkle in his eye.

Julia trembled as she repeated the gesture, and couldn't help herself from saying, "Thank you."

To her amazement, the great creature spoke back, "It is we, the Ramo, who thank you, child of Ross. Welcome here, you are!"

Julia repeated the gesture with the other Ramo, then Grandfather who had stood off to the side said, "My grandfather, Luti Mikode, holds the staff. Lakka is his apprentice." Then he said, his voice full of drama and concern, "Daughter of Ross thinks you attacked her father all those years ago. Did you?"

Luti Mikode looked at Lakka with an expression of "who me"? Then let out a chuckle from deep in his belly. A rolling low-pitched rumble of amusement. Then he said, "If attack we did, dead he would be. Only to scare we wanted. Ran he did. We took a piece of mountain, threw it down there," he said pointing down the trail. "He did," he said, indicating Lakka was who tossed the giant boulder. Lakka looked at Julia and gave a slight shrug of his shoulders. Then the most amazing thing happened, something no one but Julia had ever witnessed. Grandfather, Luti, and Lakka began to laugh. And they laughed with an innocent joy like three youngsters playing a practical joke. Julia couldn't help but be caught up in it, and she giggled, at ease and relaxed.

Grandfather said, "You should have seen your father the first time we came back here. I almost had to drag him up the trail. Remember, Luti?"

The great Ramo had settled back to his usual stoic demeanor and said, "Tremble he did, when greeting we made. He dropped a thing. Jumped back when I reached to pick it up. Told me to keep it he did."

Luti Mikode glanced sideways to Lakka who removed a thong which held a pouch around his neck. He opened the pouch, took something out, and gave it to his master. Luti Mikode held his hand out to Julia and said, "Love your father Ross, I did. Want you to have this, he would." She held out her hand as the great Luti Mikode gently opened his and released a still-shiny brass object into her palm. It was a compass, and there was an inscription on the cover. She looked closer and read the words, "*MAY YOU ALWAYS FIND YOUR WAY HOME. DAD*"

"This was given to my father by his father when he went off exploring. I read that in his journal. I never thought I would hold it," she said quietly.

"Words to live by are those. Yours now, it is," Luti Mikode said, and he brushed his hand softly against the side of Julia's face.

Julia remembered she had something to return to the proper owner as well. She lifted the strap of her side-pack off her shoulder and reached in for the bundle it held. She could not resist the urge to see it one more time, so she carefully unwrapped the fibers. The beautiful canary yellow diamond gleamed like a beacon of sunlight shining from within.

She held it out to Luti Mikode and said, "This is the most beautiful stone I have ever seen. It belongs with you, Luti Mikode. Samantha Lewis was right."

The great Ramo leader replied, "With me, no. Stone of Third Eye is for all people. Even you, daughter of Ross. See it your father did, in the mountain. You come, show you we will. Guide you, that will," he said pointing to the compass.

"Now, go we must. Daughter of Ross, find your treasure within."

In less time than it takes for a leaf to fall, they were gone, and just as silently. Julia stood there next to

Grandfather for a moment in silence, then she said, "Those were the same words my father said to me in my journey with the Vine of Soul."

"There are no coincidences in matters of spirit, my child. You lead the way back."

# CHAPTER FORTY-THREE

Julia left Grandfather at the bottom of the trail, next to the big boulder. He did not want her to drive him back to the village, saying, "Our paths now go in different directions, my child. I have walked mine for many years, and I know it well. What path will you walk? Where will it take you? Go," he said pointing down the ragged road. "Find your true path, and if it brings you back here, I will be waiting for you." Without another word or gesture, he turned and began the two-hour walk back to his hut.

Julia sat in the old pickup truck for a minute. She glanced down at the compass which she had laid on the passenger seat and thought of her father. With a sigh, she started the engine and headed south.

The three-hour drive back to Auki was uneventful and a bit boring. It wasn't until the road began to swing to the west, that it was improved enough to make decent time. She checked in to the Auki Lodge, and after a short nap and a hot shower Julia checked her messages. There was only one new one from the company. It was from Alex.

*Alex Taylor,*
*Chief Financial Officer, Lucarana Mining*
*Dear Miss Witherspoon,*
*Please be advised that the courier from the company has been instructed to meet you at H.I.A.'s Gate Three tomorrow at 9:00 AM. Your reservations have been made for the Flight 122 from Gwaunaru'u Airport. Departure is 8:00 AM.*

*His name is Michael Williams, and he will drive you to a room reserved in your name at the Heritage Park Hotel. It is only three blocks from the Parliament Building where the closing will be held in the Land Jurisdiction Office in Room 2A, on the second floor. It will commence at 1:00 PM, as you already know.*

*Funds in the amount of $250,000 U.S. dollars have been wired to ANZ Bank. The account needs only your signature and a code to be accessed. These funds represent the initial bonus due you as per my instructions from Peter Allaire and the board.*

*For any other financial requirements, please contact me via the satellite phone during normal business hours. The direct number, you already have.*

*Regards,*
*Alex*

Julia reread the letter twice. The tone and content were all business. "I guess he got the message," she thought to herself.

The next morning, she drove the rental truck back to the airport and boarded Flight 122, twenty minutes before departure. She sat in her seat while the twin turboprops began to hum, thinking of everything that had happened since she last sat in the very same plane, only seven days earlier. She had come to this island seeking vindication for her father and validation for herself. She had found both. Strangely, though, she realized that she did not feel the triumph she would have expected. Why was that? Unconsciously, her hand went to the front pocket of her jeans where the small compass had replaced the switchblade. The melody of Tom's song and the lyric "old Algiers" continued to haunt the background of her thoughts.

The short flight to H.I.A. was over in a blink, and with her two carry-ons she walked through the doors of the shuttle gate and into the terminal building. A voice behind her said, "Miss Witherspoon, excuse me. My name is Michael Williams. I'm here to pick you up."

Julia turned around and met the courier, a handsome African American man in his late twenties, professionally dressed in a dark suit, and having a military bearing to his presence.

"I was told to expect you. Nice to meet you," Julia said extending her hand.

"Let me take your bags, ma'am. The car is just outside in temp parking. We should get moving."

Michael Williams held the door to the black Mercedes sedan for Julia, then deposited her two bags in the rear seat.

As he wheeled the car out of the terminal he said, "The Heritage is only fifteen minutes away, and is very nice. I stayed there last night. Is there anything you need that might require a stop before we get there?"

"Yes, thank you for asking!" Julia replied. "I didn't expect to be doing what I'll be doing today and brought nothing to wear except for the bush and casual dining. I checked out some shops online last night, and Pacific Clothing opens early and looks like they'll have what I need."

"I see. Let me get the directions," he said, pulling over and reaching for his phone.

Williams pulled in front of the large, obviously well-stocked store, judging by the window displays, and said, "Take all the time you need, Miss Witherspoon. Until I board my flight back to Toronto, I am at your disposal."

Julia reached for the doorlatch and said, "I shouldn't be too long, but I've got to look the part, right?"

Julia browsed the aisles which were surprisingly well represented by the latest in women's fashion, including business attire. A well-versed salesgirl with an eye for detail and style helped her pick out a double-breasted long-sleeve khaki blazer with a white top and white cotton pants. A matching khaki bag and light brown three-inch heels completed a look that was not too formal yet not too casual. Turning around in front of the full-length mirror she knew that her looks would draw attention, and she began to relish the idea of being in front of the cameras. She decided to wear the clothes out of the store to get used to their fit,

"Miss Witherspoon!" Michael Williams said. "I must say, what you picked out is stunning! You look more like a movie star than a mine boss!"

"Thank you, Michael. We'd better get to the hotel. I think I took a little longer than I intended."

It was now almost 10:30 in the morning. She checked into her room and put her bags on the low stand at the foot of the bed, hanging her blazer on the doorknob of the closet. She walked to the window and pulled the drapes back and looked across the beach out to the ocean beyond. Julia Witherspoon, despite any outward appearance, was in emotional turmoil. She now knew for certain that her father was not attacked by vicious giant apes, but rather, he chose to stay and learn from them and Grandfather. The more she thought about it, the more she realized that the father who returned to Canada embodied the wisdom and mannerisms of Grandfather, although she had no way of understanding that at six years old. It was something she heard often though as she was growing up. Friends, who had known her father from before he left, always remarked on how he had changed, how different he was, and most had drifted away.

"How would Dad have felt about what I'm going to do?" she wondered. "And what about Tom?" Last night she did something with a man that she had never done before, and never thought she would ever do with any man. She told him she loved him, and he confirmed he felt the same. She indulged the idea that Tom could come back to Mala and find something to do while she worked for the company, but that was a miserable fantasy, and she knew it.

"Oh well, time for a hot shower and a bite to eat. That'll get me ready to meet the cameras and seal the deal." In the shower, Tom's guitar melody floated through her mind, and the sparse lyrics he barely sang, "...watch the sunrise on a tropic isle" stuck in her head.

After she dried her hair and got back into her new outfit, she texted Michael that she would be in the café overlooking the pool. It was 11:15, and her phone lit up with a message from Michael saying, "Roger that."

Michael sat down at her table, placing a titanium

attaché case on the floor between his legs. He joined her for coffee but passed on the cranberry scone she was enjoying.

"Are you ready for your big debut, Miss Witherspoon?"

"I guess so, but I've never spoken to a large group of people, much less in front of cameras, so I'm a bit nervous. I imagine they'll just ask me about Lucarana. Who we are and the history of the company. Stuff like that. I should be able to handle it, and by the way, you can call me Julia."

"Whenever I speak before an assembly, I make sure to anticipate as much incoming as possible. It helps with confidence and calms the nerves.'

"What do you speak to groups about?" Julia asked, relieved to have something to take her mind off the countdown.

"I was recruited out of M.I.T. where I specialized in advanced biometric security design. I worked for...uh, the government for a few years, then opened my own shop. I only work for well-heeled clients, like your company, Miss Witherspoon. Speaking of which, we should get going. It's 11:35 now, and there are some things I need to discuss with you before the signing begins. It's just a short walk to the Parliament Building. Shall we?"

They left the beachside hotel and began walking the three blocks towards the center of the city. As they rounded a corner, the imposing Parliament Building came into view, now just a block away. But what they saw in the street in front of the building caused them both alarm.

"Michael, what's going on? Who are all those people

with signs? What are they all doing?" Julia asked, her voice rising in pitch.

"I'm not sure, ma'am. Just keep your head on a swivel and stay right behind me."

They approached the government building and to her amazement Julia soon realized that the crowd was there to protest her, or at least the actions the company she represented was about to take. There were more than one hundred people on the street and many were carrying signs. Most were chanting slogans, although she couldn't make out what they were saying. But she could read the signs. One said, "MALA FOR SOLWATA." Another read "SAVE OUR ISLAND," and the more profane ones began with "MINERS SUCK" and "CANADIANS GO THE HELL HOME," but they got worse, much worse. And worst of all, cameras were at the scene, and they started rolling when the two arrived. Security police were discreetly standing in the shadows, hoping for a peaceful arrival of the V.I.P. but certainly prepared for anything.

Julia Witherspoon and Michael Williams faced a gauntlet. One which there was no way to avoid. They began their march to the stone stairs, which would deliver them to the safety of the Parliament Building, but the crowd wanted its moment they had waited for and blocked their way. Michael Williams was himself an imposing figure, and the titanium briefcase latched to his wrist was a powerful deterrent when he swung it in front of him. He wasn't trying to hurt anyone, just sending a message. Julia was jostled, and then something revolting happened. She was spit on. Afraid and disgusted, she reached in her pocket for her switchblade, bringing it out concealed in her hand.

At that moment, the crowd parted enough for a local

celebrity to approach the pair. She was an attractive woman, about forty years of age. She held a microphone in her hand and a cameraman trailed behind her. She stuck the microphone out and said, "Excuse me. Excuse me, Miss Witherspoon. May I get a comment? How do you feel about all this?"

Julia turned to Michael and spoke in a hushed voice, "Michael, how did they know I would be here? What should I do?"

"Someone must have leaked the meeting. Not everyone appreciates mining. I think you should smile at the camera, answer a question, and then say you don't want to be late. I'll be right behind you."

Julia turned back to the reporter as the crowd instinctively quieted to hear what she would say. She stalled to collect her thoughts by saying, "What did you ask me? I couldn't hear you."

The ambitious and aggressive reporter said, "My name is Robin Clarke and I'm with TTV. How can you justify your company raping the beautiful island of Mala, Miss Witherspoon?"

Julia was taken aback by the question, but recovered and said, "I hardly call a tiny, modern mining operation in a corner of such an immense parcel of land 'raping' the island. My company has every intention of preserving the rest of the lease for the enjoyment of all native islanders."

Not to be deterred, the reporter fired back, "Is that why the rest of the parcel has been sublet to the most vicious logging operators in all of Oceania?"

"I don't know anything about that, Miss Clarke. I'm sure it's just the rumor mill at work. Now, if you'll excuse me, I have a meeting to attend."

Thankfully, and with the constables having moved in

closer, the crowd allowed them access to the steps. When the doors closed behind them, Julia released a deep breath she had been holding, and tried to regain her composure.

"I sure as hell hope that Lucarana didn't do what that reporter implied," she said, although she vaguely remembered something about that as she skimmed emails from the company.

"We have a room just down the hall from Two-A where the closing will take place. I told you earlier there were some things I needed to discuss with you before the meeting gets underway."

They got off on the second floor and Williams held the door to the small conference room they had reserved. They both sat down at a round table in front of a window that had a view to the sea. Michael Williams held one side of the titanium attaché case up to his eye, and the handcuff keeping it attached to his wrist automatically opened. He did the same thing to the small round lens on the other side and they both heard a click as the locking mechanism was released. He set the case down in front of him.

"I will be waiting right here for you when you are finished signing all the documents," he began. "This is the satellite phone the company has given you. It has been pre-programmed with all the numbers you might need to reach anyone in the company. The operating instructions are in the box. I am familiar with this phone, and it's easy to use."

"That will be a big help!" Julia replied.

"Next, here is the passcode to give to David Walsh, CEO of ANZ Bank. As you can see, he will take a shot of it with his camera, and by the time he does, I will have verified the closing to your company, and they will authorize him to give you access to your account via the code."

"OK, I got it," Julia acknowledged.

Then Williams pulled a large file folder out of the case, which he then closed and moved to the side. "This file contains the original closing documents that will return with me after they are signed off on." He opened the file folder, which was upside down to Julia. The cover was glossy, with some kind of picture on it.

"This is the formal lease agreement for one hundred years on the tract, for the price which you know is fifty million dollars. Most of the rest is boiler plate stuff, which you have already been sent in attachments from your legal department," he explained.

Julia said, "I've skimmed through most of it. Like you said, a lot of boiler plate."

"This is the agreement stipulating that no less than seventy-five percent of the workers be native islanders. Apparently, this deal was sold as an opportunity for high-paying jobs, although as we saw, there was obviously a lot of push-back. There's a lot of other minor understandings which require your signature, but those are the most important ones. Except for this last one."

"What's that Michael?" Julia asked with a little trepidation.

Michael Williams, remembering the exchange of words with the reporter said, "It is the agreement between Lucarana Mining Company and Oceana Logging."

"Agreement? For what?' Julia blurted out.

"For a twenty-year lease on all non-mine-specific land, which will be conveyed to your company in twenty minutes. Someone who had access to all this paperwork must be an environmentalist and leaked everything. The Clarke woman was telling the truth."

Julia stood up and walked to the window. She looked out at the sea. Memories flooded through her mind in rapid succession. She realized that she was being shown, in the blink of an eye, all the events in her life that had led her to this exact moment in time. Her father never coming back from the hospital. Working in the far-north fields. Finding his journal. Seeing the yellow stone for the first time. Then returning it. It all spooled across her inner vision as if in fast forward.

Her thoughts were interrupted by Michael Williams clearing his throat. "Ma'am, it's almost one and in an hour the right of rescission expires. If you don't have any questions to ask me, you'd better head on down there. I'm sure everyone is waiting."

After saying that, he slid the file folder with the glossy cover across the table to her, turning it so she could pick it up in the correct position.

She looked down at the folder, trying to understand what the company had put on the cover. Then she realized what it was. It was a birds-eye view photograph of the giant open pit mine at Lookout Lake. An enormous series of winding truck lanes spiraled into the earth following the kimberlite ever deeper below the surface. It was a gigantic wound stretching for miles across an otherwise barren terrain, and in truth, Julia had never been revolted by it because there was nothing but grizzles and wolves for hundreds of miles in any direction.

"But what about Mala?" she thought to herself. "What will that island look like after we get rolling?" She turned to Michael Williams and said, "You're right, Michael, I've got to get down there. First though, I need to use the lady's room." She took off her khaki blazer and folded it over the chair placing the portfolio next it. "I'll be right back. I don't want to have to excuse myself in the middle of everything," she said taking her purse.

Julia Witherspoon turned right out of the conference room and walked in the opposite direction of room 2A, past the restrooms and towards the sign that said "Stairs" over the steel door at the end of the hall. She slipped through the door and removed her high heels, walking barefoot down the stairs. She exited through the side of the building and turned away from the crowd she could still hear out front, leaving her new high heels and purse on the sidewalk for the first lucky girl to discover, a nearly four-hundred-dollar gift. She hailed the first cab she saw. The haunting melody again played in her mind, only this time it was soothing to her.

Julia sat in the cab and opened her phone. She hit the Google icon and spoke softly into the microphone, "Patsy Cline. Algiers. Name of Song." She just had to know. The little blue circle spun around and around. Then the screen lit up.

"You Belong to Me"

# EPILOGUE

Julia Witherspoon stood in the soft sand looking out to sea past the man-made island where thatched huts stood like nests a mere half-dozen steps above the waterline. The small wavelets soaked her new tan capri pants she had bought at Pacific Clothing, along with numerous other items designed for island living, before boarding the plane back to Auki. She extended the rental agreement on the pickup truck for a year, prepaid, to the delight of the tiny rental company. Now she could take her time figuring things out.

It occurred to her that she had accomplished exactly what she set out to do just under two weeks ago, and her life had changed profoundly. Just not in the way she hoped it would when she left. She did retrace her father's footsteps. In fact, she was standing in almost the exact same spot he'd stood when he decided to go home and be a father. But, of course, Julia didn't know that. What she did know, was that her old life was extinguished when she turned right out of the conference room door instead of left, a couple of days before. She still had a hard time believing she did it.

"Now what?' she thought to herself. "I followed Dad here, but he left to go back home. Is that what I'm supposed to do?" She shook her head, no. The conversation she was having with herself was almost as animated as if she were talking to someone else. "He left to raise me," she mused. "What's in Canada to go back to? Nothing!" she concluded.

She looked out to sea and noticed three lights skimming just above the waves. She had noticed them before and when asked, it was explained that they are common, and no one pays attention to them. One by one they dipped into the ocean and disappeared. "Interesting," she thought. "I'll have to look into this. Maybe it will give me something to do."

Then her thoughts turned to the last day of her childhood. She remembered the exact day and the exact time it ended. Her father was pulling her up a hill on a toboggan, two days before Christmas, just before noon. It would be their last run, then they were going to his favorite café for hot chocolate and grilled cheese sandwiches. She couldn't wait, it was her favorite. They never made it to the café. Instead, her last memory of her father was him clutching his chest and falling in the snow. An ambulance took him to the nearest hospital, and a police officer took her home. She was only ten years old. Once again, she was alone.

Julia shook her head, trying to clear it of memories that would never clear. Then, she thought of Thomas, and "You Belong To Me" bubbled to the surface of her mind. They had said they loved each other their last night together, but did she? She closed her eyes and just stood perfectly still in the warm tranquil water. When she opened them, she knew she had her answer. "I can't imagine life without him," she thought to herself. "Now, how do I make that happen?" She remembered the last thing Grandfather had said to her before he walked back to his village. "If your path brings you back here, I will be waiting for you."

Julia turned to walk through the village to the hut with the blue door. It was as good a place as any she could think of to begin her new life.

Made in United States
Orlando, FL
10 February 2023